MURDER
ME
TWICE

A Detective Joe Ezell Mystery

Book One

P.J. Conn

Cover and Book design by eBook Prep
www.ebookprep.com

First Edition, December 2015
ISBN: 978-1-61417-809-5

ePublishing Works!
www.epublishingworks.com

DEDICATION

MURDER ME TWICE is dedicated to Jeffrey C. Ingwalson who gave me an irresistible idea for a book, and to Sally A. Morrison who loves a good mystery. You guys rock.

THE
DETECTIVE JOE EZELL
MYSTERY SERIES

Murder Me Twice
Stairway To Murder

CHAPTER 1

Los Angeles, June 1947

A distant siren woke Hal in the dead of night. Drenched in sweat, his heart racing, he shook off the tangled bedclothes to stumble into the kitchen for a glass of cold water. It didn't help. The nightmare came often, and even without a trigger he'd be plunged into the murder, nearly choking on the coppery scent of her blood pooling on the sidewalk. He'd once had such an orderly and ordinary existence until one evening after work he'd gotten off the Red Car one stop early. He'd simply longed for a few minutes to himself before going home, but the break in his routine had sent his whole life spiraling out of control. If only he could go back and undo that one tragic mistake, she wouldn't have died, and wouldn't now haunt his dreams with gunshots and terror.

Los Angeles, late January 1947

Hal looked out the window and cursed the rain. He'd lost track of how many days he'd gotten up to gloomy gray skies. Faye was the most attentive of wives and thought whenever it rained he ought to leave for work fortified with a steamy bowl of hot oatmeal. He hated oatmeal and doused the spongy lukewarm mass with raisins and brown sugar to add some much needed taste. When she turned back to the stove, he dripped on maple syrup.

Faye was too sensitive a woman to bear even a hint of criticism, so he'd drink his orange juice, down one cup of her awful weak coffee and do his best to finish a bowl of her wretched oatmeal. Thank god he'd convinced her a division manager often had luncheon meetings and there would be no need for her to make him lunches. That meant he could look forward to one palatable meal a day. He was often asked how he managed to stay trim when he worked at a desk. With Faye's menus, it would be difficult to gain even an ounce of weight a year.

She kissed his cheek and handed him his briefcase while her gray Persian cat, Mr. Cuddles, regarded him with his usual evil eye. Hal hated the spoiled beast, but Faye doted on the heavily furred feline so he did his best to get along with her beloved pet, but Mr. Cuddles made no such effort in return.

He'd read the *Los Angeles Times* on the Pacific Electric Red Car into town and search for good news and some humor in the comics. Most of them weren't nearly as funny as they'd been before the war, but he gave thanks every day that he'd survived. He hadn't seen any action stationed in Washington, D.C., so it hadn't been difficult, but still, he was enormously grateful, nonetheless.

His firm occupied the whole fifth floor of a starkly modern skyscraper located a convenient two blocks from the train station. He always arrived at work early, before the sidewalks were crowded, and his overcoat, hat and big black umbrella kept him dry until he pushed his way through the gleaming brass revolving door.

"Good morning, Mr. Marten," Joe, one of the elevator operators greeted him. "Looks like we've got us another rainy day."

"It's good for the farmers and crops," Hal replied.

"That's what I like about you, Mr. Marten. You're always looking on the bright side."

Hal sold insurance, and he couldn't afford to be gloomy. "It's the only way to be."

He got off on the fifth floor for the California West Insurance offices and said hello to Brian Babcock and David Holmen, who'd also come to work early. They were right out of college and eager to make their mark in the world. His interest was solely in their sales figures, but he smiled as though seeing them at their desks was the highlight of his day. He unlocked the door to his office, hung his overcoat and hat on the oak hat rack in the corner and carried his dripping umbrella into his private bathroom. He sat at his desk and checked his calendar for the day.

He'd meet with his salesmen at nine and then compile reports until noon. George Sharp, the vice president for sales, often complimented him on his reports and for having a gift for relaying information in a concise way. Other division managers buried facts under a dozen sleep-inducing pages, while his reports were a beacon of clarity. He was on track to make vice president before he reached forty. He got up and adjusted the blinds on his office windows. Even on a gray day open blinds made his office brighter, and he needed every drop of sunlight he could find.

His secretary, Lorraine Adams, was a dear woman with a desk right outside his door. She was barely five feet tall, preferred dresses with lace collars, and was the best secretary in the building. He wrote himself a note to buy flowers for her desk when it finally stopped raining.

"Mr. Marten?"

One of the early boys stood at his door. He smiled and welcomed David Holmen in. "Do you need something before the nine o'clock meeting?" he asked.

"I have a question about my vacation, and I didn't want to waste everyone's time then."

Hal laughed. "So you'll just waste mine now?"

David blushed deeply and stood up straighter. "No, sir, of course not. I'm hoping to get married this summer, and I wondered if it's too early to put in a request for the last week in June."

"Mrs. Adams keeps the vacation book. Ask her about the date when she comes in. June is a popular month, but if you have a wedding planned—"

"I haven't proposed yet, but I thought if I had a June vacation, it would be an incentive to have the wedding then."

"Excellent planning, Mr. Holmen," Hal replied. "It ought to impress your girl. A man with your vision can go far with California West."

"Thank you, sir. I certainly hope so."

Hal hid his smile until the young man had returned to his desk. He'd been a captain in the Quartermaster Corps during the war, and had gotten used to young men saluting and addressing him as sir. With fair hair, blue eyes and a slim build, he'd looked good in his uniform, even if he hadn't felt like a soldier. He got up to glance out the window, but the rain hadn't let up. He walked around his desk three times and sat down to review his notes for the meeting.

After another day, remarkable only by its ordinariness, Hal got off the Red Car one stop early. He'd noticed the Golden Bear Lounge on the corner months ago, but he'd not frequented bars on the way home even before he'd married Faye. Today, he felt compelled to break the monotony of his routine and went on in. There was a bar closer to home, The Square Deal Café. The front windows where painted black and whenever he walked by, he was enveloped in a smoky haze, and the jukebox was so loud the music could be heard from across the street. Clearly, it wasn't his type of place.

The Golden Bear Lounge was quiet, and comfortably dim with dark mahogany paneling. Deep green leather booths lined the wall opposite the bar. He left his hat, overcoat and umbrella on the coat rack near the door and joined the half-dozen patrons seated on stools at the long bar.

The bartender had a handlebar mustache right out of the last century and parted his hair in the middle. Hal had never enjoyed barbershop quartets and hoped there weren't three waiters about to join him in song.

"Name's Mitch," the bartender announced. "This is my mom's place, so don't get rowdy."

Hal hadn't gotten rowdy his whole life and laughed at what he hoped was a joke. He asked for a beer and sipped it slowly. The two men seated closest to him were bragging about their service in the Pacific during the war, and Hal strained to hear their accounts of the action they'd seen. Their voices rose and fell with the excitement of their stories, and he caught only half of it.

The nearest man turned to Hal. "You serve during the war?"

"Yes, I was in the Army Quartermaster Corps," Hal replied.

"Where were you stationed?" Mitch asked.

"Washington, D.C."

The two veterans laughed. "Bet you never fired a shot," one said.

Hal had heard that remark so often he had a ready reply. "No, I didn't, but you must have been grateful to have food and supplies."

The older of the two men guffawed. "The army food kept me from starving to death, that's all I'll give it."

"Don't let them bother you," Mitch offered, and continued polishing the mahogany bar with a clean towel.

"I'm used to it," Hal replied. "After a soldier has bullet holes shot through his clothes, it's natural he won't have much respect for a man who's merely battled moths."

Mitch had a loud booming laugh and everyone seated at the bar leaned forward to get a good look at Hal. That's when Hal saw the woman. She was seated in the last booth and dressed in a black suit and little black cocktail hat with a veil covering her eyes. She had to be waiting for someone, but she got up and walked out alone. From the pride in her posture, she didn't strike him as the type who'd forgive a man for being late, or even worse, standing her up.

Hal could easily imagine a big man coming in and shouting her name. Mitch would tell him to get out and things might get ugly. Hal had wanted only a beer, not the chance to be in a bar fight. He laughed to himself, finished his beer before any mayhem ensued and caught the Red Car for the short trip home. He unwrapped a peppermint he'd taken from the bowl at his favorite restaurant for lunch and chewed it up quickly to keep Faye from guessing he'd stopped for a drink. He'd liked the bar, and thought he might stop by again, and soon.

Thursday nights, Faye served meatloaf with mashed potatoes and green beans. It was difficult to ruin mashed potatoes, so hers weren't too bad, and the green beans were out of a can, but the meatloaf, well, a brick would have been equally tasty. He loved to take his wife out to dinner on Saturday night. She regarded it as a special treat. He considered it a matter of survival. Mr. Cuddles ate the finest of cat foods on the back porch while they dined, and he often thought the cat had the better meal.

Their one-story stucco Spanish style duplex had arched windows, a red tile roof and a lush magenta bougainvillea framed the front door. Sundays were quiet at their place. Mr. Cuddles slept all day on his cushion by the front window, as he did every other day. Hal read the Sunday paper and worked the crossword puzzle while Faye finished whatever sewing project she'd begun that week. She loved to sew and model her new clothes, but she had the worst eye for color and pattern he'd ever seen. He'd thought of going with her to her favorite fabric store to offer an opinion on the material. She liked to shop during the week, however, so far there hadn't been an opportunity.

Her sewing had improved with the new Singer sewing machine he'd given her for her birthday. He'd thought it an odd present for a man to give his wife of less than a

year, but it was what she had truly wanted. She'd
unwrapped the box with a childlike glee and covered his
face with kisses. She'd wanted to make him a shirt, but
he'd encouraged her to make something she could wear
herself.

When he made vice-president, he'd insist she shop at
Bullock's or I. Magnin rather than wear clothes she'd
sewn herself. She could still sew curtains, or clothes for
the children they hoped to have. They hadn't had any
success on that score as yet.

She was affectionate, but he wished there were more
passion in their lovemaking. Sex was new to her and
perhaps he was doing a poor job of teaching her how to
enjoy it, although she always snuggled against him when
they got into bed. He'd have to peel off her nightgown,
she never came to bed without it, but she had a lovely
figure he wished she'd be proud to display. She had a
cute birthmark on her right shoulder that resembled a
cat's head with the pointed ears. It made her laugh when
he called her his kitten, and he did enjoy being with her.
It was just that he'd thought being married would be
more fulfilling than it had turned out to be. Maybe when
they had kids things would improve.

The next week the weather improved slightly, but there
had been floods farther north. Floods meant claims
would be coming in, but California West believed
customers remained loyal if they were loyal to them. It
was simply a matter of shaking out the claims, because
sadly, there were always a few people who took
advantage of any chance to profit from fraud.

Despite the busy week, in slow moments Hal thought of
the woman in the bar. There was a world of sophistication in
the way she moved. Her suit had been expensive and her
saucy hat perfect for the cocktail hour. She had beautiful legs
too. He wondered whom she had expected to meet and why
he had not showed. Only a fool would keep a woman that
lovely waiting alone in a bar.

Thursday night, he made his second trip to the Golden Bear. Mitch remembered him, but the talkative veterans were gone and there were new people seated along the bar. Hal surveyed the other patrons without giving himself away, and when he looked into the mirror behind Mitch, he found the woman he'd hoped to see seated in the last booth.

She was dressed in navy blue tonight with a new cocktail hat slanted on her dark upswept curls. The veil shielded her eyes, and he wondered if they were a striking blue, or perhaps an exotic green. She wore black kid gloves and sipped a martini.

The radio behind the bar was tuned to a station playing big band music. Les Brown's hit, "Sentimental Journey," with Doris Day singing, provided an evocative melody for such a lovely woman. He wondered where she'd been that day, and where she'd be going if no one came to join her. When Mitch spoke, he'd been so lost in thought, it startled him.

Mitch rested his arm on the bar. "Have you been reading about the Black Dahlia murder?"

"Yes," Hal replied. "What a gruesome case. What sort of man would kill a woman and cut her body in half?"

"I keep thinking about the young mother who was out for a walk with her baby in a stroller, and found her, half here, half there. The murderer made no effort to hide the body, so he must have wanted her to be found."

A man seated two stools away, whose eyebrows were startling white tuffs, cleared his throat, but his voice remained gravelly. "It has to be a man. Women don't butcher each other like that. You think he'll go after someone else?"

"I'm afraid so," Mitch offered. "A man couldn't be that violent and go back to listening to ball games."

Hal caught sight of the woman in the corner of his eye as she stepped out the front door. She'd been only a flash of dark blue, but her parting brought a quick sense of loss. He hid it well, and continued to sip his beer.

Faye didn't like having liquor in the house, and he wasn't much of a drinker so he hadn't minded the ban on spirits. He couldn't imagine her mixing up a pitcher of martinis for him when he got home. He stifled a laugh so no one would believe he was amused by the gory story of Elizabeth Short, the young woman known as the Black Dahlia, but even with the dreaded meatloaf for dinner, his mood remained upbeat going home.

Faye turned in front of him showing off her new dress. "What do you think?" she asked.

She had sewn several dresses from the same pattern and this time had chosen a floral print that would have been more appropriate for a bedspread. "I like the color," Hal responded with all the tact he could muster. "Would you call it peach?"

"Peach or apricot," she replied. She tied her purple apron around her waist and went into the kitchen to finish preparing dinner. It was Wednesday night and that meant macaroni and cheese with a slice of ham left over from last night. She never used enough cheese on the watery macaroni, but it helped to wash down the piece of dried ham. Sometimes she added a spiced peach. He hoped this was one of those nights.

He leaned back in his easy chair and closed his eyes. Everything was going well at work, and his days passed quickly. It was the nights that were beginning to wear on him. Their duplex had been freshly painted before they moved in. Even if he'd had any useful skills to make repairs, which he didn't, they weren't needed for upkeep. The pale beige carpeting was new too, and Faye vacuumed daily to keep it clean. She was a terrific housekeeper, but that was a given in his mind, not a reason to rejoice.

"Dinner's ready, sweetheart," Faye called. "I remembered the spiced peaches you like."

"Thank you." Hal stood and tried to look forward to tasting something she couldn't ruin. Tomorrow would be

Thursday, and he couldn't wait to stop by the Golden Bear again. He bet the woman in the veiled hat couldn't cook worth a damn either, but no man would possibly give a damn.

Thursday, the evening held a bitter chill, but Hal still got off the Red Car a stop early and walked to what had become his favorite place. The veterans were back and nodded to him as he sat down near them at the long mahogany bar. He drew in a deep breath, and told himself, as he had all week, that he deserved a few moments to relax before going home at least once a week.

He waited until after Mitch had served his beer to send an idle glance toward the booths along the wall behind him. Two were occupied, and the woman he'd really come to see sat alone in the last booth. Tonight she was dressed in a startling red suit, with a matching veiled hat. He tried not to smile too wide, but he couldn't deny he was thrilled to see her.

Mitch followed Hal's glance, rested his arms on the bar and leaned close to whisper, "She's in here once a week, orders one martini and leaves as alone as she came. I figure she lost someone in the war and has a drink to remember him."

She certainly wasn't dressed like a grieving widow that night, but Hal nodded as though he agreed with Mitch's assessment. "No one ever talks to her?" he asked.

Mitch straightened up. "Lots of men have approached her, and while I can't hear what she says, it's enough to send them running. Try it if you're feeling brave."

Hal took the comment as a dare, left his glass on the bar and walked to her booth with the same easy confidence he displayed in his office. "May I join you?"

She looked up at him through her hat's lacy veil, and her bright red lipstick made her smile doubly warm. "I'm on my way out, and the booth's all yours."

Her voice was pitched low, like a movie siren uttering

a provocative line, and unable to think of a clever response in time to inspire her to stay, Hal stood back as she brushed by him. He noted how gracefully she moved on her red high heels and swallowed hard rather than drool. Elated that he'd spoken to her rather than being defeated by her casual dismissal, he returned to his stool and picked up his beer.

"Well?" Mitch asked.

Hal shrugged. "She was polite, and merely said she was on her way out."

"Maybe you should come in earlier next week," Mitch offered with a sly wink.

Hal took a long swallow of his beer rather than respond, but he was sorely tempted to do just that. He never left the office early, but he might make an exception just once. The challenge would be to find the charm to inspire the pretty lady to stay.

CHAPTER 2

On Sunday afternoon, Hal quickly grew bored with reading the *Los Angeles Times* and tossed the crossword puzzle aside. "Why don't we go to the movies?" he suggested.

Faye looked up from the new dress she was hemming by hand. "I suppose we could go, if you want to."

Hal couldn't recall a single time she'd offered what he'd welcome as a much needed break in their stifling routine. He picked up the paper to check movie times. There was a nice theatre within walking distance, and they could make the matinee if they hurried.

"The *Ghost and Mrs. Muir* sounds good." He'd already made up his mind and went to the closet for their coats.

Faye set the dress aside, smoothed out her grey wool skirt and orange sweater. "Do I need to change my clothes?" she asked.

"No, you look beautiful as always," he assured her. He helped her with her brown tweed coat and thought it was one of her best purchases. It had probably been on sale rather than her first choice. With curly brown hair and hazel eyes, she was such a pretty girl, and he leaned down to give her a quick kiss. He took her hand as they walked to the theatre.

"Can we buy popcorn?" she asked.

"Of course," he agreed and bought two red and white striped boxes. They found seats on the aisle near the center of the theatre where he preferred to sit. They had just gotten comfortable when the newsreel began. He was so relieved to be out of the house he paid scant attention until the cartoon. Bugs Bunny was silly at best, but he laughed with the rest of the audience. There was a good crowd for a wintery afternoon.

In the feature film, Rex Harrison starred as Captain Gregg, and Gene Tierney as Mrs. Muir, a widow who'd bought the supposedly haunted Gull Cottage. Natalie Wood played her little daughter. Hal found himself intrigued by the prospect of a love affair involving a lonely young woman and a handsome ghost, but the pair weren't truly together until the end of the film when Mrs. Muir died and Captain Gregg appeared to take her hand. When the lights came on after the credits, he was surprised to find Faye in tears.

"Didn't you like the story?" he asked.

She wiped her eyes on her lacy handkerchief. "I loved it, but it was just so sad."

"Not if you think of them as being together in the hereafter," he responded. He brushed away the last crumbs of popcorn from his lap and helped her snuggle into her coat. They held hands as they walked home. "Next time I'll find a comedy if you'd like that better."

"But I loved *The Ghost and Mrs. Muir* even if it was sad. It seemed like a story that could really have happened."

"You believe in ghosts?" Hal asked, clearly skeptical of their existence.

"There are places that are truly haunted, I read about them all the time," she countered.

"It must be difficult to prove," he answered.

"Not to the people who've actually seen ghosts. They're often so terrified by the experience they never forget it."

He loved it when she showed some spirit. "Should we

go looking for some on our vacation? There must be a haunted hotel somewhere in California, maybe up in the Gold Rush country."

"I didn't say I wanted to see one!" she exclaimed. "Now let's hurry, I'm getting cold, and I need to put the chicken in the oven."

Hal hurried his step. She continually overcooked the chicken, but that night he'd check on it a dozen times if he had to and make certain it was roasted to perfection rather than incinerated. He laughed in spite of himself.

"What's so funny?" she asked.

"Nothing really," he assured her, but he succeeded in helping her produce a delectable chicken that evening and was grateful all through the meal.

Faye went to the library on Monday and came home with an armful of books written by authors who claimed to be experts on ghosts. Hal liked to read nonfiction accounts of the war, or novels set during the strife, while Faye went for much lighter fare. He didn't tease her about the books, but he dismissed them as entertaining fabrications rather than the truth.

They were seated in the living room Tuesday night reading when Faye looked up. "I'm reading about the Tower of London which is positively filled with ghosts. It's said people often see a headless Anne Boleyn."

Her eyes were lit with excitement, but Hal couldn't help himself. "If the ghost has no head, how do they know she's Anne Boleyn?" he asked.

Faye bit her lip. "That's a good question, maybe by her clothes?"

"Yes, probably," Hal agreed. He returned to his book grateful she'd found an interest other than sewing unattractive clothes. She described another ghost in the Tower, and he nodded and smiled, but he wished she'd see through the silly accounts rather than gush over the foggy apparitions.

He took her out to dinner to celebrate Valentine's Day,

and gave her a gold bangle bracelet with a heart charm along with flowers and candy. She surprised him with a pair of pajamas she had sewn herself, and he pretended to be pleased. He was grateful they were made from pale blue cotton rather than a hideous print that would have disturbed his dreams.

He tried them on and found they were a size too large, but that was a small complaint. He picked her up in an enthusiastic hug. "Thank you. These are the most comfortable pajamas I've ever worn."

"Oh good, I'll make you another pair," she responded happily.

He gave her a loving squeeze rather than reply, but as long as he didn't have to wear her creations out of the house, he'd consider himself lucky.

The following Thursday night, the beautiful woman Hal had come to see had again worn black. He hadn't had to leave the office early, merely to leave when everyone else did rather than remain late to plan for Friday. He went straight to her booth.

"Do you believe in ghosts?" he asked.

She smiled as she glanced up at him. "Of course. There are several people I intend to haunt."

She nodded slightly, and he took it as an invitation to take the seat opposite hers. He slid into the booth. "So you believe it's possible?" he inquired.

"I intend to make it so," she responded, her voice deliciously low and intimate.

He watched her sip her martini and lick her bright red lips. It was the most erotic thing he'd ever seen, and the bar suddenly grew uncomfortably warm. "What do you have planned, footsteps, opening and closing doors, rattling chains?"

"Too ordinary," she dismissed with a wave of a gloved hand. "I'm thinking of glowing lights, chilling mists, and familiar songs when no radio is playing."

"You're making me shiver just talking about it."

She regarded him with an indulgent smile and then checked her watch. "Time to go. Don't ever follow me," she cautioned.

"Why not?" he asked. But she left without responding. He reached for her glass, tasted her martini and made a face.

Mitch came over to fetch the glass and clean the table. "Too much for you?" he asked.

"Are you referring to the martini, or the woman?" Hal asked.

Mitch responded with his rich rolling laugh. "Both."

Hal followed him to the bar and ordered a beer but it tasted like water after the breath-taking sip of gin. It prompted him to compare the woman in black to Faye, and he was instantly ashamed of himself for doing so.

When he got home, he found Faye had added mushrooms to her meatloaf to give it a strange chewy texture. He wondered about getting a dog that would sit under the table and eat the scraps he could sneak him. He doubted he could walk the dog often enough to keep him from growing obese though and discounted the idea. He drank water with his meals, and Faye didn't comment when he got up to refill his glass.

"How was your day?" he asked as he returned to the table.

"Pretty ordinary. Mrs. Espinoza, Carmen, from next door, came over to ask me to help her change a ceiling light bulb. She's afraid to stand on a stool when she's all alone."

"So you climbed up on the stool?" he asked.

"Yes, it doesn't take a minute to remove the fixture and switch the bulbs. It isn't like working on high tension wires." She giggled at the thought.

"No, I suppose not, but I hope you were careful."

"Well, I didn't want to wait for you to come home. You've better things to do with your evenings than change light bulbs for Carmen."

"She's a nice lady, and I wouldn't mind," he responded.

Searching for something more to say, he settled on the library books. "How is your ghost study going?"

She had eaten the last bite of her meatloaf and hesitated with a green bean on her fork. "I found the most fascinating place, the Winchester House. Have you heard of it?"

"No, tell me about it." He added another dash of salt to his mashed potatoes.

"It's in San Jose, so maybe we could visit it someday. Sarah Winchester built it after she'd lost her only child and her husband. She turned to a medium in hopes of contacting them and learned there was a curse on the family because of all the people who had been killed with Winchester rifles. The medium told her to move west and create a house for the spirits. Sarah came to California in 1883 and started building; she even included a séance room."

"Did the spirits move in?" he schooled his features rather than laugh out loud.

"Yes, they did. It's a fabulous Victorian house, and the ghosts told Sarah to keep building. It has 160 rooms, and thirteen bathrooms. She liked the number thirteen. There are six kitchens, forty staircases, many of them going up the ceiling, forty-seven fireplaces, two thousand doors, some open on blank walls, and ten thousand windows. Construction continued until Sarah died in 1938. I guess money was never a problem for her."

"Apparently not, but the house would be something to see," he agreed. "So the place has ghosts?"

"People have heard organ music when no one is playing, voices, cold spots, sometimes wavering lights and people no more substantial than fog. Weird goings on, but visitors swear it's true."

"I'm sure they do."

Faye shrugged. "I don't care if you don't believe it, I do."

"I didn't say I didn't believe it, Faye. I'd just like to see a ghost for myself is all."

She got up to carry her plate into the kitchen. "They can't be ordered like dishes on a menu."

"Certainly not," he called to her. He finished his water and carried his plate and glass into the kitchen and set them on the counter beside hers.

"You didn't have to help clear the table," she scolded softly.

"I wanted to," he replied. She made a playful wave to send him out of her kitchen, and he went into the living room and picked up his book about the naval battles in the Pacific. He'd found it particularly interesting, but his mind wandered to the beautiful woman in the bar each time he turned a page.

They often listened to radio programs in the evening. Faye loved the *Adventures of Ozzie and Harriet,* while he preferred the mystery shows. He loved *Inner Sanctum* with its spooky creaking door opening, and the *Adventures of Philip Marlowe*. It seemed everyone was having an adventure, except him.

On Sunday, Hal took Faye to see *The Bachelor and the Bobby Soxer.* She loved Cary Grant, and thought the comedy also starring Myrna Loy, Rudy Vallee and Shirley Temple thoroughly entertaining. She nearly skipped along beside him as they walked home.

"I loved that movie, could we go again?" she asked.

"If you want to, but didn't you find it difficult to believe Shirley Temple could be Myrna Loy's little sister?" Hal asked.

"It's a movie, Hal, and the actresses are just playing parts. Comedies are supposed to be funny, and you shouldn't analyze them as closely as you do your insurance contracts."

He conceded the point. "You're right of course. Teenage girls do get crushes on older men, so that Shirley was so fond of Cary made sense."

"Any woman would fall in love with Cary Grant," Faye added with a wistful sigh.

"Certainly," he agreed. "He's far more charming than Rudy Vallee, so Myrna Loy couldn't resist him either." They had continued their conversation about Cary Grant movies over dinner, and he congratulated himself for again saving the chicken from absolute doom in the oven. Altogether, it was a pleasant day, even if it lacked the delicious excitement he'd felt talking with the veiled woman in the Golden Bear. After making love with Faye that night, he laced his hands behind his head, stared up at the ceiling and wondered if his mystery woman would tell him her name.

In the office on Thursday, Hal was presented with so many challenges he couldn't clear his desk and leave at his regular time, let alone early. He watched the clock and cursed under his breath. Finally deciding he couldn't contain all the damage one of the new salesmen had made in a single day, he grabbed his overcoat and hat and left. On the Red Car home, he debated whether or not to stop at the bar when he was certain the woman he'd longed to see all week would already have come and gone.

With the faint hope she might possibly have waited for him, he went in almost afraid to look at the last booth, but it was empty. Once in the door, he couldn't turn around and leave, so he slid into his usual seat at the bar and ordered a beer.

Mitch served him and leaned close to whisper. "Didn't see her today. Maybe she's found somewhere else she likes better."

Hal shrugged rather than groan at that miserable possibility, but he was afraid he'd scared her away. He heard someone down the bar mention the Black Dahlia and thought any woman who'd been so horribly murdered would surely return as a ghost, if there were such a thing.

When he got home, he apologized for being late. "I'm sorry. One of the new salesmen failed to calculate the payments accurately on several policies he'd written. He was so proud of the new clients he'd signed, but I insisted he contact them and explain the errors, which were entirely his, not California West's. Quite naturally, they weren't pleased and wanted to speak to me as his supervisor." He seldom discussed business with Faye, and was relieved when she showed minimal interest now.

"I'm sorry you had such an awful day. I added black olives to the meatloaf, and took it out of the oven so it wouldn't be ruined when you were late."

"I am sorry," he repeated.

"It wasn't your fault." She reached up to kiss his cheek and served his least favorite of her dinners.

The olives did add a bit of flavor even if they didn't entirely counteract the rubbery mushrooms. She always prepared plenty of brown gravy, which thank goodness came out of a can, and he added an extra spoonful tonight.

"I found another ghost," she revealed with a delighted smile. "In 1932, an actress, Peg Entwistle, who'd made only one movie, *Thirteen Women,* which sounds like bad luck right there, jumped to her death from the H in the Hollywoodland sign."

"Really? Was she making a statement about Hollywood?" he asked.

"That's reasonable to assume. Maybe she had a lot of talent and didn't get the breaks she'd hoped for. Poor thing. People say they see her and sometimes smell her gardenia perfume. The Hollywoodland sign is close enough for us to visit."

"Let's wait until the summer when it will be a lot warmer out than it is tonight."

Disappointed, she sat back in her chair. "I should have thought of that. Peg's ghost wouldn't like the cold weather any better than we do."

"Probably not." The papers were filled with conjecture about the Black Dahlia murder, but they'd never discussed it. Faye was all sunlight, and while she might be enchanted by ghost stories, she'd be horrified by a real murder. Murder wasn't a polite topic for dinner conversation anyway.

CHAPTER 3

Hal stood at his desk shuffling his work for the day when his secretary came to the door. "Do you have a minute to see Mr. Babcock?" she asked.

He grimaced slightly. "Sure. Tell him to come on in." Brian entered, looked even more sheepish than he had last Friday. "You needn't apologize again, Brian. Let's just start the week fresh. I'm confident you won't repeat the same mistakes," Hal assured him.

"I sure hope not, but I've thought all weekend that maybe I'm just not cut out to sell insurance."

"Do you have something else in mind?" Hal gestured toward the chairs facing his desk and Brian took one.

"No, I enjoy meeting people and sales seems to be a good fit for me, but maybe just not insurance." He looked down at his newly polished wingtips before looking up at Hal, his expression filled with gloom.

"All right, but you'll need a reference. You've spent only six months with California West, and I could only state that you were here. Why not give it a year? A new employer would be more impressed by your commitment to your first job, and I'd have more to compliment you on in a reference."

Brian nodded thoughtfully. "All right, if you think I should."

"I do, and by then, you might decide you'd prefer to stay here with us rather than look for a job elsewhere."

The salesman rose and took a step toward the door. "Thanks, Mr. Marten. I'll do my best not to disappoint you this week, or ever again," he quickly added.

After Brian had returned to his desk in the outer office, Hal made a note of their conversation in the new salesman's file. He relied on his notes when he wrote performance reviews and was certain Brian would now take meticulous care with policy costs. There was a real value to commitment of any endeavor, of course, but he quickly suppressed the need to consider his own.

He bought a bouquet of mixed flowers for Faye before boarding the Red Car, and she was so thrilled by the gesture he regretted not doing it often. He followed her into the kitchen and watched her fill a crystal vase with water. "Be sure to trim the stems, and the flowers will stay fresh much longer."

Faye took her kitchen shears and snipped a stem. "Like this?"

"Perfect." He kissed her cheek and got out of her way. They had a comfortable routine, and there was a value to sticking with it, but as he looked around the familiar furnishings of the living room, he wanted so much more. "Faye?" he called. "Why don't we look at new furniture on Saturday?"

She peered out of the kitchen. "You don't like what we have?"

"I'm just tired of it," he admitted readily. "Maybe all we need is a new chair or a lamp."

"Whatever you want, my love," she replied and hurried to put their chicken and egg noodles on the table.

Hal knew exactly what he was doing: seeking a cheap thrill with a new woman rather than doting on his wife as he should. He and Faye hadn't known each other long before they'd married, and while they got along well, it was mainly due to her passivity rather than to a true accord. She was pretty with a cheerful disposition, and he would never hurt her by being unfaithful, but a conversation in a bar was just harmless fun. He told himself that repeatedly, but when Thursday arrived, he couldn't wait to get to the Golden Bear.

She was seated in the back booth, dressed in her blue suit and cute veiled hat. She smiled as he approached, and he sat without asking permission. "I'm Hal Marten, and we should exchange names if nothing more."

"Pearl LaFosse," she replied before sampling her martini.

"Hello, Pearl." He thought it the perfect name for her. She was a sophisticated young woman, with an enchanting elegance and as graceful as a string of pearls. He'd not seen her wearing any though. "Do you have sisters, Ruby and Opal and…."

She licked her lips and shook her head. "I'm an only child."

"So am I," he replied.

"That means we're both used to getting our own way," she said. "It's a tragic pairing I'm afraid."

"I could pretend to have a brother or two," Hal offered agreeably.

"It's too late, I already know the truth."

Hal hadn't told her the biggest truth: that he had a wife at home waiting to serve him a nearly inedible meat loaf. For the moment, it didn't matter to him at all. She picked up her purse, and eased out of the booth before he could stop her with a question so intriguing she'd want to stay.

"Good bye," she whispered, and all the men in the bar turned to watch her walk out the door with an enticing feminine sway.

Saturday was a crisp cool day, and Hal and Faye went furniture shopping. Hal wasn't certain what he wanted, but when Faye fell in love with an over-stuffed chair upholstered in a hideous purple print, he couldn't go along. "I'm afraid it's too big for our living room." He walked around it and lifted the seat cushion. "I should have measured the room before we came. Let's do that before we buy anything so we won't find ourselves with something that doesn't fit in the space we have."

Faye ran her hand fondly over the back of the chair. "Would it fit in the bedroom?"

That she couldn't see the chair for the monstrosity it was appalled him, but he forced down a frustrated groan. "We need to measure it too. Let's go get some ice cream before we go home."

"Ice cream? We haven't gone out for ice cream since we were dating." Distracted by the thought, she took his hand and left the furniture store with a brisk step.

Aunt Lucy's Ice Cream Parlor had a black and white tile floor, white wrought-iron chairs and marble topped tables. Although the charming shop offered more than a dozen flavors, Faye made her choice quickly. "I'd like a single scoop of vanilla, please."

"You'd not care to try something new?" Hal asked. "Maybe the peach?"

"I'm sure it's delicious, but I want vanilla."

Hal nodded to the clerk who scooped up her order. "Give me chocolate chip," he asked. They took a table in the window, and he ate his ice cream as slowly as humanly possible while she played with her spoon between bites.

"May we take some home?" she asked.

"If you'd like to. You have plenty of money for household expenses, don't you, Faye? If you need more, we can easily revise our budget. I don't want you to think you shouldn't buy ice cream if you'd like some. Or anything else, cream puffs, or whatever."

"Cream puffs?" she covered her mouth with her napkin to muffle a giggle before it became an unladylike snort. "I don't usually serve dessert. I suppose I could learn how to bake pies. It would be just like following any other recipe, wouldn't it? "

The mere thought of her tackling pastry was almost

more than he could bear. Surely he'd choke to death on her first crust. "I'm sure it is, but it would be much healthier if we saved desserts for the weekends and ate more fresh fruit during the week."

"Do the spiced peaches count?" she asked.

"Yes, they do, and fresh peaches will be delicious in the summer." They continued talking about fruit as they finished their ice cream and bought a quart of vanilla ice cream to take home. He added a jar of chocolate syrup to give the bland flavor a kick and began thinking about what movies were playing for tomorrow. He just wanted out of the house rather than to spend another placid afternoon at home.

Thursday, Hal had a question ready for Pearl and slid into her booth. "What's your favorite ice cream?" He held his breath, hoping she'd offer a flavor worth tasting.

Giving the question serious consideration, she turned the slender stem of her martini glass slowly in her gloved hands. "Anything with lots of chocolate. Some chocolate chip ice cream has only a sprinkling of chips, and I like it with a multitude of tiny slivers spread all through it. I love rocky road if it has lots of walnuts and marshmallows, chocolate swirl, if it's heavy on the swirl, or chocolate alone if it's thick and rich."

The way she'd looked at him as she stressed the word *thick*, sent his blood straight to his groin. He could barely breathe, let alone speak. "Chocolate sundaes are good," he finally got out.

She licked her pretty red lips. "Banana splits are my favorite. It's the only time I eat bananas." She glanced at her watch. "Time to go."

His thoughts were so befuddled he couldn't think of a polite way to ask where she had to be in such a rush. He just sat, unable to stand in a gentlemanly fashion before she walked away. There was a carving of a California golden bear by the entrance, and she reached out to touch his raised paw as she slipped out the door.

Mitch came to pick up her martini glass before Hal had taken a sip. "Do you want to finish this?"

"No thanks, not this time." He followed the bartender to the bar and found a young Chinese man seated on his usual stool. The fellow was slim and handsome with golden skin, and wore his black hair slicked back. His dark suit was well-tailored and an expensive gold watch hung loose on his wrist. Hal took the stool beside him.

"Lou King," the man said, and slid his business card toward Hal. "I'm a bail bondsman, should you ever have need of one."

Hal picked up the card. "I hope not, but I'll keep it just in case. Hal Marten, I'm with California West Insurance." He handed Louis one of his cards. The firm had a silhouette of a giant sequoia as their logo.

"Insurance?" Louis nodded thoughtfully. "A beneficial concept when one lacks a large and affluent family."

"Even if you're blessed with an abundance of wealthy relatives, there's undoubtedly an insurance need you've overlooked."

Lou nodded thoughtfully. "I'll keep your card should one arise," he responded, and slipped it into his suit coat pocket. "It was nice to meet you, but night court keeps me busy, and I need to be on my way."

Mitch came to their end of the bar. "Before you go, Lou, what do you suppose the bail will be when they finally arrest someone for the Black Dahlia murder?"

Lou stood and straightened his coat sleeves. "There will be no bail set for such a gruesome case, and even if there were, I'd not handle it."

"Why not?" Hal asked, genuinely curious. "Do you make your decisions based on the crime, or do you have to believe in a man's innocence before you'll handle his bail?"

The Chinese man responded with a rueful smile. "I'm a businessman, and guilt or innocence doesn't concern me, but I don't want something as sinister as the Black Dahlia murder contaminating my files. Good night."

"Good night." Hal drank only half of his beer before leaving for home and hoped he'd not need another excuse for being late.

Faye had been circling locations on a map of the gold fields, and when Hal came through the front door, she jumped up and hurried into the kitchen. "I found lots of haunted places in the Gold Country, love. We could visit them all in a single trip."

Hal hung up his coat and hat before surveying the map resting on her heap of library books. "It does look as though they're close. Maybe it's all the same ghost who's commuting on a celestial plane between these places."

Faye put Mr. Cuddles on the back porch with his dinner and brought the silverware to the table. "Can't be. Some are men and others are women. You've heard of Sutter's Mill where gold was discovered?"

"Sure, it's what brought the gold rush."

"Well, there was a doctor who had his own hospital nearby and while he did his best, often prospectors were too sick by the time they arrived at the hospital, and they died there."

"And are now ghosts?" he asked.

"Some are. The hospital is long gone, but there's a restaurant nearby that might be built over a burial ground. Sometimes the owner hears footsteps when there's no other person around. Others see a young woman there in a long dress, just a vague image, but people always describe the same girl."

Hal took his place as she brought in their plates. A photo in a cookbook might make the meatloaf crowded with mash potatoes and green beans look appetizing, but one taste would shatter the illusion. He waited for her to take her seat. "What about all the dead prospectors, aren't they floating around too?"

"There, and in other places, too. A lot of them met with misadventure," she countered impatiently. "You ought to read the books so we can plan the trip together."

"Sure, when I finish the one I'm reading, I'll start on them," he promised.

Surprised, she cocked her head slightly. "You mean it?"

He reached over to squeeze her hand. "Of course. If we're going to tour the Gold Country, I'll have to know where we're going." He didn't interrupt her again as she related another tale about a cemetery ghost that protected a crumbling tombstone where a family of three lay buried. It was a great spooky story perfect for a radio mystery, but he didn't look forward to standing out in a deserted cemetery waiting for a ghost to appear. He'd insist upon giving the effort a time limit, and thereby avoid the problem.

On Saturday, Hal measured all the rooms in their duplex and completed sketches showing where everything presently sat. "You see, that chair you liked would barely fit through the door, let alone in a corner of the living room or bedroom. Maybe we ought to just buy a couple of new lamps for the end tables by the sofa."

Faye turned on one. "Isn't the light bright enough now?"

"It isn't the brightness that's the problem, sweetheart. The lamp base is simply uninteresting. We bought things too quickly before we moved in so we'd not have to sit on the floor and read with a flashlight."

"Sometimes you're so silly, Hal."

Silly was not a word anyone else would ever use to describe him, but he smiled as though he were amused rather than insulted. "There's a new lamp store I pass every day on the Red Car. It might be a good place to begin rather than a department store."

"Could we stop again at Aunt Lucy's for ice cream?"

"We could. Will you try something new?"

"Why should I? I love vanilla, you know that."

"I certainly do." The Packard he'd owned before they'd gotten married sat in the garage most days. Faye drove it to the market, and they used it on the weekends, but the mileage remained low. It was a comfortable car that would make a trip through the back roads of the Gold Country bearable, but next year, he'd plan an adventure that would be a lot more fun. Maybe they'd drive to Arizona to see the Grand Canyon, anywhere new would suit him just fine.

CHAPTER 4

Carmen Espinoza came out her back door to empty her trash and saw Faye seated on her back stoop wiping away tears. The plump little woman set the wastebasket on her porch and slipped through the gate separating their yards. "Good heavens, what's happened, child? Has someone died?"

Embarrassed to have been caught weeping, Faye stood and wadded her handkerchief between her hands. "No one I know of. I'm just not sure what's happened, but Hal has changed. He's so restless now, and before he was such a steady sort. It's why I married him."

"Come have a cup of tea with me," Carmen invited, "and maybe we can sort this out."

Faye followed her neighbor through her back door. In Carmen's side of the duplex, the rooms were reversed to their side, and it always made Faye a bit dizzy to visit her. She sank into the sofa and picked up one of the floral needlepoint pillows Carmen delighted in creating. She rested her elbows on the pillow while Carmen prepared the tea. "I'm not sure where to begin," she called to her.

Carmen had already had the teakettle on the stove and entered carrying a tray with two cups of tea, and a small crystal bowl of sugar cubes. "Do you take sugar?" she asked.

"No, thank you, plain is fine." Faye took her cup and blew across it to cool the golden tea. She waited for Carmen to take the chair on her right. "Hal is a very responsible man. That's why he's been promoted several times. He can be depended upon to handle whatever assignment he's given, no matter how difficult."

"That's an excellent trait in a man. I adored Arnold, my first husband, but Lord help us, it was a challenge for him to get through the day."

Faye's eyes widened. "Your first husband? How many have you had?"

"Only three," Carmen responded with a shrug. "Arnold was killed in a car accident that was entirely his own fault. His attention wandered, and wham, he was gone."

Faye took a sip of tea. It had a cinnamon flavor she liked. "I'm so sorry. Were you very young?"

"Twenty-two when I lost him. My second husband, Carlos, he was as steady a man as you describe your Hal to be. We had three sons, delightful boys, who are a big help to me now that they're grown. Carlos had a weak heart, and when I lost him, one of his friends was so anxious to offer comfort, I thought we'd have a happy marriage. Unfortunately, he proved to be a heavy drinker, and I divorced him and went back to using Carlos's last name."

Faye stared at her neighbor. They'd talked on several occasions, but their chats had never grown this personal. She could easily imagine Carmen being slender and pretty when young, but she was still amazed the white-haired woman could have been married three times. "You do have a lot of experience with marriage then, don't you?"

"Yes, I most certainly do. Now you say Hal has grown restless? Tell me how."

"He used to be content to stay home on the weekends, but now he's always looking for somewhere to go. We go shopping, but never buy much. We've always gone out to dinner on Saturday night. I love Clifton's Cafeteria, but now he chooses a different place each week. It started with a restaurant in China Town, then a Mexican restaurant. We went for Italian food last week. Does that strike you as odd?"

Carmen pursed her lips. "Well, he does appear to be looking for variety, but that's not a bad thing."

"I suppose not, but still, it worries me. He used to be content to work the crossword puzzle on Sunday, but now he's decided we ought to go to the movies. We saw *The Bishop's Wife* this week."

"With Cary Grant as the angel? *Arsenic and Old Lace* was my favorite of his, but I love whatever he stars in, don't you?"

"Yes, I do," Faye admitted shyly. "We usually talk about movies after we've seen them, but this week, Hal just laughed and said we're as likely to see an angel as a ghost. Do you believe in ghosts?"

Carmen hesitated to reply and took a long swallow of tea. "Well, I've never seen one myself, but other people have."

"Exactly! We're planning to go up to the Gold Rush country on our vacation and look for some."

"Ghost hunting? Although Hal doesn't believe in them?"

"No, he doesn't, but I do, and I'm planning the trip. If we stay in The Cary House in Placerville, we're likely to see ghosts. Almost everyone who stays at that hotel does."

"Really? I'll look forward to hearing all about your trip. A nice vacation will give you a chance to relax and enjoy yourselves. Maybe your husband is concerned about something at work and simply doesn't want to burden you with it."

"Do you really think that's all it could be? The other night, I woke up, and he wasn't in bed with me. He was standing in the living room looking out at the street. I didn't know what to say, so I went back to bed and left him alone."

Carmen reached out to touch Faye's knee. "That's probably very wise. I doubt he was thinking of another woman when you're such a pretty girl. In fact, you can dismiss that thought as absurd. Would you like more tea?"

Shocked, Faye sat back. "I've never even considered another woman." Horrified by the possibility, she began to cry with huge gulping sobs.

"Oh dear, I'm so sorry. I shouldn't have said such a thoughtless thing. Please forgive me. Maybe what Hal needs is a hobby, like playing tennis or golf. Does he have an interest in sports?"

Faye wiped her eyes. Her lashes were long and dark, and she didn't wear mascara or it would have run clear to her chin that morning. "Sports? Well, don't most men like sports?"

"Yes, but maybe he needs to get out and play himself to run off the energy that's made him so restless. I don't mean to be indelicate, but what about s-e-x? Are things going well there?"

A bright red blush filled Faye's cheeks. "Very well, at least I think they are. If anything he's become more ardent. That isn't bad, is it?"

"No, of course not," Carmen assured her. "You mustn't expect Hal to be the same man every day. Sometimes he's bound to be preoccupied by problems at work, and other days, he'll be more carefree. You don't feel the same way every day, do you?"

Faye sniffed. "Pretty much, yes." She finished the last of her tea and stood. "Thank you, I need to stop crying right now so my eyes won't be puffy when Hal gets home tonight. It would upset him if he thought I'd sat home crying all day."

"Hal sounds like a wonderful husband, dear. Hang onto him."

"Oh, I intend to." Faye went out the back door, and stopped to look at their small backyard. A gardener came each week to mow the lawn front and back, but it could use some color. She'd ask Hal about it that night and see what he said.

Hal was amazed Faye had come up with the idea on her own, and he needed a gulp of water before he could reply. "You're right, the yard would be much prettier with a flower border. Let's go to the nursery on Saturday and see what they suggest. March shouldn't be too early to plant flowers in southern California."

"You like the idea?" she asked.

"Yes, of course, I do. Whenever you think of something you'd like to do, just tell me. You're here all day with only Mr. Cuddles for company, so you'll see what needs to be added long before I will."

Faye regarded him with a wide, loving smile. "You're a wonderful husband, Hal. You know that, don't you?"

"Thank you, you're a wonderful wife," he replied, but his heart sank even as he spoke the words.

That Thursday, Pearl was dressed in a gray suit with black trim and a matching veiled cocktail hat. She looked as beautiful as always, and Hal could no longer contain his curiosity. "You're always dressed in the latest fashions. Do you work for a ladies' magazine or with a designer, or perhaps you're one yourself?"

She sent a lazy glance toward the men seated at the bar before she smiled at him. "Thank you, but I simply wish to be presentable. There must be a great deal involved in designing clothes, or running a magazine. It must be exhausting."

"I'm sure it is," he replied, sorry his question hadn't prompted her to confide more. He didn't want to just stare at her, but her red lipstick made her mouth so alluring, it was difficult to look away. "Creative people love their work though, don't they? Do artists complain about the effort it took to complete a painting?"

She dipped her head and looked up at him through her veil. "Never, they have too much pride in the finished work they're eager to display. I'm reading Irving Stone's book about Vincent Van Gogh, *Lust for Life*. It's a rather tragic tale."

Greatly relieved she'd offered a topic he could pursue, he leaned in slightly. "Tell me about Van Gogh." He loved to hear her talk, her voice was soft, as though revealing secrets, and sometimes fell to a sexy breathy whisper. He forgot all about time, but all too soon, she glanced at her watch, and was ready to go. He rose, but she shook her head, silently forbidding him to follow. He carried his beer to the bar, and Lou, the bail bondsman, had again taken the stool he thought of as his.

Mitch dried a clean glass on a towel. "Looks like you and the lady are fast becoming friends. Why don't you leave with her?"

Hal shrugged. "We both have places to go."

"Does she have a husband?" Lou asked.

"She's never come in here with him if she does," Mitch offered. "She's always alone."

Lou nodded thoughtfully. "That doesn't mean she doesn't have a husband who works late." He turned to Hal. "Whatever you do, avoid becoming involved in a love triangle. Believe me, they're always more trouble than they're worth."

"And you'd know?" Hal asked with a skeptically raised brow.

Lou laughed. "I earn my living providing a service to people who've fallen into desperate situations. I'm warning you about a particularly nasty one to avoid. Consider it a favor."

"Thanks, I will." Hal swallowed the last of his beer and left in time to catch the next Red Car home. Pearl always wore gloves, so she could be hiding a wedding ring, but he thought it more likely that Mitch was right, and she'd lost a husband or lover in the war. No one in the bar knew he had a wife though, so if there were a love triangle brewing, he'd be the one creating it.

* * *

That evening Mr. Cuddles jumped into Hal's lap and eyed him coldly. He raised his hands rather than pet the ample-sized feline. "Faye, what does he want?"

"Probably just a snuggle. He's finally warming to you, Hal. Give him a few pats before you put him down."

Hal set his book aside and stroked the cat with a light tentative touch. His fur was silky smooth and not unpleasant, but Hal simply didn't like the yellow-eyed beast. He lifted him and was surprised by how much he weighed. Mr. Cuddles jumped out of his grasp, and landed on the carpet with a thud. The pampered pet walked away in a proud strut to his preferred perch by the window.

"How long have you had Mr. Cuddles?" he asked his wife.

"I got him as a kitten four years ago. He should live to be at least twenty, if we're lucky, maybe even longer."

Appalled the cursed cat would be around nearly forever, Hal left his chair, went into the kitchen for a drink of water and out into the backyard for some fresh air. He needed to measure the flowerbeds before they went to the nursery to be certain they bought enough flowers. It was too dark now, but he'd remember to do it first thing Saturday morning.

Faye followed him out into the yard. "Chrysanthemums would be good for the yard, wouldn't they?"

"Yes, they're pretty, but they might be better in the fall. The nursery should have spring flowers, pansies, snapdragons, something pretty even if they won't last through the summer." They had only a small slab of concrete by the back door rather than a nice patio, but it was enough to inspire him. "We could use a couple of outdoor chairs and a table so we could sit out here on warm evenings. Let's see what we find on Saturday after we've been to the nursery."

"Sure, I love to go shopping with you." She took his hand as they returned to the house, and squeezed his fingers before letting go.

* * *

Hal drew doodles on the edge of his calendar. Meetings he'd have to attend, or lead himself, were noted in block letters. The deadlines for monthly sales reports due in California West's headquarters in San Francisco were noted in red. The men he oversaw were achieving at a pace that would put the office above their monthly goal for March. He'd congratulate them, but he was also concerned they were doing so well headquarters would raise their quota. He tapped his pencil on his desk in a staccato rhythm. He couldn't tell his crew to slow down, but he didn't want them to burnout on the job either.

He got up to look out the window. The day was windy and clear, a good day for selling insurance, as every day was. He drew in a deep breath and released it slowly. There was far more to life than work, however, and he'd warn his salesmen against neglecting their personal life. Volunteer work always looked good on a résumé when a man came up for a review or promotion, and he'd mention that too. He returned to his desk and took out a sheet of paper to make notes for a sales meeting that would have nothing whatsoever to do with sales.

Pearl was dressed in dark blue that night. As Hal joined her, he longed to spend more time with her than a few precious minutes once a week. Faye would believe him if he told her volunteering for a charity would enhance his résumé, and it would give him an excuse for coming home late on Thursday nights. But the thought of lying to his wife made him sick to his stomach.

"Why so serious?" Pearl asked.

Rather than waste a minute with the truth, Hal forced a smile. "Just a thought of something I should have included in notes for a sales meeting, I won't bore you with it. What are you reading this week?" He relaxed when she mentioned an author he knew and their conversation flowed as smoothly as he'd hoped, until she glanced at her watch. He wanted to ask her to stay, but when he was expected at home, he couldn't. "I wish we had more time."

"So do I," Pearl responded, and she brushed her hand over his shoulder in a soft caress before heading toward the door.

Faye invited Carmen to come over and enjoy their new patio furniture. The redwood chairs had bright floral padded cushions to make them comfortable, and the small round redwood table was the perfect size for a pitcher of lemonade and glasses.

"It's warm enough this morning to sit outside, isn't it?" Faye asked.

"Yes, let's enjoy the pleasant weather before it grows too hot. I love the pansies you've planted. I ought to buy some too."

"Thank you." Faye bit her lip, but couldn't contain herself for long. "Hal has bought a couple of new suits. He wears a suit everyday for work, but he's become more concerned about his appearance. Maybe it's all in my mind, but since you mentioned another woman…"

Carmen raised her hands. "Please, I never should have said such a silly thing. I spend too much time listening to the soaps on the radio, and they need constant turmoil among the characters to keep everyone listening and buying detergent. It doesn't mean that your Hal is two-timing you the way the soap opera characters always are. If a businessman needs a new suit or two, there's nothing even remotely sinister about it."

"You don't think?" Faye poured Carmen a glass of lemonade. She lacked the patience to squeeze lemons, and it came in a bottle at the market and was quite good. She poured herself a glass too.

"No, I don't. Does he come home late at night with lipstick on his collar and smelling of perfume?"

Faye laughed in spite of herself. "No, he's here every night for dinner, although sometimes he prepares for Friday meetings and is home a few minutes later on Thursdays."

Carmen took in the pretty yard. "A man needs more

than a few minutes to pursue another woman."

"Maybe he meets her on the Red Car," Faye suggested.

"There's no romance going on with people riding the Red Car," Carmen assured her. "They're crowded and someone is always getting on or off."

"At his office then," Faye proposed.

"Has he described his secretary?" Carmen asked.

"Yes, Mrs. Adams is a grandmother who's been with the company for years. I don't think she'd appeal to him."

"Go look in the mirror, Faye. You're far too pretty to worry over other women."

"I know, but..."

Carmen turned in her chair to face her young friend more directly. "You need to put your mind at rest. There's a detective who has an office near the market. Do you have enough money set aside to hire him for a day or two? That would probably be all you'd need."

Faye nodded. "I've seen the sign on the window above the drug store, Discreet Investigations."

"Yes, that's the place. Now have you been listening to Our Gal Sunday? It's my favorite on the radio. I love the idea of an orphan from Colorado marrying a titled lord. Not that we see many wealthy Englishmen in this neighborhood."

"No, not a one," Faye agreed. "I like that show too." She drew in a deep breath to relax and enjoy their pretty yard, but while they continued to talk about the characters on popular radio serials, she couldn't recall even one who'd ever hired a private detective.

CHAPTER 5

Joe Ezell took the name of his firm, Discreet Investigations, seriously. He bought his suits right off the manikins in the windows of the Salvation Army thrift shop. He didn't particularly care about the fit if the clothes were close to his size. Some of his jackets were too large and some trousers a bit short, but they were good enough for undercover work. In cold weather, he added an overcoat that had seen more than a little wear. People remembered a man in an expensive suit, but his goal was to go unnoticed in a crowd. His work required a lot of walking, and his one extravagance was a pair of fine leather oxfords. They were a necessity as he saw it, and no one ever looked at a man's feet.

Despite possessing little in the way of natural talent, he'd once hoped to become a golf pro. WWII had ended his dream by keeping him away from the game for too long. He'd served in the Coast Guard on the Greenland patrol. In addition to protecting the cryolite mines that were needed for refining aluminum, they forecast the weather for Europe. With few outlets for entertainment, he'd begun reading mysteries. He thought Dashiell Hammett's Sam Spade detective stories were the best, but he liked Agatha Christie's Hercule Poirot too. At the end of the war, he'd found few jobs available for forecasting the weather, and had become a detective instead.

He'd found a private detective's manual written by a man who'd been with the Pinkerton Detective Agency. It provided the basics, and he'd studied and passed the test for a private investigator's license. With his new knowledge combined with what he'd learned from detective novels, he considered himself fully prepared for the job and had opened Discreet Investigations last fall. He'd thought a classy name would attract clients who could pay well, but so far, the clients who had trickled in had had modest budgets, which unfortunately forced him to do likewise. It did leave him time to play golf, however.

Most of his cases involved gathering photos of a straying spouse to provide grounds for a divorce. It usually involved spending hours doing surveillance from his car, lying in wait, he liked to call it, to get a photo of someone trespassing outside their marriage vows. A few cautious people had come to him before they got too deeply involved with someone new.

That's how he'd met his girlfriend, Mary Margaret McBride. She'd been his first client. She was a nurse at the VA hospital and had been engaged to a handsome sailor she'd met there. She didn't want to misjudge him, but she wasn't certain she could trust him either.

Joe had found her fiancé stepped out on her so often he'd taken a dozen photos of him leaving a variety of women's apartments. He became an accomplished photographer from that case alone. He hadn't believed women would actually greet a man at their door dressed in filmy negligees like they did in the movies, but some sure did.

Upon hearing his report, Mary Margaret had promptly jettisoned her unfaithful fiancé and fallen into Joe's arms that very week. She was a sweetheart and cooked the best pot roast he'd ever tasted. When she'd hinted that she'd welcome a marriage proposal, he'd convinced her to give herself plenty of time between engagements to be certain she knew exactly what she wanted in a man. He thought they might marry some day, but he was in no hurry to make it any time soon.

When Faye Marten peeked in his office door, neatly stenciled with Discreet Investigations in gold, he'd stood to welcome her. All he had was a desk and swivel chair he'd bought at a secondhand store, and oak chairs from the same place. He'd bought a new Underwood typewriter, because he needed the best for his reports. While also new, the four-drawer gray file cabinet standing in the corner contained a scant dozen files. He couldn't afford a secretary, but it looked like a detective's office to him, and so far, the furnishings had been convincing enough for his clients as well.

"Come in and sit down," he greeted her. "I'm Joe Ezell, and I'd love to help you solve whatever problem you might have." He motioned her into one of the straight-back chairs facing his desk and took his own padded chair behind it.

Faye looked around the sparsely furnished office and shrugged slightly. "I'm not certain I even have a problem."

Joe used yellow legal pads to note a client's initial information and reached for one and his pen. "Let's begin with your name."

"Faye Marten, that's with an e, not an i. My husband's name is Hal, Harold really, but everyone calls him Hal. He's with California West Insurance."

The detective asked for her address and telephone number as well. "Now tell me, Mrs. Marten, what brings you here today."

She fidgeted in her chair and grasped her purse more tightly. "You may think this is very silly of me."

"I take all problems seriously, my dear. When did you notice, or become aware of what might be a problem?"

"Several weeks ago, I guess. I've no evidence at all,

nothing to bring in or point to really, it's just an uneasy feeling that my husband has changed."

"In what way?" Joe asked.

Faye related the same concerns she'd shared with her neighbor, Carmen. "What I want I suppose, is simply reassurance that nothing is wrong, and that Hal is the same man he's always been."

"Of course. You shouldn't doubt your misgivings, however. Why don't I observe your husband, discreetly, of course, for a few days and see if anything is amiss." He requested all the information he'd need, learned about Hal's service during the war, and was pleased she'd thought to bring a photograph he could slip into his pocket. He explained his fees, and gave her a reassuring smile.

"Do you want to be paid now?" Faye asked.

"Fifty dollars should cover my initial expenses. Will it be a problem for you?"

"No, not at all. Hal is very generous, and I'm thrifty, so I've more than enough set aside for whatever I want to do."

"That's very wise of you," Joe remarked. She handed him cash, and he wrote her a receipt and walked her to the door. "Just continue your life in your usual manner, and let's meet again at this time next week."

"Thank you, Mr. Ezell. Good-bye."

Joe closed his door behind her and leaned back against it. From what she'd said, her husband was either in his office, or on his way to and from there. They were together on the weekends, so there weren't any of the huge gaps in time that his other clients had reported. If Hal Marten were straying on Faye, he had to be damn quick about it. He laughed to himself, because it didn't matter whether he caught the man in the act or not, he'd already been paid.

Faye passed the building custodian on her way out. He was a burly black man with a near blinding smile. "Have a nice afternoon, miss," he said.

"Thank you," she replied and went on her way, still uncertain whether or not she'd done the right thing in coming to Discreet Investigations.

That night, Joe ate at Mary Margaret's apartment. She'd prepared the pork chops with corn bread dressing he loved. "With cooking this good, I swear you should open a restaurant. You're sure to make a fortune."

Mary Margaret was petite, five feet two inches tall with fiery-red hair and freckles, which everyone said made her look as cute as a bug. "And where would I find the resources for such an enterprise? I could hardly save it from my nurse's salary."

She was always so practical, a trait Joe feared he frequently lacked. "If you invited the president of a bank to dinner, he'd be sure to give you a loan."

"Which I'd have to pay back, and what if other people didn't love my cooking as much as you do? Then I'd have to close the restaurant, but the bank would still expect me to repay the loan. Where would I be then? No, it's far too risky a venture for me."

"I understand," he agreed thoughtfully. He'd found the phrase worked wonders whether he actually understood her reasoning or not. "Let me ask you something. If all a woman has is a feeling her husband is cheating on her, should she trust it, or shrug it off?"

"Trust it," Mary Margaret insisted. "I take it you're referring to a case, the details of which I don't expect you to divulge, by the way."

"Thank you. People usually come to me with strong suspicions, just as you did. A suspicion is more substantial than a mere feeling, isn't it?"

"Could be. Women tend to trust their intuition for a good reason."

"I suppose that's true," Joe admitted. "It's just difficult to know where to look if all the client has are *feelings*, and no clues, or facts, I can actually investigate."

"I'm sure you'll do your best."

"I'll give it my best shot. May I please have a little more stuffing?"

She kissed him and served him a delicious second helping. "Anything else I can do for you?"

Joe regarded her with an appreciative smile. "Let's wait until after dinner, but maybe we could save the dessert for later."

"Don't make it too late," she teased. "I have to be at work early in the morning."

He nodded. "So do I, but sometimes missing a little sleep is worth it."

She leaned in close. "Prove it."

He did.

Joe took to every investigation with a keen zest for his newfound profession. Early the next morning, he parked his car near the Marten's duplex and followed Hal, discreetly of course, to the Red Car station. The man walked briskly, with real purpose, and Joe had to hurry to keep up. He boarded the train after Hal, took a seat several rows behind him and pretended to look out the window while he watched him. Hal opened the first section of the *Los Angeles Times* he'd carried from home, and folded the newspaper neatly to allow him to read without disturbing the man seated beside him.

Joe carried a small notebook and jotted down his first impressions of Hal Marten. Hal was better looking than he had appeared in the small photograph Faye had given him. His gray suit fit his trim build handsomely, his shirt was snowy white, and his tie a maroon and gray stripe. Joe had only gotten a quick look at the man's shoes, but they held the same gleaming polish as a military officer's.

Once they reached the train station downtown, Joe wove his way through the crowded sidewalk to keep Hal in sight. When he reached his office building, he entered, and went to the bank of elevators. Joe walked on by to the coffee shop on the corner. He went in, sat down at the counter and had a cup of coffee and a hot cinnamon roll that was fresh from the oven and absolutely luscious. He wiped his fingers on his napkin and added a few more thoughts to his notes. So far, Hal had impressed him as being thoroughly professional.

He waited until ten o'clock to enter Hal's building and rode the elevator to the fifth floor. From the glass double doors at the entrance of the California West office, he could see men seated at multiple desks, many talking on the telephone. Faye had said Hal had his own private office, so Joe didn't see him, and he didn't want to call attention to himself by walking in to request information on life insurance. Instead, he went out for a walk and came back at noon to follow Hal as he walked alone down the street to a café that looked expensive. From what Joe could see, the place did a lively luncheon business. He waited ten minutes to be certain Hal would have been seated, and then went in to look at the menu. He saw Hal seated at a table alone, eating a sandwich, and turned around and walked out before Hal could catch sight of him.

He always had a book in his pocket and went down to MacArthur Park to read until time to follow Hal home. There was less vigor in Hal's step on the return to the Red Car station, which made him easier to follow. When they reached their station, Joe waited for Hal to head for home before he went in the same direction to get his car. He'd type up a detailed report for Faye Marten, but so far, he'd seen nothing to cause her any worry whatsoever.

He'd wait until Thursday afternoon to watch Hal a second time and maybe whatever caused him to arrive home a few minutes late would prove to be incriminating.

On Thursday, Hal watched the clock all afternoon and swore it often stood still. He couldn't be seen bolting out of the office ahead of his salesmen, so he had to remain at his desk several minutes after closing time, until they had all left for home. His secretary was always half out the door at six, and he wished her a good evening when she said good-bye.

Once he'd left the California West office, he had to wait so long for an elevator, he considered racing down the stairs, but finally the doors opened on one, and he rode down to the first floor. He hurried and caught the Red Car he'd hoped to catch, and arrived at the Golden Bear Lounge several minutes earlier than his usual time.

Pearl had worn her red suit, and looked as delicious as a cherry pie. "You look beautiful as always," he said in greeting.

"Thank you. I brought the Irving Stone book on Van Gogh, and thought you might want to read it."

She handed him her copy of *Lust for Life*, and Hal grinned as he accepted it. He was inordinately pleased that she'd brought him the book, and he'd tell Faye a salesman had loaned it to him. "Thank you. I'm sure I'll enjoy it." They conversed so easily now, and he relaxed and sat back in the booth. Mitch brought him a beer, and he thanked him.

"Do you like mysteries?" she asked, her voice a seductive query.

"I do. I listen to several on the radio, but haven't read one in a while," he told her.

"I picked up an Agatha Christie book, *Body in the Library*, because it has such an intriguing title. Rather than a gruff detective, there's a sweet little old lady, Miss Jane Marple, investigating the crime."

"How did the body come to be in the library?" he asked.

She responded with a mere hint of a giggle. "That's the whole story, and I've read only a few pages. One morning, an English couple awaken to find a stranger, a beautiful girl in an evening gown, dead in their library. The wife asks her friend Miss Marple to come and solve the crime."

"And, of course, she will," he said.

"Of course, no one would buy a writer's mysteries if he or she, failed to solve the crime. That's the essential element in mysteries, isn't it?"

"I suppose so." It was so easy to discuss their expectations for a novel, but all too soon, Pearl excused herself and left. He turned to watch her pat the carved bear's paw on her way out, but waited in the booth rather than join the men seated at the bar. He wished he knew where she was going in such a hurry, but if he asked her such a pointed question, he'd probably not see her again. He wouldn't risk it, and hoped someday she'd take him into her confidence and tell him on her own.

Joe had followed Hal into the Golden Bear and taken a stool at the bar. The bartender was friendly, and the easy conversation among the clientele made him feel welcome. He sipped a beer and kept his eye on Hal in the long mirror behind the bar. Hal had met a rare beauty, but they had only a brief conversation before she left. Joe laid his money on the bar intending to follow her, but he strolled out a few minutes later so it wouldn't be obvious. He looked both ways up and down the sidewalk, but she'd vanished. He hurried to the corner, but didn't find her walking down the side street either. She must have had a car parked close by, or someone had picked her up.

Disappointed he'd lost her, he went on to the train station to wait for Hal, who appeared within a few minutes. Joe rode home with him and hung back as Hal left the train at his stop. Hal went straight home, and Joe got into his car, and pulled out his notebook to make a few notes. He'd found the reason why Hal got home late on Thursdays, and he'd seen the woman pass him a book. Their conversation looked more casual to him than intimate. Perhaps she'd hidden a message in the book setting up a more romantic date. She could have written a love letter revealing feelings she'd concealed in the bar. Or maybe they were planning some criminal caper, but that was highly unlikely.

His first thought when he'd seen her was that she was a high-priced call girl. If so, Hal must expect far more than a brief chat. He prided himself on his surveillance work and was chagrined that she'd eluded him before he could follow her home. He could come back next Thursday and leave before she did to enable him to keep a better eye on her, but before he did any more work on the case, he needed to discuss his observations with Faye Marten. He dreaded the consultation, however.

Faye arrived early for her appointment at Discreet Investigations and waited on the bench in the hallway outside the office to collect herself first. She wanted the truth, but feared it would be too awful to hear. Rather than be late, she pushed herself to open the detective's door.

"Good afternoon, Mrs. Marten, please, come in." Joe stood to greet her with his most charming smile, and immediately felt guilty for not projecting a more serious demeanor.

He'd bought an electric coffee pot and offered her a cup, but she shook her head. "No, thank you. I'd rather just get this over with. What did you discover about my husband?"

She sat with her shoulders hunched, her hands clasped in her lap, clearly fearing the worst. To put her at ease, he began with the first page of his neatly typed report. "I followed your husband last Tuesday, and he went straight to his office, left to go to a café for lunch, which he ate alone, and he returned to work until closing time. I rode the Red Car with him both ways, and he had no interest in any of the other passengers."

"That's what I'd hoped," she offered, "but what about on Thursday? Did you follow him then?"

Joe had to swallow hard and take a drink of coffee that had already grown cold. He'd have to carry his mug down to the restroom at the end of the hall to empty and rinse it, which would be a thoughtless interruption.

Maybe he ought to get a plant so he could water it with cold coffee, if it wouldn't kill it. Alarmed by how far his thoughts had strayed, he quickly refocused his attention.

"Thursday after work, your husband rode the Red Car, but got off at one stop before his usual station. He went across the street to the Golden Bear Lounge."

"He stopped at a bar?" Astonished, her eyelashes nearly swept her brows.

"Yes, it's a nice place, not a dive." He paused and resumed his effort to be thoroughly professional with the remainder of his report. "He sat in a booth that was already occupied by a young women wearing a stylish red suit and veiled cocktail hat. Frankly, she looked as though she were on her way to some elegant party. She had dark hair worn in an upswept style. Does she sound like anyone you know?"

Huge tears filled Faye's eyes, and she pulled a handkerchief from her purse to dry them. "No, I don't know anyone like that. Could you overhear what they were saying?"

"No, but I did see her pass him a book. He left the Red Car at his usual station carrying it. Did he bring it home?"

She nodded. "He said someone in his office had loaned it to him, but from your description, she isn't one of his agents."

"No, I think not. I had hoped to follow her, but wasn't able to. Would you like me to observe your husband again next Thursday? I'll wait outside the Golden Bear, follow the woman if he sees her again and learn where she goes."

She shook her head. "No, I don't want to hear anything more. If he's meeting another women and keeping it from me, then our marriage is already as good as over."

Most clients were already so angry when they came to him seeking evidence to justify their rage, he seldom saw tears, but Faye Marten presented an entirely different type of encounter. "My dear, if you love your husband, please be patient. This could prove to be merely a brief flirtation, not a full-blown affair. If you confront your husband, you might push him into this other woman's arms. Frankly, she looked as though she had expensive tastes. Your husband has a good job, but does he earn enough money to entertain women on the side?"

"No, certainly not. We often discuss our budget, and he puts money into a savings account each month. He doesn't hide the bankbook, so I can check the balance whenever I wish. He's a serious person who doesn't waste money playing cards or betting on horses."

"He also impressed me as being a serious individual," Joe offered. "Perhaps this woman is someone he knew before the war. She might have merely wanted his advice on a problem she's facing."

Her eyes narrowed as she grew skeptical. "If that were true, he wouldn't have lied about where he got the book."

It was an acute observation he wished she hadn't reached. "I suppose not. Have I answered all your questions?" he asked.

"Yes, but now I'm sorry I ever came to you. Thank you, anyway, Mr. Ezell." She rose unsteadily to her feet, and he walked her to the door.

"Would you like to take a copy of my report?"

"No, I'd just brood over it. Good-bye."

"Should you ever need me again…."

"I won't. In the future, I'll know better than to pry into my husband's life."

Joe closed the door behind her, and returned to his desk to make a few notes on how their conversation had gone so he could do better the next time such an uncomfortable situation arose. He was tempted to go back to the Golden Bear on his own and follow the classy woman just to satisfy his own curiosity. It would probably be a waste of time, and he hoped he'd be working on another job by next Thursday.

There was enough time that afternoon to go out to the driving range and hit a bucket of balls. He did some of his best thinking while working to improve his swing, even if his overall game remained deeply disappointing.

Unwilling to go home just yet, Faye returned to the bench outside Discreet Investigations. She bit her lip rather than cry, but if Hal had lied to her about why he was late on Thursdays, or about a book, then she doubted she could trust his word about anything. That her husband wasn't the trustworthy man she'd thought he was broke her heart and home was the very last place she wished to go.

The custodian finished cleaning the restroom and came down the hall pushing his mop and bucket. Faye looked so forlorn, he stopped beside her and whispered, "Are you all right, miss? I could bring you a drink of water."

"No, thank you. It wouldn't help."

"You been talking to Mr. Ezell?" he asked.

She nodded. "Now I wish I hadn't."

He parked his mop and bucket against the opposite wall. "I'm Cleotis Cotton, and everyone calls me CC. Maybe it's because I've got such big ears, but I'm real good at listening if you'd care to tell me why you're so sad."

She looked up at him and didn't think his ears looked all that large. He had such a kind expression, and engaging smile, and she was in desperate need of sympathy. Gulping back her tears, she explained why she'd come to Discreet Investigations, and what Joe had reported. She'd hoped her concerns about her husband would prove to be unfounded. Now that her worst fears had been realized, however, she was desperate to get rid of the woman in red.

She dried her eyes on a tissue. "I don't suppose you know a hit man?" she asked.

CC took a step back. "That's a mighty strange question for such a sweet little lady to ask. These things have a way of working themselves out without any need for violence."

"So I should just go on home and pretend I don't know Hal's meeting a beautiful woman at the Golden Bear Lounge?"

"I know that place," he answered.

"Do you think I should go there next Thursday afternoon and catch them together?"

"Oh no, you ought not to stir up more trouble than you've already got, young lady. Just go on home and fix your man a fine dinner and make him forget he ever knew another woman."

Faye rose slowly. "I doubt pretending nothing's wrong will work, but I suppose I could try it for a little while."

"That's right. Just go on home and have yourself some ice cream, and you'll feel better right away."

"I'll have to buy some ice cream on the way. Thank you, CC. Talking to you really was helpful."

He gave a slight bow. "My pleasure. You have yourself a nice afternoon now."

She hadn't thought she could, but maybe eating ice cream and pretending everything was as it should be was all she could do for the time being. Her head ached so badly she didn't see how she could do anything more for now, but she wasn't sharing Hal with another woman, not now, not ever.

Cleotis entered Joe's office to empty the trash. "How are you this afternoon, sir?" he asked.

Joe looked up and sat back in his chair. "I'll tell you, CC, I really like having my own business and the work I'm doing, but once I give a client my report, I can't help but wonder what will happen next."

"Is that a fact?" The custodian waited by the door.

"If I find a man is cheating on his wife, well, maybe not cheating, but looking like he wants to, how do I know what the wife will do with that information?"

"Are you talking about that pretty little lady who just left?"

"You saw her? Sweet girl, but her husband has eyes for

what looked to me like an expensive call girl."

"Then he's definitely on the wrong path, and someone ought to do something about it. Does she have a daddy who can set her husband straight?" CC asked.

"She didn't mention any family, so I guess not. I'll just have to hope for the best for them."

"You fond of mysteries, sir?"

Joe laughed. "Not the ones I can't solve."

The custodian emptied the office wastebasket into a large can in the hall, returned and replaced it by the desk. "I don't suppose you can keep investigating?"

Joe got up to stretch. "No, that would merely be snooping, and I need to devote my time to new cases that will pay the rent."

CC began to close the office door on his way out. "Makes sense. You have yourself a nice afternoon now."

"Thanks, CC. See you tomorrow." The telephone rang, and to avoid looking desperate, Joe waited three rings before he answered. "Discreet Investigations," he said with a firm confidence. The man calling asked for directions to his office, and Joe jotted down the prospective client's name so he'd be ready when he got there. He went down the hall to rinse his coffee mug, and eager to take on a new case, he dismissed all thought of Faye Marten's wandering husband.

CHAPTER 6

Hal thought Faye seemed remarkably subdued that night, and it wasn't like her. "Are you not feeling well? You're not usually so quiet."

"What? Oh no, I'm fine, just looking forward to the summer when we can take our vacation trip."

He smiled and nodded. "It should be fun even if we don't see any ghosts."

"We're going where everyone says they are, so unless they're hiding, we're sure to find at least one."

"Let's hope it's a quiet, friendly ghost then." Clearly she was excited by the trip, and he'd make certain she had a good time. He always did. Each time he went to the Golden Bear Lounge, he put himself another step closer to the worst kind of mistake. He had to put a stop to it now. That decided, he squared his shoulders and told himself the coming Thursday would be his last stop at the bar. He just needed to see Pearl one last time to say good-bye.

Thursday was overcast with a threat of rain that held off all day. After lunch, Hal made notes for what he wished to say to Pearl. It wasn't nearly as easy as preparing remarks for a sales meeting, but he felt he ought to say something profound. Even if not deep, then something meaningful to let her know she'd touched him, even if they'd only had a few brief conversations. He certainly understood himself better for it.

When his enlistment was over at the end of the war, he'd hoped to make up for lost time, marry, have a family and move up the corporate ladder with a good firm. California West offered the most opportunities for advancement, although the work seldom posed a real challenge. He'd met Faye and thought her adorable. Neither of them had families to attend their wedding at the courthouse, but he'd thought they'd create a beautiful one of their own. They still would, he was sure of it. If he needed more than Faye could possibly give, then he'd damn well join civic groups that would keep him occupied without offering any damning temptations.

That settled, he passed the afternoon with his usual mix of work and left right on time. When he reached the Golden Bear, he nodded a hello to Mitch, Lou King, the bail bondsman, and the veterans as he walked back to Pearl's booth. She was dressed in the black suit with her frivolous veiled hat, and so beautiful she took his breath away.

Now he could ask the question he'd been afraid to until now. "Where are you going in such a rush when you leave here?"

She sipped her martini, and licked her bright red lips. "Why do you ask?"

"Because I've always wondered, and I won't see you again." There, he'd said it out loud, and he meant it.

"Are you going away?"

"No, but I've obligations I should see to after work." He feared he sounded cold, and that wasn't his intention at all. "Meeting you has been a wonderful surprise, but it's time for me to concentrate on other things."

"You needn't apologize," she replied, her tone as intimate as a kiss. She raised her martini glass. "Here's to friendship."

Mitch set a beer in front on him, and Hal raised it to add to her toast. "This was much better than friendship."

She responded in a husky sigh, "Hal, you are the sweetest man. I wish you good luck in all you mean to do."

"Thank you. You still haven't told me where you go," he reminded her.

"No, I haven't, but a woman should always keep a bit of mystery." He rose with her, and she reached up to kiss his cheek. "Good-bye."

He had to bite his lip to choke back a moan as she moved out the door on her spiked heels. She had a dancer's grace, and he'd never asked if she loved to dance. It was too late to ask her anything, and he felt overwhelmed with loss. He had just carried his beer to a stool at the bar when the sound of gunfire exploded in the street.

"Nobody move!" Mitch shouted. "If there's trouble outside, we're not inviting it in here."

One of the veterans moved off his stool. "Someone may need help."

"I'll go with you," Hal offered.

Mitch moved out from behind the bar. "Fine, play Boy Scouts, but wait a minute to make certain the next shot doesn't hit one of you."

"That's fair," the veteran offered.

Hal looked at the clock behind the bar and waited exactly one minute. There had been no more gunfire, so he walked to the door, opened it a crack and looked out. There was no one in the street, but Pearl lay on the sidewalk, blood streaming from what was left of her face. "Dear God," he cried. "Call the police. Pearl's been shot." He went to her, but she was so obviously dead, he could do nothing more than kneel at her side and hold her small, gloved hand.

It had begun to rain by the time the police arrived, and they covered Pearl's body with a blue tarp. Hal felt sick to his stomach and couldn't bear to think of her lying on the cold sidewalk. He hated to leave her alone, and reluctantly went back into the bar as ordered. A detective with the Los Angeles Police Department, Jacob Lynch, insisted upon taking everyone's name and personal information before they were allowed to leave.

Hal used the payphone on the wall by the men's room to call Faye and let her know he'd be late. He tried to come up with an excuse before she answered, but the phone just rang and rang. Thinking he'd dialed the wrong number, he took more care a second time, but again, Faye failed to answer. It wasn't like her not to be home, and it worried him. He took a stool at the bar, but refused Mitch's offer of a drink on the house.

Mitch wiped away a tear. "She was such a beautiful woman, who could have wanted her dead?"

"Maybe they were after her purse, and she fought them," Lou King offered.

"Her purse lay beside her," Hal said. "She never told me where she was going, but…."

"You think someone she knew killed her?" Mitch asked.

"I don't even want to think about it," Hal responded, but he couldn't get the horrible sight of her lying in a pool of her own blood out of his mind. It just kept repeating like a flipbook he'd race through again and again until the pages bruised his thumb. When Det. Lynch came to him, he offered his name, address and the telephone number at home and at work and hoped he'd be done with it. "Am I free to go?"

Lynch looked to be in his late forties, with a slight sprinkling of gray in his dark hair. He wore a well-tailored overcoat over his suit, and his manner was coolly professional. "I need only a few more minutes of your time." He reviewed his notes. "When the first officers arrived, you identified the deceased as Pearl LaFosse. What was your relationship to her?"

Uncertain, Hal shrugged. "We'd just spoken here a few

times. I wouldn't call it a relationship."

Lynch jotted a note. "All right, but clearly you're disturbed by her death."

The regulars seated at the bar all looked equally distraught to Hal. "We're all way past disturbed," he stressed. "You might be used to seeing young women shot dead in the street, but we're not."

"Just be patient with me a little longer, Mr. Marten. Did you hear an argument, loud words of any kind before the shots?"

"No. Pearl walked out the door, and a few seconds later we heard two shots and found her dead."

"What can you tell me about her?"

Feeling utterly empty, Hal took a deep breath and released it slowly. "Nothing really. We talked about artists, books, but nothing personal."

Lynch looked at him askance. "You looking to hold book club meetings here?"

"No, of course not, it was just casual conversation. I need to go home. My wife didn't answer the phone, and I don't want her to worry that I've been in an accident."

Lynch handed Hal his card. "If your wife doesn't turn up in an hour or two, give me a call."

"I doubt that she's missing," Hal countered. "She probably had to make a quick trip to the market is all."

Lynch looked at his watch, and it was nearly nine o'clock now. "Kind of late for grocery shopping. Did she know about you and Pearl?"

"What? There is, or was, no 'me and Pearl'. I just came in once in a while to have a beer on the way home from work."

"Your wife okay with that?" the detective inquired.

Hal noticed Mitch edging closer and lowered his voice. "She was fine with it. I never stay more than a half-hour or so. I wouldn't still be here at closing time."

"That's right," Mitch added. "He's not a man to linger."

"All right then," Lynch responded. "Go on home, but if your wife isn't there with dinner waiting, give me a call."

Hal understood what the detective was implying and completely dismayed, he had to suppress a cold shudder. "You can't think she had anything to do with this."

"It's too early in our investigation to say. Do you own a gun?"

"No, I wouldn't have one in the house." Hal felt as though he were sinking ever deeper into a wretched quagmire of his own making.

"Fine. Just let me know if your wife doesn't turn up tonight."

"I'm sure she will." Hal nodded to Mitch and headed for the door. The coroner had come for Faye's body, but Hal walked carefully around the place where she'd fallen and rushed to catch the next Red Car for home.

There weren't any lights on in their side of the duplex, and as Hal came through the front door, he switched on every one he passed. Faye had baked the meatloaf and it sat in its Pyrex dish, covered just the way she'd baked it. She'd peeled and sliced the potatoes and left them in a pot filled with water ready to boil. The cans of green beans and gravy were unopened on the counter.

"Faye?" Thinking she might have fallen ill, he hurried to their bedroom, but the bed was neatly made, just as she'd left it that morning. A quick check of the bathroom showed only a tiled room with shiny fixtures and towels neatly hung on the racks.

Mr. Cuddles meowed loudly, and wove his way through Hal's legs forcing him to move carefully to avoid tripping over the big cat. "What's the matter with you? Can't stand having to wait for dinner?"

Ignoring their pet's pitiful meows, Hal searched for a note, but couldn't find one. He went next door to Carmen Espinoza's hoping Faye might have gone to help their neighbor. "Hello, I hate to bother you, but I came home late, and Faye isn't here. I wondered if she might be with you."

Carmen opened the door to invite him in, but he

remained on the porch. "I haven't seen Faye since this morning when she was out in your backyard watering the flowers. We exchanged hellos and went on about our own business. Could she be with a friend?"

Faye had never introduced him to any friends, and he wasn't sure she had any. He looked up the street, but it was too dark for her to be out for a walk. "No, I don't think so. I'll just stay home and wait for her. Thank you, Carmen."

"Have her call me when she comes home so I won't worry. She has my number."

"I'll do that." He went around to the garage and found their Packard gone. Faye had never been angry with him, and he sincerely doubted she could have been so upset with him arriving home late tonight that she'd have gone to the movies alone, or anywhere else for that matter.

He went inside and opened a can of cat food for Mr. Cuddles. The ungrateful cat woofed it down, and then turned his back on him and sauntered to his pillow by the window. "You are such great company," Hal called after him. "Anyone ever tell you that?" The cat closed his eyes and ignored him.

Hal's stomach had been clenched in a tight knot since he'd found Pearl dead, and he couldn't bear the thought of food. He put the meatloaf in the refrigerator along with the pot containing the potatoes and set the cans of green beans and gravy in the cupboard. He hadn't noted the time when he'd gotten home, but made a note of it now. He hung up his overcoat and suit jacket, but couldn't just stare at the wall while waiting for his wife to appear. Pacing the living room wasn't satisfying either.

By eleven o'clock, Faye should have been home even if she'd gone to the movies, and he pulled Detective Lynch's card from his pocket. He hesitated to call him, but if something had happened to Faye, he ought not to wait until tomorrow morning to report her missing. He reached for the telephone.

CHAPTER 7

Jacob Lynch glanced around the neatly kept living room. "This looks like a furniture showroom. Do you actually live here?"

"Yes, of course we do." Hal was suffering through the worst day of his life, and he had only a weak grasp on his temper. "Both my wife and I like to keep things in good order. Is it a crime?"

"Settle down, Mr. Marten. What did you find when you first came home?"

Hal was a long way from settled, and he needed a moment to organize his thoughts. "There were no lights on, which struck me as odd. Faye had begun preparing dinner in the kitchen, but apparently left before finishing."

"Do you mind if I have a look in the kitchen?" the detective asked.

"No, it's this way." Hal had left the lights on, walked in and leaned against the counter beside the sink.

"You said your wife had been preparing dinner?"

Hal explained what he'd found. "I put everything in the refrigerator so it wouldn't be ruined."

Det. Lynch pulled open the refrigerator and checked inside. It was as neat as the rest of the house with the perishables stacked in glass containers on the shelves, and the crisper drawers full of fresh vegetables and fruit. He slammed the door shut. "If you suspected something was wrong, you should have left the food where it sat."

Annoyed, Hal quickly put the meatloaf on the top of the stove with the pot of potatoes. He grabbed the cans from the cupboard and placed them on the counter. "There, that's what I found. It doesn't look like a crime scene to me."

"I'll give you that, but don't tamper with any other evidence in the future."

Hal spread his arms wide. "What evidence? Nothing is out of place."

"Which is suspicious in itself. Do you mind if I see the rest of the house?"

"No, go right ahead. The bedroom and bath are through the other door in the living room." Hal returned the meatloaf and potatoes to the refrigerator and waited rather than give the detective a tour. Faye's books on ghosts were on the coffee table with the map folded neatly beneath them. He didn't think there was anything out of the order in checking books from the library, but he doubted the detective would see it that way.

Det. Lynch continued making notes as he returned to the living room. "I notice someone has been reading up on ghosts. Is that you?"

"No, we went to see *The Ghost and Mrs. Muir*, and Faye loved the story. We're planning to drive up to the Gold Country this summer, and she hoped to see one."

"Would you say she often dwelled on morbid thoughts?"

"No, not at all. Faye is a remarkably even-tempered and pleasant person. She doesn't regard ghosts as evil."

"Do you own a car, Mr. Marten?"

"Yes, a Packard, but it isn't in the garage."

"You should have told me that sooner." The detective shook his head. "Did you plan to mention it before I left?"

"Yes, of course. From what I can see, my wife was preparing dinner, but was interrupted by something, or someone, and left without leaving me a note. Maybe she expected to return shortly, but hasn't been able to call."

The detective finally spotted Mr. Cuddles curled on his pillow. "Is that a real cat, or a stuffed toy?"

"No, Mr. Cuddles is real, but he doesn't take to strangers, so don't try and pet him."

"I'm not even tempted," the detective replied under his breath. "What about family? Does your wife have family living close that she might have gone to see?"

"No, she was an only child, and her parents were older when she was born. They're both gone now."

Lynch nodded thoughtfully. "Now I know you're concerned, Mr. Marten, but could your wife have gotten a call from a former boyfriend and gone to meet him?"

Hal caught himself, but he almost laughed because Faye was too reserved a young woman to be out partying with an old beau. "No, her high school boyfriend was killed on Iwo Jima. She hadn't been dating anyone when we met."

Lynch went to the sofa. "It's been a long day. Do you mind if I sit?"

"No, make yourself comfortable." Hal took the wing chair beside the sofa, but was almost too anxious to sit quietly and shifted his position nervously.

"How did you and your wife meet?" Lynch asked.

"At UCLA extension classes. I took an accounting class that would help me at work, and Faye was enrolled in some fashion course. We spoke while getting coffee one night during the break, and then began looking for each other and started dating. We were married last summer."

"Does she belong to any clubs or organizations that meet at night?"

"No, she stays close to home. I don't believe she had a happy childhood, and she enjoys having her own house. She spends a lot of time sewing new clothes."

"That's why she was taking a fashion course, I assume?"

"Yes, from what she said, it was a history of fashion, not instruction on design."

"Your wife has your car," the detective responded. "I'll check and make certain she wasn't in an accident. Give me the license plate number."

Hal supplied it. "I'd not even thought of an accident." He rubbed his forehead. "This has been such an awful night, and I'm not thinking clearly. I should have called the hospitals before calling you."

"I'll have a man check," Lynch promised. "We'll give you a call if we find her, or if she comes home, telephone me right away."

Hal stood with him. "I will, but I don't know what I'll do with myself while I wait."

Lynch nodded toward the coffee table. "You could read up on ghosts."

Hal showed the detective out without responding to his sarcastic taunt. He went into the kitchen to put the coffee pot on the stove, and watched the clock as he wondered where Faye could possibly have gone. That she might have been badly injured in a traffic accident was too awful to contemplate, but he began to hope she'd be found in a hospital and soon.

He reached for a coffee cup from the cupboard, and was repulsed clear through by the dried blood crusted on his shirt cuff. The cup slipped from his hand and shattered as it hit the floor. It was all he could do too keep himself from breaking into as many jagged pieces. He took out the broom and dustpan to clean up, but he couldn't bear to remove the shirt bearing the last traces of Pearl LaFosse he'd ever have.

He was still wide awake when the detective called him at 2:00 a.m. Faye hadn't been found in any of the local hospitals, and no unidentified young women had been admitted. There had been half a dozen traffic accidents, but all the participants had been accounted for, and a

Packard hadn't been involved in any.

"What do we do now?" Hal asked.

"It's been my experience that people usually turn up in a day or two," Lynch responded.

"Other people maybe, but Faye is too responsible a person to go off on her own without leaving me a note or talking to me on the phone. Something has to be very wrong."

"That may be true, but without any idea of where she might be, we don't know where to look. I'll call you tomorrow. Are you planning to go into work?"

Hal hadn't thought of the office once. "No, I'll call in sick. You can reach me at this number."

"I'll do that, and remember what I said. Most people turn up on their own. You might check her clothes and see if anything is missing. That will give you something to do with your time."

Insulted anew, Hal had already hung up the phone when he remembered the Black Dahlia. Elizabeth Short had been missing for a week before her body had been found in two ghastly bloodless pieces. From what he'd read of the case, Elizabeth liked to go out to party and dance and had obviously met up with the wrong partner. Faye wouldn't have gone out dancing. She wouldn't have even known where to go, and murderers wouldn't be out wandering respectable neighborhoods ringing doorbells and hoping a beautiful young housewife came to the door.

He managed to safely fill a second cup with coffee and while waiting for it cool sufficiently to drink, he remembered when someone went missing, the police always listed what they'd been wearing. He prayed Faye would appear at any minute, but in case she didn't, he ought to check her side of the closet. The problem was, he'd lost count of how many dresses she'd made in similar styles and couldn't name what was missing. Her purse was gone, as were the pair of black pumps she wore nearly every day. Her tweed coat wasn't in the hall closet, so he continued to think she'd been called away and would soon return.

He couldn't sleep and made a cheese sandwich to silence his stomach's plaintive rumblings, but it tasted like cardboard. Unbothered by his mistress's absence now that he'd been fed, Mr. Cuddles raised his head occasionally to yawn as he watched Hal pace the living room.

"I suppose she told you where she was going," Hal called to him, but as always the cat kept his secrets.

Finally growing exhausted, Hal stretched out on the sofa and fell asleep as soon as he'd closed his eyes. He awoke with a start early the next morning and checked the time. He had a horrible headache and had overslept, but his secretary wouldn't be at the office for another hour so he hadn't been missed yet. Mr. Cuddles, however, was perched on the arm of the sofa regarding him with an evil eye as he waited for his breakfast.

"Give me a minute to wake up and swallow some aspirin," he called to the cat, but Mr. Cuddles meowed pitifully, clearly not in a waiting mood. "All right, come on." There was half a can of cat tuna in the refrigerator left from last night, and he served him a goodly clump.

He seldom had headaches, and washed down three aspirin to make certain he'd taken enough. He showered, shaved, dressed in casual slacks and a shirt he wore for the weekends. He hung the blood-stained shirt in the closet. When Faye got home, she would have more to explain than he did, and he'd worry about the stained shirt later.

He brought in the newspaper, made coffee, toast and scrambled a couple of eggs. He was a much better cook than Faye, and he should have insisted he do the cooking until she learned how. Why had he kept quiet and suffered through so many tasteless meals? There had to be a tactful way to urge her to take a cooking course. He'd simply worried too much about hurting her feelings to speak up as he should have.

He called the office to tell Lorraine Adams he wasn't feeling well and wouldn't be in. She suggested he drink lots of hot water laced with lemon and honey. He thanked her and said he hoped to be at work on Monday, but he doubted he should return to his desk if Faye were still missing. He washed his dishes and put them away. Satisfied the kitchen was as spotless as Faye always kept it, he poured a second cup of coffee and opened the paper.

Pearl's murder was in the Metro section with a grim photo of her body lying beneath the tarp. There was only a brief report of a shooting death outside a popular bar and a request for tips to be sent to the police. Waiting notification of kin, Pearl's name wasn't given. When the telephone rang, Hal was so badly startled he nearly spilled his coffee in his lap.

"I'm assuming you've not heard from your wife, and I've no news of her either," Det. Lynch began, "but I thought you might like to come with us to see where Miss LaFosse lived. I know you're without your car, so we'll pick you up."

"Staying here isn't helping anyone any, so of course I'll come." He longed to learn whatever he could about Pearl and pulled on a jacket so he'd be ready to go. "You'll have to amuse yourself today, Mr. Cuddles." The cat appeared to be unchallenged by the thought.

Hal left Faye a note to tell her he'd been too worried to go into work and to stay put until he came home. He left it on the kitchen counter where she'd be sure to see it if she arrived home before he did. Grateful for any excuse to leave, he waited on the front porch for Det. Lynch who soon arrived in a black Ford sedan driven by a uniformed officer.

Hal joined him in the back seat. "Have you been to her place?" the detective asked.

Exasperated by the detective's ridiculous question, Hal chose his words with care. "No, of course not. We'd just talked a few times at the Golden Bear. There was nothing more."

"She had no identification in her purse, just a twenty dollar bill, a red lipstick, and a key with a tag from the Starlight trailer park."

"What?" Hal couldn't believe Pearl would have lived there. Trailer parks had sprung up all over Los Angeles in the years after the war when housing was in such short supply, but he couldn't imagine a woman as elegant as Pearl being content in the close confines of a trailer.

"She didn't seem like that kind of a girl?" the detective asked.

"I don't know what to think. I've driven past the Starlight Park, but never given it a second glance."

They drove through the gate, and stopped by the manager's gleaming Gulfstream trailer. "Let me do the talking, Mr. Marten. You're here because I thought you might recognize something important, not because I'm desperate for your company."

Hal didn't care why he was there. The park had been open only a few years and most of the trailers were new. Some had a rounded teardrop shape and looked as though they could be hitched up and rolled out with little notice while others were long and wide and clearly built to stay put. There were tiny lawns in front of the nearest trailers, and a flower garden or two surrounded by rocks painted white. The entrance way was a long clean street with side streets branching off to the left and right. It was a pretty place, but still, it just didn't fit his idea of Pearl.

The detective returned to the car. "The manager sat down and cried when I told him Pearl was dead. Apparently they'd been close. She'd listed no next of kin when she'd moved in, and he had no idea who should be notified. Maybe we'll find an address book or letters in her trailer." He gave their driver the directions to a Gulfstream on the first road to the left. There was no lawn, nor flower border. In fact, compared to the other trailers parked nearby, Pearl's looked vacant.

Lynch left the sedan, climbed the three steps and unlocked the door with the key from Pearl's purse. "Let me take a look inside first, before you come in."

Hal got out of the sedan and leaned back against it. The sun was out, but it was not yet warm. A woman hanging her laundry on a clothesline two trailers away looked his way, and he nodded a silent greeting. She ignored him, picked up her basket and returned to her trailer.

The detective leaned out the door and gestured for Hal to come on in. "It doesn't look as though she lived here," he said. "There are some clothes in the closet, several pairs of high heels, hats in boxes, but there's nothing in the refrigerator, and only a toothbrush and toothpaste in the bathroom."

The small living room at the front of the trailer had upholstered benches and a table with rounded corners between them. A philodendron in a turquoise ceramic pot sat in the middle of the table. The plant looked freshly watered, and Hal touched the soil and found it damp.

"What are you doing?" Lynch asked.

"Pearl must have watered it yesterday. Do you mind if I take it home? Otherwise, it will just wither and die now that she's gone." Had it only been a day? His sorrow felt far too deep for such a short time.

"Yeah, sure. Take it. Look at the closet and tell me if these are Pearl's things."

She'd been wearing her black suit yesterday, and he recognized the gray, blue and red suits on the hangers. There was a purple dress he'd not seen, but it looked like something she'd wear. Her hats were in boxes on the shelf, and her beautiful high-heeled shoes were carefully aligned in a row on the floor. "Yes, these are hers."

"Check the drawers," Lynch asked.

The trailer was as expertly designed as a ship captain's cabin and not a single space had gone unused. Hal opened a drawer, found nothing and opened the others in what would have been Pearl's dresser with the same result. "There's nothing here."

"This looks to me like a dressing room rather than a home," the detective confided. "Wait here while I speak with her neighbors."

Hal was too nervous to sit, and continued exploring the trailer. The bathroom had a shower, but the aqua towel didn't look as though it had ever been used. The bedroom had a bed with a beige spread and blanket. The crisply pressed white sheets were neatly tucked in so the bed hadn't been slept in Wednesday night. There were more drawers along the walls, also as empty as those near the closet.

He quieted his mind, but felt nothing of Pearl's presence. She'd said there were people she'd like to haunt, and he wished he'd pressed her for reasons. If she were out haunting anyone, she hadn't swung by the trailer on her way, or he felt sure he would have sensed her spirit. She'd possessed an innate sparkle he couldn't believe had died with her.

If the trailer key was the only one she carried, where had she spent the rest of her time? He wondered if she lived with someone who'd always be home waiting for her. His first guess would be a wealthy man who could afford her pretty clothes. Perhaps she had lived with a roommate, or her mother, or an invalid aunt. Only the philodendron seemed real. He went outside and sat down on the top step.

The police officer leaned against the front of the sedan. "You knew the victim?" he asked.

Hal shrugged. "Barely. I'd no idea she lived here." He watched a young man approach them, stood and stepped down to the concrete walkway in front of the trailer.

"I'm Jed Riley, the manager here." He wore gray slacks, a multicolored knitted vest over a white shirt and brown loafers. His eyes were red, and he carried a handkerchief. "I can't believe Pearl is dead. Why would anyone have shot such a kind and pretty woman?"

Hal waited for the officer to respond, and when the man didn't, he offered his own opinion. "I really don't care why, all I want to know is who did it, so he can be caught and sent to prison for the rest of his life."

The manager blew his nose on his handkerchief. "Yes, of course, I want that too."

The detective had disappeared down the row of trailers, and Hal felt free to do some investigation of his own. "Did Pearl spend much time here?"

"No, I seldom saw her. Once she told me her trailer was a retreat, I believe that's the word she used. She always paid her rent on time, in cash."

Clearly the man had had a crush on Pearl and would miss her terribly. "What about mail? Did she receive any here?"

"No, I told the detective the mailman leaves the mail for me to sort and put into the mailboxes inside the gate. She might have gotten an occasional flyer, something everyone received, but nothing personal."

Hal knew her mail had to have gone somewhere. "It must be a big responsibility running a park as large as this," he offered.

"Oh it is, but I enjoy dealing with people, and there's always one problem or another to keep me busy. Nothing major, you understand, just little things here and there."

Lynch rounded the corner and approached them with a quick step. He looked surprised to see the manager. "You have my card, if anyone comes to ask about Pearl, or tries to enter her trailer, call me immediately."

The young man's eyes grew wide. "Do you think the murderer might come here?"

"He could, so don't crowd him. Just call me."

"Oh, I will first thing," Jed promised with an emphatic head bob.

Hal went back into the trailer to fetch the philodendron. He was relieved Jed didn't insist he'd take care of it himself. He set it on the floor of the car beside him as they drove away. "Did you learn anything?"

Lynch shrugged. "I couldn't find anyone who knew Pearl. A few said they'd seen a woman come in or go out of the trailer, but none had ever spoken with her. Usually there's a busybody nearby who makes it their business to know everything about everyone, but I couldn't find one."

"What about the post office?" Hal asked. "Would they know where her mail was delivered if it didn't come here?"

Lynch pursed his lips. "What were you doing, interrogating the manager?"

"I wouldn't call it an interrogation. I just wondered is all."

"Next time wonder to yourself."

"Yes, sir." Hal looked out the window, searching the streets for Faye as they drove to his neighborhood. "Will you wait while I check to see if my wife is home?"

"I will," Lynch responded.

Hal set the plant on the front porch as he fished his keys from his pocket. He opened the door and was met with a disappointing silence. He went on in and found his note where he'd left it. Mr. Cuddles was ready for lunch, but he owed the detective a response first. He went to the door and shook his head. Lynch waved and drove off.

"All right Cuddles, lunchtime." He gave the cat the remainder of the can of cat food. Faye kept a dozen cans in the cupboard so she'd not run out, and apparently the cat didn't mind a steady diet of tuna.

There were cans of soup, and he heated some chicken noodle. It was hot, and he supposed would taste good to someone who wasn't completely numb. He added crackers and cheese and thought it a meal. He finished the crossword in the paper and got up looking for something else to do. He went out into the yard and the snapdragons and pansies they'd planted looked good and didn't need water.

Carmen Espinoza came out into her backyard and waved. "Faye didn't call me. Did she get home very late?"

Hal walked over to the low chain link fence that separated their yards. "She hasn't come home, and I've no idea where she could be. Even if you didn't speak with her yesterday, had she recently mentioned somewhere she was meaning to go, or someone she needed to see?"

"Why no, other than the gold rush trip you're planning, and she'd not have gone that far on her own. I hope she's not lying unidentified in a hospital nearby."

"So do I, but the police checked, and she isn't a patient anywhere."

"She's just up and disappeared?" Carmen asked, clearly puzzled.

"No, she wouldn't have simply left without taking her beloved Mr. Cuddles. She means to come home, or at least she did when she left."

"Oh dear. What should we do?"

Carmen was a sweet woman, but he had nothing to offer. "Other than wait, which is nearly impossible, I don't know."

She reached out to touch his sleeve. "I'll pray for you."

He thanked her and turned away, but she called him back. "Did Faye keep a diary?" she asked. "There might be something helpful in it if she did."

"I don't think so, but I'll look." He went back inside and while he feared he was invading his wife's privacy, he went through her side of the dresser. She kept her lingerie neatly folded, and thinking it would be a good place to hide a diary, he slid his hands under her things all the way to the back of the drawer. He found only a detective's business card, and the office was close enough for him to walk.

He went to the telephone and called the number on the card. "Hello, my name's Hal Marten, and I believe my wife may have contacted you recently."

Joe Ezell straightened up in his chair with a startled jerk. No one he had been paid to investigate had ever turned around and come looking for him, and he didn't know how to respond. "I don't discuss my clients, Mr. Marten."

"Well, in this case you should. My wife's missing, and I think you might know where she's gone. I'll be there in a few minutes."

"What do you mean she's missing?" Joe asked.

"Is there any way to misunderstand? She's disappeared. We'll discuss it when I get there." He hung up before Joe could argue and yanked on his jacket. With everything else that had gone wrong, a surly private detective was the last straw.

CHAPTER 8

Joe Ezell feared there was no way to avoid talking with Hal Marten, and he'd try and make the best of it. He quickly made a fresh pot of coffee and reviewed the file containing what little information he'd gained for Faye Marten. If she'd been so disheartened by his report that she'd left her husband, he certainly didn't deserve the blame. For once, he might have an answer as to what had happened after he'd ended a case, but this wasn't good news at all.

He got up to look out his window but didn't see Hal Marten coming before he knocked on his door. He quickly let him in. "Mr. Marten?"

"Yes, I don't care how *discreet* your investigations might be, my wife didn't come home last night. The police can't find her and believe she'll turn up on her own, but I don't. She had your card in her dresser. Tell me why."

Joe gestured toward one of the two visitor chairs. "Please, have a seat." He took his own place behind his desk, grateful it formed a sturdy barrier between them. "You've no idea where she's gone?"

Hal took a chair. "None whatsoever, or I wouldn't be here. Why did she hire you?"

"I didn't say that she had," Joe hedged.

Hal banged his fist on the desk so hard Joe jumped in fright. "Do you want trouble with the police?"

"No, of course not," Joe exclaimed.

"Then tell me what you do know, or I'll give your card to the detective I've spoken with, and he'll interview you."

Joe raised his hands in a conciliatory gesture. "Let's take a moment to compose ourselves, Mr. Marten, and then I'll tell you what little I know."

Hal spit out his words between clenched teeth, "I am composed." He very seldom lost his temper. In fact, he'd been praised at California West for the cool adept way he handled problems. Today, he possessed none of his usual restraint.

"Would you like coffee?"

"No, I wouldn't like coffee."

Joe squirmed in his chair. He couldn't think of a way to avoid telling Hal what he knew, so he drew in a deep breath, stopped stalling and got on with it. "Your wife came to me because she thought you might be having an affair."

"What? Are you serious? What prompted her to believe such a ridiculous thing?"

Joe stared up at the ceiling, but found no helpful advice written there. He opened Faye's file and ran his finger along the list. "She described you as having become restless and always wanting to go somewhere when previously you'd been content to stay home. She mentioned you'd bought new suits, and…."

"Is that it?" Hal leaned forward in his chair. "What did she hire you to do?"

"She said you often came home late on Thursday nights."

Hal swore under his breath. "Yes, I usually stay at my desk a while after my salesmen leave to prepare for Friday morning meetings. Did she actually believe I stopped at a brothel on the way home?"

Joe drew in a deep breath. "No, of course not, but I followed you to the Golden Bear Lounge last week, and mentioned in my report that you'd spoken to a beautiful woman there."

Hal felt his heart lurch. "She paid you to spy on me?"

"Please, Mr. Marten, all I did was observe you for a day or two. I told her a simple conversation in a bar didn't amount to anything, and advised her to work on your marriage."

Hal got up and began to pace. "What wonderful advice. The beautiful woman, Pearl LaFosse, was shot and killed last night when she left the Golden Bear, and my wife has disappeared. What do you think now?"

The detective's voice became a hoarse croak, "My god!"

"Exactly. The detective on the case thinks it's an odd coincidence, don't you?"

Joe balanced his elbows on his desk and cradled his head in his hands. "Your wife didn't strike me as a woman who'd resort to violence, or I'd never have taken her case."

"My wife isn't in the least bit violent," Hal countered. "Last night the police insisted upon questioning everyone who'd been at the bar, making me late to get home. Maybe after what you'd told her, she feared I'd stayed with Pearl, and she didn't want to be there when I finally arrived."

Completely flummoxed, Joe shrugged. "I don't know what to tell you."

"I didn't come here for advice. I want you to find Faye, and fast."

Joe sat back. "She's not been missing a day yet, and she'll probably come home on her own."

Hal put his hands on Joe's desk and leaned toward him. "That's what the police say, but I'm not going to wait until whatever trail there might have been grows cold."

"All right fine. She's most likely gone to stay with family or a girlfriend. What names can you give me?"

Hal sank into his chair. "She has no living family, and she never mentioned any friends."

"Doesn't that strike you as odd?"

"Odd how?" Hal asked.

"Your wife is very pretty, personable, why wouldn't she have made friends, perhaps among your neighbors?"

"She's well-acquainted with the woman who lives next door, but Carmen has no idea where Faye is. Faye isn't reclusive, not at all. She simply prefers to spend her time at home."

"Doing what?"

"She likes to sew."

"There's a lead right there," Joe announced. "Do you know where she shopped for fabric? She might have made a friend among the clerks."

Hal's headache was coming back, and he rubbed his temple. He'd seen the green bags from the store and recalled the name. "It's Fiona's Fabrics, right around the corner."

"I know it. I'll go over this afternoon and see what they know about your wife. Do you have a photo of her I could show around?"

Hal pulled one from his wallet. "Don't lose this, I don't have many of her."

"Really? Don't you have photos from your wedding?"

"No, we were married at the courthouse and left to celebrate rather than wait for the free-lance photographer taking photos to get to us."

Joe held the photo by the corner. "This is a good photo of Faye. She's smiling and looks real sweet. I'll be careful with it." He waited for Hal to ask about his fees, but he just sat there staring at him. Joe cleared his throat. "We should discuss my fee. I'll need a retainer, shall we say fifty dollars?"

Hal stood, pulled the wallet from his hip pocket and pulled out the bills. "I'd like a receipt."

"Of course." Joe opened the top drawer on his desk and removed a receipt book. He hadn't used it much and hoped Hal Marten didn't realize he had only limited experience. He wrote the receipt with a firm hand and handed it to Hal. "I'll keep the duplicate in the file. If Faye's there when you get home, call me, and I'll refund your money."

Hal went to the door. "I wish to hell my wife had never come to you."

Joe let him go without responding, but he did too.

Hal nearly ran into Cleotis Cotton as he left the Discreet Investigations office. "I'm sorry. I should watch where I'm going."

"No harm done, sir. You have a nice afternoon now."

Hal glanced over his shoulder. "Thanks, you have one too."

Cleotis opened Joe's office door and looked in. "A man just left here in an awful rush. Did you give him bad news?"

"No, but he gave me some. Do you remember that pretty girl who came in last week?"

"Yes, sir, I do."

"That was her husband, and she's disappeared."

"You mean she's up and left him?"

"I don't know, maybe. Apparently the police believe she might have shot a woman leaving the Golden Bear Lounge last night. I told her that was where her husband stopped on Thursdays."

CC leaned against the doorjamb. "Oh my, that's very bad news."

"What an understatement." Joe stood and picked up the notebook he used in his investigations. "I need to find her before the police do."

"You do that, Mr. Ezell. I wouldn't want anything bad to happen to such a nice lady."

"Neither would I, CC. See you tomorrow."

"Good-bye, sir. You have a nice afternoon now."

Joe walked into Fiona's Fabrics and instantly recalled going shopping with his mother in just such a warm, comforting shop. Bolts of colorful fabric were displayed on shelves along the walls. File cabinets were filled with clothing patterns, and standing racks held buttons, zippers and thread. His mother was a talented seamstress who often made prom gowns for high school girls. It seemed like a long time ago. He went up to the counter and waited while the clerk cut some blue and white gingham fabric for a dark-haired young woman and rang up the sale.

The clerk was tall and thin with frizzy red hair caught in a knot atop of her head. Her glasses were tethered around her neck with a beaded cord. She wore more make-up than needed, but Joe didn't care to see her without it. When she was free, he introduced himself. She offered her hand.

"Fiona Walters, owner of this proud establishment. How may I help you?"

He showed her Faye Marten's photo. "She shopped here often, and I'm hoping you can help us. She didn't come home last night, and her husband is afraid she's met with some misadventure. It's also possible she just didn't feel like going home."

Fiona grew thoughtful and pursed her lips. "I remember Faye. She's one of my best customers and while I don't carry anything I'd describe as gaudy, she does like prints in bright colors."

"That's very interesting," Joe replied. "I'm hoping you might have gotten to know her well enough to offer a suggestion of where she might be."

"We might have exchanged a few words about the weather, plenty on fabric, of course, I can talk all day long about fabric, but we weren't close. She was friendly, never crowded the counter when the store was full, but I've no idea where she might be. Her husband must be worried sick."

"Yes, he is. Please keep my card, and if you remember anything that might be helpful, give me a call."

Fiona pinned the card to the bulletin board behind her,

and then turned to face him with a quizzically raised brow. "Could Faye have had a good reason to go missing?" she asked.

Joe never gave the specifics of a case, and especially not when he might have contributed to its disastrous outcome. Still, her question alarmed him. "Did she ever come in with a black eye, or with obvious bruises?"

Fiona frowned slightly, then paused to greet a woman who'd entered the store. "No, Faye has beautiful fair skin, and I never saw any sign that she'd been abused."

"That's good news. I hope she comes home soon."

"Should I call you if she comes in?" she asked.

"It's likely she would have gone home first, but yes, do give me a call if you have the time."

She nodded, and left the register to answer a customer's question about patterns. Joe was disappointed that Faye hadn't grown close to Fiona, or at least exchanged phone numbers. He dreaded having to call Hal Marten to report his lack of progress.

When he returned to his office, he made a list of places Faye might have frequented. Even a woman who sticks close to home goes out sometimes. Holding his breath, he dialed Hal's number, and he answered on the first ring.

"This is Joe Ezell. I had no luck with Fiona. She remembers your wife and the fabrics she bought, but nothing in the least bit enlightening."

"Damn."

"Exactly my feeling too," Joe replied. "Did Faye have her hair done at a salon? Women often share secrets with their hairdresser that they wouldn't tell another soul."

"No, her hair has a natural curl, and she told me once that hairdressers were a waste of time and money. I dropped off and picked up the dry cleaning on Saturdays, so she didn't go there. She did the grocery shopping every week. The clerks are friendly; they're paid to be. Maybe she stuck up a friendship with one of them and just never mentioned it."

Joe wrote down the name of the market. "I'll go right now. I might need another day to catch all the clerks on their shift, but it's possible one of them knows something. Keep thinking about what routine she had, where she went each week…"

"The library," Hal offered. "She's been going to the library for books about ghosts, and someone might remember her."

"Ghosts?"

"It doesn't matter why now. Do you want me to check the library while you go to the market?"

"No, it's better if a person not so closely connected to the case asks the questions. People will be more open with me than they would be with you."

Joe hung up grateful the conversation had gone better than he'd hoped. He needed to pick up a few things at the market, and went to the one where Faye had shopped. He introduced himself to the manager and showed him her photo.

The manager studied it closely. "She does look familiar, but I don't know her name. Go ahead and ask around. Someone in the bakery or meat department might know her."

Joe thanked him and began in the back of the store in the produce section. The clerk putting out fresh heads of lettuce shook his head. "Sorry, I don't know her. Is she in some kind of trouble?"

"No, not at all," Joe responded. He had more luck with the butcher.

"Yes, I know Faye. She comes in for the same order every week, ham, ground beef and pork for meat loaf, a roasting chicken. I encouraged her to try our pork chops, but apparently she isn't one for experimenting." He laughed at the thought.

The butcher was a large man with an apron stretched over his broad stomach. He seemed to be a good-natured sort, but not a man Faye would have confided in. Joe thanked him and hoped for better luck at the bakery counter where there were women clerks.

The woman adding freshly baked rolls into the case stopped to look at the photo Joe showed her. "Sure I know her. She buys a loaf of white bread every week and has us slice it for her. Occasionally she'll buy parker house rolls, but it isn't often."

Joe sighed. Fiona knew fabrics, the butcher knew meat, and the bakery lady knew baked goods, otherwise Faye was invisible to them. "While I'm here, give me a dozen of those rolls and what about one glazed donut." He paid for his purchase and ate the donut when he returned to his office. There was nothing better than a freshly baked donut, but it provided scant compensation for his lack of progress.

He licked the glaze off his fingers. It was nice to take a delicious break from the case, but he couldn't stop worrying. For all they knew, Faye might have shot Pearl LaFosse and headed for the Arizona border. She might bleach her hair, change her name and marry a geologist before they caught up with her.

He called Hal again. "Sorry, no luck at the market. Did Faye ever mention anyone living in Arizona or Oregon?"

"Not that I recall. Do you think she's left the state?"

"We don't want to think the worst, of course, but she might have rather than stick around to answer questions."

"If she hadn't gone missing, no one would be asking any questions," Hal argued.

"True, but she might not have been thinking very clearly if she'd shot Miss LaFosse."

"She couldn't have. We don't even own a gun, so where would she have gotten one?"

"Excellent question. Your wife apparently stayed pretty close to home, so I'll check with the local pawnshops. I don't suppose you found a receipt for a weapon?"

"No, all I found was your card, but if Faye has turned into a master criminal, which I refuse to believe, she'd have destroyed it. She'd not have left her pet cat, Mr. Cuddles, here with me if she were leaving for good."

"That's something to consider. When do they pick up your trash?"

"You want me to search through our trash?"

"Couldn't hurt, and I should have suggested it earlier. People make notes, and she might have jotted down a name or address, something that will be useful. I'll get back to you after I visit the library tomorrow."

"Thank you."

Joe poured himself another cup of coffee and thought the day hadn't ended too badly after all. When CC came by to empty the trash, he was in a more positive mood than he had been earlier in the day. "Do you like donuts, CC?"

"Oh yes, sir, I love them."

"Next time I'm in the market I'll get you one."

"You needn't do that." CC grabbed the wastebasket and carried it out to the large trashcan. He returned it to the office and set it down gently. "Did you find the missing lady?"

"All I've found is where she isn't," Joe confided. "I still hope she'll return home on her own."

"I'll hold that thought too. Have yourself a nice afternoon now."

"You too, CC."

Joe kept his golf clubs in his car, and he left the office intent upon spending more time at the driving range. It was a great place to take out the frustrations nearly overwhelming him that day.

Hal had been reading *Lust for Life*, the book Pearl had given him. He kept thinking of her and had to re-read the opening paragraphs over and over. He ran his hands across the cover as if he could still feel her touch, but the book held no promises of any kind. He laid it aside and went to search through the trash.

He glanced toward Carmen's duplex and hoped she

wouldn't come out while he was riffling through the week's garbage. Faye cooked such conservative amounts of food there weren't piles of discarded leftovers. There were the newspapers rolled into a neat clump, and a few tissues with pale pink lipstick prints. He caught sight of a piece of paper near the bottom of the can and leaned in to get it. It was a list of the yardage needed for a new pattern. He tossed it back into the trash.

He went inside and washed his hands, then thought to look under the sink for yesterday's trash, but all he found was a wrinkled paper towel. It was going to be a very long night, and because they ate spaghetti every Friday night, he put a pot on the stove to boil water for the pasta. He wouldn't add the meatloaf though, just a few fresh vegetables and sauce would be more than enough.

Early Saturday morning, Hal felt a weight ease onto the end of the bed. He sat up expecting to find Faye had finally come home, but it was only Mr. Cuddles making himself comfortable. "You aren't allowed on the bed," he reminded him, but too frustrated to deal with the blasted cat, he lay back down and punched his pillow. He couldn't get back to sleep before his alarm went off, and he got up expecting another wretched day.

He'd just finished eating breakfast when Detective Lynch knocked on the door. He moved back to invite him in. "Have you found her?"

"No, but we've found your Packard abandoned in South Central. You can pick it up later from the impound lot."

Hal's knees grew weak, and he sank down on the sofa. "Do you think someone kidnapped Faye for our car?"

Lynch's impassive expression veiled his thoughts. "The keys were in it, so it seems likely, unless your wife usually runs with a crowd in South Central."

"Of course she doesn't." They were a long way from the colored section of town, and there was nothing wild about Faye, unless she'd shot Pearl, which he couldn't accept. "She must have gone out on an errand, and run into the wrong people."

"Apparently. Although there's no sign of a struggle, so if your wife came to any harm, it wasn't in your car."

"If she'd been hurt, you would have found her in a hospital, wouldn't you?" Hal asked.

"Yes, we would have."

"Or she could be lying dead under a pile of debris in some alley," Hal offered.

"It won't help to let your imagination run wild, Mr. Marten."

"Tell me something that will help," Hal countered crossly.

"I think it's time to release her case to the press. Do you want to offer a reward for information?"

"I couldn't offer enough to make it worthwhile." Hal sat back and looked toward the window and found Mr. Cuddles completely disinterested in their conversation. For some appalling reason, he wanted to hug the damn beast, but he fought off the embarrassing impulse.

"Fine, we'll simply appeal to the public to look for her. Do you have a photo we could use?"

Hal got up to go into the bedroom and returned with a high school photo. "She doesn't look any older, so this will do. Please return it."

"Will do." The detective opened his notebook. "Can you describe her, age, height?"

"She's twenty-six, five foot five, curly brown hair, hazel eyes, and has a slender figure. As you can see, she's very pretty, and I want to bring her home."

"Of course. Stay here if you can, so if she calls, you'll know where she is."

"I'll need to pick up my car first."

"Fine, do that, and then stay here."

As soon as the detective left, Hal called Joe Ezell and asked him for a ride to the impound lot. "I want you to look at the car. You might see something the police missed."

"I'll be there in five minutes."

* * *

The impound lot was located in a scruffy neighborhood neither of them had ever visited. The lot spread over a whole city block and was surrounded by a high chain link fence topped with barbed wire. Grass peeked through multiple cracks in the worn asphalt paving. There were rows and rows of vehicles, some forlorn wrecks. Hal checked in with uniformed guards at the gate and signed for the Packard.

An eerie silence hung in the air, and frightened Faye hadn't been found with the car, Hal drove away as fast as the speed limit allowed with Joe following in his Chevrolet sedan. When they arrived home, he parked the car in the driveway rather than the garage so they could examine it more easily.

"Open the trunk," Joe asked.

"The police would have checked it, wouldn't they?"

"Of course, you needn't worry we'll find Faye's body inside."

Hal popped open the trunk. "The spare tire is gone." So disgusted he could barely think, he stood and looked away rather than scream the obscenities filling his throat.

"Guys who'd steal a car, apparently with your wife in it, wouldn't be likely to leave anything valuable behind," Joe said. He ran his hands over the trunk liner and searched the trunk thoroughly, but it held nothing more than the jack and tire iron.

"Let's imagine how this happened," the detective offered.

"I'd rather not," Hal countered.

"Fine, I'll just go over the interior." Joe began with the back seat searching for anything that might have dropped to the floor or fallen between the seats. "Do you always keep the car this clean?"

"Yes, I don't want Faye to be ashamed to drive it."

Joe opened the passenger door and checked the map pocket, but all he found was a neatly folded map of Los Angeles. The glove compartment held only a package of tissues and a pencil. There wasn't anything of interest to be found on the driver's side either. The floor mats were clean as though the men who'd hijacked the car had wiped their feet before climbing in.

He slammed the driver's door and brushed off his hands. "Clean as a whistle. Did your wife ever leave the keys in the car while she shopped?"

"I don't think so, but I always drove when we were together. What are you suggesting?"

"Let's say kids found the car with the keys in the ignition and took it for a joy ride. Who would your wife have called for a ride home?"

"She would have called me to tell me someone had stolen the car," Hal offered.

"Not if she knew you'd already left your office."

"She would have been surprised and angry, and would have marched right back into wherever she'd stopped to call the police and report it."

"They don't appear to have any record of a call from her, do they?"

"The detective might not have checked. I'll call him."

"You do that, and I'll head on over to the library."

Hal parked the car in the garage and pulled down the door. He'd hoped they'd find Faye with the car, and that she had apparently been left behind somewhere doubled his worry. He went inside to call Detective Lynch, who replied in a bored monotone that of course they had checked for any calls to the police that might have come from Faye. It had simply been too routine a procedure to mention.

Hal hung up and went into the kitchen to fix lunch. Mr. Cuddles followed. He took the cheddar cheese from the refrigerator and cut the cat a small slice. "Do you like cheese?" he asked.

Mr. Cuddles swallowed it and meowed loudly for more. "All right, I guess you do." He gave the cat another small bite of cheddar and took a dish of cat tuna out to the back porch where the cat would stay until Hal opened the door.

Hal wasn't hungry, but thought he ought to maintain whatever routine he could until Faye was found. He made himself a grilled cheese sandwich just the way he liked it and sat at the kitchen table to finish working the crossword puzzle. It would be a very long afternoon, and a sad one when he thought of Pearl. She'd been such a fascinating woman, and he couldn't believe anyone could have wanted her dead.

Joe Ezell hadn't been to the local library since he'd graduated from high school and nothing much had changed, except for the librarian. Miss Sandra Sloan was an attractive blond, rather than one of the sweet gray-haired ladies he recalled from his youth. He introduced himself and showed her Faye's photo.

"She's been checking out books about ghosts. Do you remember her?"

"Of course, I remember Faye," the librarian responded. "We like it quiet here so students can study, but she takes the request so seriously she whispers when we talk, as though we were exchanging state secrets."

Joe feared this was going to be another conversation where he'd learn only what the speaker cared about, and little about Faye, but he did his best to inspire something more. "She didn't come home Thursday night, and her family is trying to find her. Did she ever mention a place she'd like to go, or somewhere she hoped to visit?"

The librarian pushed her pencil behind her ear. "She wanted to go up to the Gold Rush country in the summer with her husband, that's the only place she mentioned. Has she just disappeared without leaving a note?"

"Yes, I'm afraid so. Did you two ever exchange telephone numbers?"

"No, we talked about books, and our conversations didn't go any further. I wish I could be of more help."

"Thank you for your time. You have my card, and if Faye should happen to come by in the next couple of days, please give me a call."

"I will. Are you sure there isn't something you'd like to check out today?"

Her voice had dropped to a sultry purr, leaving Joe enormously flattered. "I have a sweetheart, but if I didn't, I'd come here often to pick up something to read." He left with a bounce in his step, but even after stopping at several pawnshops, he still had nothing worthwhile to report to Hal Marten.

That night Joe took Mary Margaret to her favorite place in China Town, the Lotus Garden. She knew all the dishes to order, and he was happy as long as they had some ribs and crisply fried spring rolls. He tried not to slurp his wonton soup. "I swear this tastes better every time we're here."

"Do you think so?" she asked. "I've always thought it was delicious. I don't expect any details, but how is the case going with the suspicious woman?"

Joe sighed and put down his spoon. "Badly, I'm afraid. She's disappeared."

Mary Margaret leaned forward. "You don't mean it."

"I do mean it. I've been looking for her, but haven't turned up a single useful clue."

"Could the Black Dahlia killer have struck again?"

"I doubt it. She wasn't a party girl like Elizabeth Short, so they wouldn't have crossed paths. Where would you go if you decided to leave town without telling anyone?"

Their waiter brought the remainder of the dishes they'd ordered, and Mary Margaret waited until he'd left them to reply. "You seem like too nice a guy to give me any reason to leave Los Angeles, so I won't make up something to send you in the wrong direction should I decide to go."

"Thank you, I appreciate the compliment. I think you're awfully nice too."

She smiled. "I'd go up to San Francisco because it's a great place to visit. A friend from nursing school lives there, and I could stay with her until I found a job and a place to live."

Joe put a couple of spare ribs on his plate, along with a spring roll. "You'd rely on a friend, that's what most people would do, but the missing woman doesn't appear to have had any."

"No friends at all?"

"Her husband has never met any."

Mary Margaret added a spoonful of fried rice to her plate. "That doesn't mean she doesn't have any."

"Why wouldn't her husband have met them? He's a nice looking man with a good job. She should have wanted to show him off."

"She might have wanted to, but maybe she's afraid her friends might not be up to his standard."

"That's a thought. Maybe she had skanky friends from high school that she'd rather he didn't meet."

"Exactly," Mary Margaret agreed, "or maybe she just wanted to keep him all to herself rather than invite any competition while they were dating."

Joe regarded her with renewed admiration. "That's probably closer to the truth. With any luck, she'll turn up soon."

"Or be found dead," Mary Margaret observed.

"That's not how I want this case to end, sweetheart. Have some beef and broccoli, and let's talk about something else." Anything else he thought to himself. There had already been one murder in this unfortunate case, and he dreaded having to deal with another.

CHAPTER 9

Sunday morning, Carmen Espinoza brought Hal a plate of waffles. "If you've already eaten, these can be saved and warmed in the oven tomorrow. Do you have syrup?"

Hal took the warm plate. "Yes, we do. Thank you, I love waffles and haven't had any in long while."

"Oh good, I'd hoped you'd enjoy them. The recipe makes more than I can eat, so I usually freeze some for another day. Faye's photo is in the morning paper asking for information about her. I hope you get some good news from it."

"So do I, Mrs. Espinoza."

"Please, call me Carmen. I'll leave you to enjoy your breakfast. Please let me know if there's anything I can do, anything at all."

"I will. Thank you again." Hal carried the plate into the kitchen and took the syrup from the cabinet beside the stove. Melted butter would be good, so he took out their smallest pan to melt some. Mr. Cuddles had already eaten his fill of tuna and begun his morning nap, so Hal left him where he was rather than exile him to the back porch while he ate. The waffles were light and golden brown, perfection really, and he wished Faye were there to enjoy them with him. He also knew Carmen had brought them over as an excuse to mention Faye's photo in the paper. He ate the waffles anyway.

He'd found the photo in the Metro section of the paper when he'd brought it in. The grainy picture wasn't nearly as pretty as she was, but if anyone had seen her, they'd recognize her from it. Not everyone got up as early as he did on Sundays, so it might be late afternoon before anyone called the police with information.

He ate very slowly, savoring every sweet crumb. When he and Faye had married, she'd been living in a boarding house and hadn't owned any kitchen things. He'd had a couple of pots and pans, a cookie sheet and some utensils. They'd bought what they'd believed every kitchen should have, but neither had thought of a waffle iron. He wondered what else he'd not missed. He washed Carmen's plate and set it aside to return later.

He wanted to go out and walk until he became so tired he'd be afraid he'd not make it back home, but Lynch had told him to stay put and wait for Faye, or news of her. He read the paper, did the crossword, and went out to the yard to water the flowers. He was close enough to hear the phone and sat down in one of their new redwood chairs and stared up at the sky. If Faye were able to come home, he thought she already would have, and he planned to return to work tomorrow rather than lose his mind waiting for her there at home.

Midmorning Monday, Detective Lynch and a uniformed officer arrived at the offices of California West. Mrs. Adams stood at Hal's office door to announce them. He immediately left his desk and ushered them in and closed the door behind them.

"Is there any news?" he asked. He gestured toward the chairs facing his desk, but neither man cared to sit.

"We caught one of the kids who stole your car. He's fourteen, no master criminal by any extent. He swears he and his friends found your car with the keys in it, and thought a joyride wouldn't get them into too much trouble. He says they never saw your wife."

Hal leaned against his desk. "Where did they find the car? Won't that give you a lead as to where she might have been?"

"Yes, it does." Lynch glanced toward the officer, who continued studying the floor. "It was parked around the corner from the Golden Bear Lounge."

"Dear God," Hal murmured. He hadn't wanted to believe Faye was even capable of murder, but this didn't sound good.

"It looks as though Faye shot Pearl LaFosse, and ran for her car, only to find it had been stolen," Lynch continued. "She was close to the Red Car line, so why didn't she just go on home and finish cooking dinner as though nothing had happened?"

Hal drew in a deep breath and released it slowly. If Faye had shot Pearl then her thinking couldn't have been all that clear. "She could have, but she didn't. How could she have explained the missing car?"

"She could have claimed it had been stolen from your garage," Lynch replied. "It happens. We need you to come to the station with us. We've some other ideas that will take too long to discuss here."

"All right, fine," Hal agreed. He told Mrs. Adams to cancel whatever appointments he'd had for the rest of the day, and he walked out with his two escorts. Every salesman's eye was on them but he ignored their stares rather than acknowledge their natural curiosity. As they waited for the elevator, he shook his head. "This has been the worst sort of nightmare. Is there any chance the boy you caught is lying?"

"Rather than start rumors circulating here, let's wait to discuss it at the station," Lynch cautioned.

The detective rode in the front seat of the car with the officer, and Hal had the back seat to himself. Last Monday had been like so many other routine days, but now a week later his well-ordered life had dissolved into utter chaos. He watched the passing scenery and envied the people walking along without his heavy burden of dread. Once at the Hollywood station, Detective Lynch led him into an interrogation room that smelled of stale smoke and sweat.

"Don't you have an office," Hal asked.

"This will do for now. Take a seat and make yourself comfortable."

Hal chose the wooden straight-backed chair closest to the door and sat down at the table. "Have you found Pearl's next of kin?" he asked.

"Your wife is missing, and you're concerned about Pearl?"

"I can worry about multiple things at the same time, Detective. As for Faye, she couldn't have simply disappeared. She has to be somewhere."

"Yes, of course, she does," Lynch agreed. He took the chair opposite Hal's and opened a file with photos of Pearl lying dead on the sidewalk.

Sickened, Hal turned away. "I'd rather not look at those."

"They're just a reminder of why we're here."

"We're here because my wife is missing, aren't we?" Hal asked. The small narrow room made him uneasy, and he wanted to get this over with and leave as quickly as he possibly could.

"That's one of the reasons." Lynch shuffled through the photos, returned them to the file, and set it aside. "Let's look at your wife from a new angle. If she shot Miss LaFosse, found her car was gone, and took the Red Car home, she might have been so horrified by what she'd done, she could have confessed the minute you walked through the door."

"Don't make up things," Hal cautioned. "She wasn't there Thursday night, and hasn't come home since."

"You told me she hadn't answered the phone when you called from the Golden Bear. You were anxious to get home and left around nine. You didn't call me until after eleven to say your wife was missing. What happened between nine and eleven?"

"Nothing happened, I fed the cat, cleaned up the preparations Faye had made for dinner, which you already told me I shouldn't have, and I waited to call you until it got too late for her to be out alone."

Lynch nodded thoughtfully. "A man might react very badly if he learned his wife had shot his girlfriend."

"Is this why you brought me here, to make ridiculous accusations you can't prove? I still don't believe Faye could have found a gun somewhere and shot Pearl, and I wish you'd stop referring to her as my girlfriend. We were barely acquainted. Aren't the police interested in facts? Your inventive suppositions are absurd. Am I free to go?"

"In a minute. Let me continue my 'inventive suppositions' just a moment longer. Men sometimes lose their tempers and hit their wife harder than they'd intended. Did you kill Faye when you learned what she'd done and dispose of her body before you called me?"

Horrified to be accused of murder, Hal drew in a deep breath and posed a ready alternative. "Of course, not. If Faye came to the Golden Bear, she might have seen whomever shot Pearl. He could have taken her with him rather than allow her to identify him to the police. That's why we can't find her, she's the murderer's hostage. The killer has to be someone who knew Pearl. Why aren't you investigating that angle rather than badgering me?" He considered mentioning he'd hired Joe Ezell to find Faye since the police couldn't, but Lynch would swiftly follow that lead to Faye's tie to the private investigator and provide her with a reason to kill Pearl. He avoided that trap.

Lynch stared at Hal a long moment. "You may have come up with a logical theory, but that doesn't mean it's the truth. Did you have an insurance policy on your wife?"

"I'm in the insurance business, so of course, I did, but it isn't as large as mine."

The detective flashed a knowing smile. "You see, we've lots more to discuss, but it can wait. The next time we talk, you might want to bring an attorney."

"You might want to bring a detective with a some common sense." Hal strode out of the station and hailed a cab. He could call one of the California West attorneys, but their field was contract rather than criminal law. He returned to his office and walked in smiling as though he'd been out for a pleasant ride rather than forced to endure a most unwelcome interrogation.

Lorraine Adams looked surprised to see him. "Did they have any news?"

"Unfortunately, no. Take a long lunch if you like, we probably won't get much done today."

His secretary smiled. "Bullock's is having a sale."

"Fine, go and look for bargains." He entered his office and loosened his tie. He hadn't been back for more than five minutes when George Sharp, the vice president for sales, called him.

"What's going on there, Marten? Your wife's photo is in the *LA Times*, and policemen are strolling through your office?"

"My wife is missing, thank you for your concern," Hal responded curtly. "The police are investigating, and they aren't disrupting the office's business."

"Well, see that they don't and hurry up and find your wife."

"Yes, sir." Hal hung up ready to go to the sale at Bullock's himself. There hadn't been even a hint of concern in his boss's voice. Wait until he learned Faye might be linked to a murder, would be linked if Detective Lynch got his way. The man was right, he did need a criminal attorney before his situation grew any worse.

He wondered if Joe Ezell could recommend one, and then remembered he'd kept Lou King's card and figured a bail bondsmen could undoubtedly give him names. He reached for the phone.

* * *

Lou King was already at the Golden Bear Lounge when Hal walked in. It was the last place he wanted to meet, but Lou insisted it was perfect. Hal took the stool beside the bail bondsman, and Mitch brought him a beer. He took a sip, and licked the foam from his lips.

"I'm afraid my wife, her name's Faye, may have seen who shot Pearl and could have become his hostage," he confided softly. "The detective on the case suspects Faye shot Pearl, and he's accusing me of killing Faye and hiding the body. I don't want to speak to him again without an attorney present who'll shut down his speculation before it grows any more absurd."

"They let you walk out of the station. That means they're grabbing for straws." Lou slid him a business card.

Hal read the name, "Gladys Swartz? Is she any good?"

"She's terrific and pursues acquittals with the force of a bloodhound drunk on a scent. Have you ever tried to walk one of those dogs? They go where they're going and you can only follow along and hope you'll somehow get back home."

"I'll remember that," Hal responded. Mitch drew close as he polished a glass, but Hal didn't care if he overheard.

"Good, there are plenty of other dogs." Lou gestured for Mitch to give him another round. "None of us knew you even had a wife until last Thursday night. Why would the police believe that she killed Pearl or that you killed her?"

"Lunacy?" Hal answered. Every time he recalled the conversation at the police station, it struck him as even sillier than it had been originally. "Does this happen often?"

"All the time," Lou swore with a raised hand. "Give Gladys a call, and ask for her advice. You'll have to pay for it, but she's well worth it."

Mitch rested an elbow on the bar and leaned in close.

"Detectives have been here asking about you, but I didn't tell them anything other than what you said last Thursday night. You haven't been coming in long, and you haven't caused any trouble. I couldn't tell them anything about Pearl other than that she came in, ordered martinis and left as alone as she came. If they're going to blame her killing on a housewife who'd never met her, they must not have much of a case. I don't see it going to court."

Detective Lynch's accusations were flying so wildly, Hal wasn't sure what would be believed. "If they can't find Faye, there will be no trial." He took a long swig of beer. "Lou, what happens to Pearl's body if no family is found to claim it?"

"You're worried about her body?" the bail bondsman asked, clearly amazed.

"Does that sound cold with my wife missing?" Hal asked. "I'm not prepared to pay for a funeral for a woman I barely knew. I just wondered what the usual procedure was."

"Unclaimed bodies are cremated."

Hal glanced down the bar and saw the man with the puffy white eyebrows, and several men he didn't recognize. It was Monday night though, not Thursday, so it was no wonder it was a different crowd. He didn't feel like staying.

"Thanks, Lou. I'll call Miss Swartz in the morning."

"It's Mrs. Swartz," Lou offered. "She was widowed during the war, and now concentrates solely on the law."

"That's exactly what I need." Hal told Mitch good-bye and left to catch the next Red Car home.

Hal scheduled an appointment late Tuesday afternoon so he could leave the office early rather than come in late. He'd expected Mrs. Swartz to be a stocky middle-aged woman who'd wear brown gabardine skirt suits, tightly laced oxfords, and frown at him over her thick glasses. He was wrong on all counts.

Gladys Swartz caught her long blonde hair in a tortoise shell clip at her nape. Had she worn it loose, she could have doubled for Veronica Lake. Her black dress was simply cut and fit her slender figure superbly. She wore only a hint of perfume, but it was a haunting, spicy scent. Her eyes were a vivid blue and held not a particle of sympathy as she listened to his story. That much he had anticipated. He concentrated on the facts: Faye had hired Joe Ezell, learned about Pearl, and now Pearl was dead and Faye had disappeared.

"You haven't been charged with any crime, so what do you expect me to do about your current mess?" she asked.

"Whatever you can," Hal responded. Her law firm's building wasn't far from where California West was located, and it was an easy walk. The office was decorated in dark woods and furniture covered in forest green leather. The bookcases were filled with legal tomes. The top of her mahogany desk was cleared of any files or papers, and she didn't take any notes.

"Lou King recommended you highly," Hal continued.

"That's very kind of him." She leaned forward, rested her arms on the desk, and laced her fingers together. "From what you say, all Detective Lynch has is imaginative conjecture. He won't come after you again until he finds your wife's body."

A sharp wince of pain shot through him. "Please don't say that," he countered. "She could be a murderer's hostage, which is awful, but I don't want to believe she's dead. She's only twenty-six, and far too nice a person to have shot anyone."

Gladys leaned back in her chair. "You keep believing that, and we'll think of her as missing until she turns up. Did you engage in any noisy arguments your neighbors might report?"

"No, never, we got along every well. We love each other."

"Love," she emphasized.

"Yes, we fell in love and married last summer. We treated each other respectfully, and I can't recall ever arguing about anything."

"Nothing at all?"

"No, nothing," Hal stressed. "Does that sound unlikely to you?"

"Yes, but that's not really the point, this is your story."

He glanced out the window, and found the coming sunset had filled the sky with a glorious pink haze. Even that spectacular beauty left him untouched. "I'd appreciate any advice you can give me, anything at all."

"You look completely lost, Mr. Marten."

"Will you charge me for that observation?"

She laughed, and then apologized. "I'm sorry. You're caught in a ghastly situation, and if you want me to be there if Lynch calls you into the station again, I will be."

"Thank you." He meant to stand, but sat just a moment longer.

"Do you have dinner plans?" she asked.

"How could I?"

"Fine, let's go to dinner and think how you can avoid being charged with murder."

Hal wasn't hungry, but going to dinner with Gladys Swartz was the best offer he'd had all day. "Fine, let's go." He finally found his legs and stood, and she came out from behind her desk.

"There's an Italian place just up the street that makes the most delicious spaghetti. It always lifts my spirits when I'm blue." She removed her jacket from the back of her chair and walked ahead of him to the door.

"How about a deep indigo?" Hal asked, and then laughed in spite of himself. "I'm sorry. I only slept a few hours last night, and I'm getting punchy."

"Then you definitely need to eat." She paused to tell the firm's receptionist that she was leaving for the day. The young woman took a quick glance at Hal and dipped her head to hide her smile.

Hal didn't notice. He followed Gladys to the elevator

and remained silent as they rode down to the first floor. "I may not be very good company," he announced as they reached the street.

"This is a strategy meeting, Mr. Marten, I don't expect to be entertained."

"Yes, of course. I'm sorry."

"Are you always so agreeable?"

"I try to be."

"So you'll avoid an argument rather than speak up?"

Hal didn't like where the conversation was going. "It depends on the situation and the subject. Some issues aren't worth pursuing."

"Excellent answer." She paused outside the Italian restaurant and gave him a chance to glance at the menu posted in the window. "Everything's good."

He'd taken Faye out for Italian food a few Saturdays ago, and the memory overwhelmed him with sadness now. "I do have to eat," he reminded himself and pulled open the door. The interior was softly lit, but it was a friendly place with red and white checked tablecloths, not somewhere a man would take a woman he wanted to romance.

The host greeted Gladys by name and ushered them to a table in a quiet corner where they could talk. "Thank you, Lloyd."

Hal waited until he'd walked away. "Lloyd doesn't sound like an Italian name."

"No, it doesn't, but he comes from a large family and maybe his parents just ran out of names."

"Probably." Hal picked up the menu and was amused by the descriptions of the selections offered. "Are the ravioli truly 'pillows of perfection'?"

"Try them and see," Gladys responded. "I'd rather not have wine tonight, but please order yourself a glass if you'd like."

"It wouldn't help," Hal answered. He had done all right in the office. He'd complimented his best salesmen and urged on the others who were in a slump. His head hurt, but it had all day. "Do you have any aspirin?" he asked their waiter.

"Of course, sir, let me get you some." He quickly returned with a little flat metal tin containing a dozen. "You may keep this, of course."

"Thank you." Hal swallowed three with some water and slipped the little box into his jacket pocket. Gladys ordered spaghetti and an antipasto salad, and he ordered a salad and ravioli.

He reached for one of the thin breadsticks in the glass container on the table. "My wife is a horrible cook," he revealed without realizing he'd spoken aloud.

"Did you eat out often?"

"Not often enough. I shouldn't have said that."

"No, you ought to tell me everything you can think of about your wife so you won't be surprised if you're questioned again. You didn't argue over her cooking?"

"No, I didn't want to hurt her feelings, but I should have signed her up for some cooking lessons rather than kept quiet about it."

Gladys tilted her head and studied him with a gently assessing gaze. "You seem like a really nice guy, Mr. Marten. That must annoy the detective to no end. He has to believe you're hiding something, because most of the people he deals with are."

Hal spread his napkin over his lap. "I'm no different. I failed to tell him Faye had hired a detective, and I hadn't told Faye I'd been stopping by the Golden Bear Lounge. I usually stayed at work later on Thursday night, maybe thirty minutes or forty-five to have everything ready for the early sales meeting Friday. I stopped at the bar on a complete whim, and went back a few times. I could never have anticipated becoming a near witness to a murder, or that anyone would ever suspect Faye of committing it."

"But she'd learned about Pearl LaFosse from Joe Ezell. She didn't accuse you of stepping out on her?"

"No, she seemed somewhat preoccupied, but I'd no

idea that she'd hired a detective until I found his card after she'd gone missing. No matter how I look at it, by stopping at the Golden Bear, I pushed the first domino, and sent the whole line collapsing one by one."

Gladys took a breadstick, snapped it in two and took a bite of the shorter end. "I used to line up dominos with my big brother, so I get your point. Blame isn't a productive emotion, Mr. Marten. Let's stick with the facts and keep our feelings in neutral."

"Does numb count?"

"Numb will do for now." She leaned back as their waiter served their salads. She jabbed a forkful and chewed it thoroughly before she spoke again. "I'm feeling more optimistic already, how about you?"

He layered small slices of cheese and salami on his fork and added a bit of lettuce. "Too soon to tell, but thanks for suggesting dinner. I don't remember eating lunch."

"Stick to your usual routine," she advised. "You'll find comfort in it."

"I doubt I should be at work, but I couldn't bear to stay at home another day and wait for Faye to show up or for the phone to ring."

"No, clearly you're better off at work if you can handle it."

"I can," he swore, but he was merely going through the motions. He finished his salad and took another breadstick. "I like these. They're fresh and crisp."

"They are." She smiled at him before eating the last of her salad. "You kept going back to the Golden Bear. Was it to see Pearl?"

"Not at first. I caught only a glimpse of her before she left, but she was elegantly dressed and looked out of place, which struck me as odd. I went back to the bar because taking a half hour for myself once a week felt good. Once I'd spoken to Pearl, and she wasn't easy to talk with, it became a challenge. I didn't mean to take it anywhere. If fact, the night she was murdered, I told her I wasn't coming back."

"Was she was no longer a challenge?"

"No, I finally realized it was stupid to pursue her when Faye was waiting for me at home. It was just a game, and I didn't want to take it any further."

"Was Pearl disappointed?"

"No, not at all. She wished me luck and walked out the door and was shot. She always checked her watch and left before our conversations ever grew lengthy. She wouldn't tell me where she was going in such a hurry, or whom she was meeting. I wish she had, because it might lead us to whoever murdered her."

"That's good," Gladys interjected. "It shows there was nothing serious between you two. Your wife may have found out about Pearl, but it didn't mean anything and was already over."

Hal waited until the waiter had served their entrees to respond. "But Faye wouldn't have known that." He tasted his ravioli, and it was as delicious as promised. "This is awfully good."

"I told you so." She wound her spaghetti on her fork to move it gracefully to her mouth without having to slurp in the last noodle. "It sounds as though it would have been completely out of character for Faye to have shot Pearl."

"That's what I've told Lynch, but it hasn't kept him from believing otherwise."

"That's because he doesn't know your wife, and you do. Would you describe her as outgoing, or somewhat shy?"

"Shy, she'd smile and be pleasant, but she wasn't the type to strike up a conversation with someone on the street. Successful salesmen have that knack, the instant appearance of friendship, and they can talk about anything with anyone. No one would ever hire Faye for a sales job, because she'd probably hide in the stockroom."

"Was she ever loud or confrontational?"

"Never. She went along with whatever I wanted to do, and I chose things she'd want to do too."

"So your only complaint was about her cooking?"

Hal kept eating while he considered his answer. "Yes, and I never spoke it aloud."

"You sound like a prince of a husband."

He looked up at her. "Is that bad?"

"It's unbelievable. Did she have complaints about you? Did you leave the bathroom a mess, wet towels on the floor, the toilet seat up, that kind of thing?"

"No, Lynch thought our house looked too neat to be lived in."

For a moment, she concentrated on her dinner, and then looked up. "Did it remind him of a set for a play?" she asked.

"No, a furniture store display room was how he put it."

She took a sip of her water. "That's downright rude, and you didn't react?"

"No, I thought he was deliberately trying to insult me, maybe provoke me into doing or saying something he could use against me."

"That's a good way to regard his observations. We can consider the police our friends when we need help, but don't let them fool you into believing they truly care about your welfare. They want to solve the crimes that cross their desks, that's their only concern."

"I understand. I just wish I knew where to find Faye."

She put down her fork and watched him eat. "You have a gentleman's manners."

"I hope so." He held her gaze, and wanted to know more about her. "Tell me about your most difficult case."

"Everything's confidential, as you must know."

"You don't have to use names," he stressed. "Just tell me about the time two men argued over who owned a race horse, something like that."

"Would you be concerned if I told another client about your predicament?"

"Probably not, but I understand. I just don't want to keep going over the same ground while Faye remains lost, or even worse, is being held hostage. I'd go through the streets calling her name if it would help to find her."

"Let's think a minute. Apparently Faye was an exemplary housekeeper. Even if her cooking wasn't very good, did she run the rest of your household without trouble? Or did she constantly forget to buy milk and eggs, or spend too much money?"

"No, she made lists and bought what we needed, and she never went over our budget. Why do you ask?"

"You know her to be a capable woman, so she should be doing all right wherever she is," she advised.

"That isn't reassuring. My whole world went to hell last Thursday night, and there seems to be nothing I can do to make everything right if we can't find Faye."

"Let's concentrate on protecting you for the time being. I always take half my dinner home in a box and eat it the next night. Would you like a box too?"

He got the message that the evening was over. Following her example, he'd take the remainder of his ravioli home. He signaled their waiter, paid for their dinner and walked Gladys back to her building where she left her car during the day. He supposed she'd send him a bill for the time they'd been together, but he'd be glad to pay whatever she charged simply for being a sympathetic ear. He rode the Red Car home, and Mr. Cuddles met him at the door.

"I didn't forget you," Hal assured him, but in truth, he hadn't thought once about getting home early to feed the cat. At least he still had one reason to come home, but sadly, a chubby feline wasn't nearly enough.

CHAPTER 10

Joe Ezell called Hal Tuesday evening, and failed to credit his sweetheart, Mary Margaret, for what he was about to say. "I've been thinking that despite the fact you didn't know any of Faye's friends, she might have had some that she preferred you didn't meet. Where did she work before you met?"

"She did secretarial work with a temp agency, so she wasn't anywhere for long."

"Do you remember the name of the agency?"

Hal tried to recall and couldn't. "I'm not sure she ever mentioned the name. She'd just say she'd worked here or there that day, often doing filing."

"What about where she lived? Could she have friends from there?"

"She rented a room from a women who was very strict about her roomers' behavior. The girls had to be home before midnight or she'd lock them out. Faye complained nobody stayed long enough to get to know. I believed it disappointed her."

"Well, then, what about high school? Do you have her yearbooks? Kids write notes to each other in them, and you might find a name we could pursue."

Hal settled down on the couch. "That's a great idea, but

Faye never mentioned having any yearbooks, and I don't recall seeing any when we moved here after we married."

"How about an address book? Did she keep track of numbers she called often?"

Mr. Cuddles leaped into Hal's lap, and he gave the beast a tentative scratch behind the ears. "She had a small one she kept in her purse, so it's not here."

"I don't want you to think I'm giving up on your case, Mr. Marten. I'll keep looking until we find her. What high school did Faye attend? I might be able to get some information there."

"She grew up in Monrovia. We never talked about high school, but I think the city has only one."

"Sounds right. They probably won't talk to me unless I tell them I'm a relative. Would that bother you?"

"Not at all if you can learn something about Faye we can use to find her."

"Thank you. I'll tell them I'm her uncle Joe, her mother's brother. I don't suppose there's any resemblance between us."

Hal closed his eyes and compared them in his mind. They both had brown hair, but Faye's eyes were hazel and Joe's brown. Their features weren't similar either. "Hair color is about it, I'm afraid, but I'm sure you'll be convincing."

"I will. I'll go over tomorrow morning and take the article from the paper to show she's missing. What was her maiden name?"

"Bell, like Alexander Graham Bell. Her full name is Faye Renee Bell." Hal refused to put it in the past tense.

"You said she liked to sew. Maybe the Home Economics teacher taught sewing and will remember her."

"If she's there. Faye graduated in 1939, so the same teachers might not still teach there."

"High school teachers tend to stay put, so I bet she will be. Maybe they'll give me a list of her teachers for her senior year, and I'll try them all."

"Call me at work whether you learn anything or not."

"Will do."

Hal hung up the phone and gave Mr. Cuddles' ears another lackadaisical scratch. The cat's warmth on his thighs was pleasant enough, but it sure wouldn't be when it got warmer. Maybe people only cuddled their cats when the temperatures were chilly. "What are we going to do, buddy?"

Mr. Cuddles looked up at him and quickly glanced away. Cleary he possessed no helpful insights either.

Joe Ezell drove the twenty miles northeast to Monrovia late Wednesday morning to miss the early traffic flowing into downtown Los Angeles. The city was close to the foothills of the San Gabriel Mountains and had been founded by a man named William Monroe who'd bought the land from "Lucky" Baldwin's Rancho Santa Anita. It was a charming city, and he found the high school on Colorado Blvd. easily enough.

The high school had Spanish architecture as so many of southern California institutions did, with graceful arches and a red tile roof. He parked across the street and walked into the office with the confident stride of a man who expects his questions to be answered. He had the article from the *LA Times* in a manila folder. The secretary left her desk to meet him at the counter.

"Good morning," Joe began. He'd rehearsed his spiel on the way to be both concise and sincere, but he wouldn't use the uncle bit unless he had to. He spoke softly to lure in the secretary's attention, spoke his piece and showed her the article. "Maybe you saw this in the paper. Faye attended high school here, and the family is trying to locate her high school friends in hopes of finding clues as to where she might be. Her name would have been Faye Renee Bell then."

The school secretary was a gray-haired woman with a substantial figure. She pursed her lips as she read the article and then shook her head. "I've been here twenty years, and I don't remember having a student with her name, and her face isn't familiar."

"Really? Would you please make a quick check of your records to be sure? She would have graduated in 1939."

The secretary sighed with the effort, but she pulled open a drawer in one of the gray metal file cabinets lined along the wall. "No, the class of 1939 didn't have a Faye Bell."

"Maybe we have the year wrong, will you look at 1938 and 1940, please."

"Well, since I've gone to the trouble of looking up one year, I suppose I can look at a couple others." She shuffled though several files and then turned to the clerk seated at a desk on the opposite side of the room.

"Hortense, do you remember a Faye Bell? I can't find her."

"Faye Bell? No I don't. Did she go by another name?"

"Her middle name is Renee," Joe reminded them. "Maybe she went by Renee."

The secretary closed the file cabinet and returned to the counter. "We haven't had any students with the last name Bell, so the first name doesn't matter. Are you sure you have the right school?"

"This is the only high school in Monrovia, isn't it?"

"Yes. The Catholic school, Immaculate Conception, only goes up to 8th grade. I think maybe you're in the wrong city."

"Could be. Thank you for your time." Joe left and stopped at a gas station to use the pay telephone on the way out of town. "Mr. Marten, I'm here in Monrovia, and the high school has no record of a Faye Bell ever attending. Are you sure she went to school here?"

Hal rocked back in his chair. "Yes, she once told me she hadn't been very popular at Monrovia High, but she'd learned a lot. How can they have no record of her?"

Joe had the uncomfortable feeling Hal Marten hadn't known his wife nearly as well as he'd thought. "The ladies in the high school office looked as though they knew the school inside out, but something isn't right here. I could check with the high schools in neighboring towns if you like."

"No, she said she went to Monrovia High, so don't waste your time looking elsewhere."

"Maybe her name wasn't Bell then. Could she have been married before she met you?"

"No, her high school boyfriend was killed in the war. They'd planned to marry when he came home."

"Do you know his name? Maybe the school will have a record of him."

"No, she never referred to him by name. It was always just 'my boyfriend'. She didn't talk about him often though, and I never asked her about him when there was no point in being jealous of a dead man."

"None whatsoever," Joe agreed. "I'll talk to you later."

"Wait a minute. Faye was born in Los Angeles, so there ought to be a record of it at the county clerk's office, shouldn't there?"

"We already know she was born, so I don't think it would help our cause, but I'll search for a record if you want to pay for it. Do you know her parents' names?"

Hal drew in a deep breath. "I never heard their given names. She always called them her mom and dad. I'm sorry. I don't want to waste your time, so skip the county clerk's office."

Joe preferred to worry over the details of a case on the golf course, but to admit it would sound unprofessional. "All right, I'll go back to my office and think about what we can do next."

"Thank you. I'll try and remember more than I have."

Hal shrugged off a cold chill as he hung up the telephone. He'd always talked about the present and future with Faye, what they were doing today or plans for something like a trip to the Gold Rush country. They'd never entertained each other in the evenings with tales of their youth. Now he wished they had.

Gladys Swartz called him later. "I forgot to ask if you're a veteran. It would help your cause."

"Yes, I was a captain in the Army, although I didn't win any medals. I was stationed in Washington D.C. with the Quartermaster Corps."

"All that matters is that you served with pride."

"Could I stop by your office later? I learned something disturbing, and I don't know what to do about it."

"Does it concern Faye?"

"Yes, and I'd rather not discuss it over the office phone."

"I'll be free at six, come by then."

Hal noted the time in his daily calendar. He'd heard nothing from Detective Lynch since they'd found his Packard on Saturday, and he considered that good. During his lunch break, he'd walked rather than stop to eat, and he returned to his office feeling somewhat calmer. He wondered if he ought to make a chart of his mood, like they did for sales. However, he'd still be skirting the bottom of the graph, and it didn't seem worthwhile.

Gladys was dressed in an attractive gray suit, and Hal realized he hadn't mentioned Faye's horrible taste in fabrics. At least the pajamas she'd made for him were a solid blue. He took the same seat he'd occupied yesterday and refrained from mentioning it. It seemed unfair to criticize Faye's tastes when she wasn't there to defend herself.

Her desktop again clear, the attorney sat back in her chair and smiled. "Tell me what you learned, Mr. Marten. No matter how minor, it might be useful in your defense should you need one."

"Which I hope I won't," he responded. He told her about Joe Ezell's lack of success at Monrovia High and watched her eyes widen.

She sat forward. "You hadn't known each other long,

and when it feels so good to meet someone new, no one looks too deeply. That's why long engagements are recommended. You accepted what Faye told you and went on doing things together. Now when you need the details of her past to find her, all your detective receives are blank stares."

"Yes, but I'm afraid it's more puzzling than useful."

"That's where you're wrong. If Faye wasn't who she pretended to be, or deliberately concealed something important from you, she could have left town with someone from her past she'd never mentioned."

"There's such a sweet innocence to Faye, that's difficult to believe," he countered.

"You don't have to believe it, and don't tell Detective Lynch what you've found either. We have to stay ahead of the police. I should have it inscribed on a plaque and hang it on the wall."

Hal nodded. "Stay ahead of the police is a fine motto, but I still don't know what to do."

Gladys stood, and he stood with her. "You're going to go home and heat up the leftover ravioli for dinner, unless you ate it for breakfast."

He smiled at that thought. "No, I saved it for tonight. Thanks for seeing me on such short notice."

"Think nothing of it, Mr. Marten. Just keep me informed, and I'll do my best to protect you should the need arise."

She walked him to her office door, and he left for home wondering if Mr. Cuddles would care to share the ravioli.

Joe Ezell had again been invited to dinner at Mary Margaret's. He brought flowers and offered to help in the kitchen. "I can chop an onion with the best of them," he swore.

"Sure you can, but everything's already prepared and in the oven." She put the colorful bouquet in a vase and placed it on the dining table. "Come on in the living room and tell me about your day."

Joe took his favorite spot on the sofa, and she curled up beside him. "It was an exceedingly odd day." Without giving away any confidential details, he described his lack of success at Monrovia High School. "Most people don't lie about where they went to high school, so this is really odd."

Mary Margaret agreed. "Women often shave a few years off their age. Could she be older than she wanted her husband to believe?"

"Maybe, but she'd never expect him to go to her school and check which year she graduated. This whole case has been strange from the beginning. It's like playing on a wobbly pool table, and the ball never rolls the way you expect."

"Maybe by the time you're a famous detective and wish to publish a book about your cases, you'll have all the answers."

"Let's hope. Something sure smells good. What are you cooking?"

"Chicken and dumplings. I hope you'll like it."

Joe regarded her with a teasing smile. "If it has anything to do with you, I'll love it."

She giggled and stood to lure him into the dining room for another of her marvelous dinners and with a sultry glance, promised so much more.

Thursday morning, Hal's boss, George Sharp, called him into his office. As a vice-president of the firm, his office was twice as large as Hal's and splendidly furnished. They occasionally met to discuss sales figures, but Hal doubted that was George's concern today.

George Sharp raised his hand to ask for a moment while he finished a telephone call, and Hal waited at the door to be invited in. George was a portly man who wore expensive clothes, but there was only so much an expertly tailored suit could camouflage, and he was at the outer limits. His gray hair formed a thick fringe around a bald pate giving him a monk-like appearance.

Hal entered when George ended the call. "Good morning," he said with all the enthusiasm he could gather, which wasn't much. He took a chair, but couldn't get comfortable.

"You look awful," Sharp responded. "How long has your wife been missing?"

"It's been a week," Hal replied, but he'd suffered a year's worth of worry.

"It's a shame, but I want you to take a leave of absence until she's found. Don't argue with me about this, Hal. You'll remain on the payroll, so don't worry about money, but your situation is too distracting for you to continue to come in as you have this last week."

Stunned, Hal leaned forward. "Coming to work is all that's kept me sane, so I'd rather stay."

"The issue isn't open for discussion."

Hal was well acquainted with George's tendency to power through a decision rather than invite comments from subordinates. It was a trait Hal considered an enormous flaw. "Who'll handle my sales crew? Many of them are new, and they need encouragement as well as supervision of their accounts."

"I'll stop by your office twice a day to oversee things. Besides, Mrs. Adams is experienced and can probably run things herself."

Hal thought Lorraine definitely could, but that wasn't the issue. "I need to work, Mr. Sharp. Really I do."

"Then spend your time looking for your wife. Stay until lunch and leave a brief description of your sales force with Mrs. Adams, and I'll take it from there."

Hal rose slowly. He would have argued all day had there been any hope George Sharp would change his mind, but it would have been easier to convince a massive boulder to dance. He didn't waste his breath on such a fruitless effort.

"Fine. I'll have it for you." He returned to his office and drew his secretary inside. "Sit with me a minute, Mrs. Adams."

"Yes, sir. What do you need?"

Hal sank into the chair behind his desk and shook his head. "Not a damn thing. Excuse me, but George Sharp insists I stay out of the office until Faye is found."

"What if she isn't?" Lorraine asked, and then slapped her hand over her mouth. "Oh no, I shouldn't have said that."

"It's what a lot of people are thinking so you needn't apologize." He told her he'd write a sentence or two about each of his salesmen for her to type. "Mr. Sharp claims he'll come by a couple of times a day to answer questions, or do whatever is needed, but he'll probably forget in a day or two. He didn't tell me not to call you, so I'll talk to you every day. I know you can handle our business as usual while I'm away, but you have my home telephone number should any real trouble arise."

Lorraine straightened up proudly. "I know what needs to be done, sir."

"Thank you. I knew I could depend on you." He'd see she received a substantial raise as soon as he returned to work. "The salesmen are sure to talk about me, but I'd appreciate it if you discouraged it when they speak with you."

"Of course, I will, sir."

She returned to her desk, and he quickly listed the names of his sales force, wrote a note to emphasize each one's strengths, and added an itemized copy of last month's figures. That would be enough to satisfy Sharp, or really, all the vice president would care to know. Hal thought about calling Gladys Swartz, but he'd not seek her advice two days in a row and risk coming across as a complete idiot.

He straightened up his office, which he always kept neat, so it didn't take long. When he was ready to go, he announced he'd be out of the office for a few days, and broke the news that George Sharp would be in charge while he was away. He noted the men's strained expressions, but no matter how concerned, none of them felt worse than he did.

"I hope to be back soon. I know you'll continue to do your best for California West while I'm away."

He left without giving anyone a chance to ask questions, strode out of the building and kept walking rather than go straight to the Red Car. Heartsick, he wandered a long while before taking the train for home. He hadn't been there five minutes before Carmen knocked on his door.

"I hate to bother you," she began. "But the police were here this morning and dug up all the pretty flowers you and Faye planted. They jabbed them back in the ground, but the yard's a mess, and I wanted you to know why."

"Thank you, Carmen. Let me get your plate, I should have returned it earlier. The waffles were the best I've ever eaten."

She waited on the porch, and pressed the plate to her ample bosom when Hal handed it to her. "I'm so frightened for Faye, but I know you didn't have anything to do with her disappearance."

"Unfortunately, the police think otherwise, but I'll speak to them before they start ripping up your yard too."

Carmen laughed, and then caught herself. "I'm sorry, none of this is funny. I stood by the fence and watched them. How could anyone think you'd bury Faye in your own backyard?"

"I'm completely unable to understand their reasoning." He bid her a good afternoon and fed Mr. Cuddles on the back porch. He closed the door to keep the cat out of his way, and again settled for soup and a grilled cheese sandwich. He began making a shopping list and put off a call to Detective Lynch until morning.

He stayed up late reading a war novel he'd been saving, rather than continue *Lust for Life*. It reminded him too much of Pearl. He set the book aside and Mr. Cuddles jumped in his lap, turned around to make himself comfortable, and stayed. "You are spoiled rotten," he scolded, but he didn't shoo the cat away. Faye had said she'd had Mr. Cuddles for four years, and he wondered if even that were true. She'd taken Cuddles to the vet for his rabies shot a couple of months ago, but he didn't know which vet that might have been, and he didn't feel ambitious enough to search for the receipt among their household expenses.

When he finally did go to bed, the cat curled up at the foot and was asleep before Hal could close his eyes. He usually fell asleep in a matter of minutes, but his mind refused to let go, and he couldn't relax. No matter how often he shifted position, he remained too tense to sleep. He lay in a tangle of sheets and blankets hurt and confused and remembered Pearl lying dead in the street and grew even more thoroughly depressed. It was past two a.m. when he got up to make some notes. He was convinced Faye hadn't left him, and the possibility she was being held as a hostage meant they'd been searching for the past of the wrong woman. Whoever had killed Pearl, had come from her life. They ought to be able to discover his identity and whereabouts from an investigation of Pearl's friends rather than Faye's. He organized his thoughts as best he could, and completely worn out, returned to bed and fell into a troubled asleep.

He called Detective Lynch at nine o'clock Friday morning, and was told he was out of the precinct working a new case. Hal left a message for him to call, but he'd not waste his time sitting at home waiting to hear from him. He waited half an hour to make certain Joe Ezell would be in his office and called him.

"Do you have any time free this morning? I need to talk with you."

Joe glanced at his empty appointment book. "I can shuffle things around. Come on over." He made fresh coffee, and laid a couple of empty file folders on his desk to make it appear he'd been working on something other than the crossword puzzle. He left the door open so Hal could walk right in.

When Hal was seated across from him, Joe offered

what little hope he could. "We've got to get a break soon. Someone will remember they saw something, or..."

"Give it up," Hal cautioned, "We're on our own. Lynch dug up my flowerbeds yesterday looking for Faye's body. If she drove over to the Golden Bear Lounge last Thursday night, she might have seen who shot Pearl and been taken hostage by the killer. When I suggested it, Detective Lynch wouldn't take the possibility seriously."

"Why? It's a damn good theory. Maybe we ought to be searching into Pearl's background rather than Faye's."

"My thoughts exactly," Hal agreed. He told Joe about Pearl's trailer. "Apparently she spent little time there, but it was the only key in her purse when she died."

"You want some coffee?" Joe asked. "It's fresh."

Hal took a cup and sat back as he sipped it. "I don't believe any family has been found to claim Pearl's body."

Joe reached for the telephone on his desk. "Let's call the coroner and ask." He had the number handy, mainly for show, and this was the first time he'd used it. "I'll tell them I'm from the Golden Bear Lounge and see what they'll tell me."

"People who'd seen her there might want to plan a funeral. I should have thought of it myself, but I've been too worried about Faye."

"That's understandable." Joe called the coroner's office with the Golden Bear story, and learned Pearl's body had not been claimed.

"Her name wasn't in the paper, so how would anyone in her family know she's dead?" Hal asked. "Maybe they didn't get together often, or weren't close."

"I'll start looking through the Los Angeles phone books. It would give us an address that might lead to a good contact."

"I didn't see a phone in her trailer."

Joe frowned. "Really? That doesn't mean someone in her family won't be in a book. Did Pearl ever seem frightened when she left the Golden Bear?"

"No, she just smiled and said it was time to go. She warned me not to follow her, so I assumed she was meeting a man."

"A jealous man?" Joe asked.

Hal shrugged. "I got the feeling it would simply be inconvenient, a bother she didn't need for me to follow her."

Joe leaned back in his chair to consider the matter. "I hope you won't think I'm out of line, but when I saw Pearl, I took her for a classy lady who might be an expensive call girl. Did she ever give you that impression?"

Hal set his empty coffee cup on Joe's desk. "No, not at all. The bartender thought she was a widow who came in to have a drink and remember her husband. She was always so stylishly dressed, I thought she might work in the fashion industry, but I didn't get a straight answer from her."

"There are plenty of designers who manufacture their lines here in Los Angeles. I wish we had a photo of her, but maybe if I ask around using her name, someone will know her."

"Good, I'll go with you."

"Let me handle it, Mr. Marten. Two men asking questions will be seen as intimidating. I'll give you a call this evening, or earlier if I discover anything."

"I didn't look for labels in her suits, and hats, when I visited her trailer. Maybe I should go out there again and have the manager let me in."

"Excellent idea. She must have bought her clothes somewhere. We'll track her through her clothes." Joe stood and Hal left to get his car.

Jed Riley, the manager at Starlight Park remembered Hal, but couldn't grant his request. "I'm sorry, but the police came back yesterday and packed up all her things, and I'll bet her plant isn't talking."

Hal had put the philodendron on the coffee table at

home and touched it each time he walked by. "No, it isn't. I wish I'd checked the labels in her clothing the first time I was here, but she'd just been killed, and I wasn't thinking clearly. Are you sure she never entertained any friends here?"

"All I can swear to is that I never saw her with anyone. That's strange isn't it? Such a beautiful woman should have had a lot of friends, male ones especially."

"I'm sure she did. We just can't find them." He left and returned the books Faye had checked out to the library. He laid them on the counter, and Sandra Sloan greeted him warmly.

"Are you Faye's husband?" she inquired.

"I am," Hal replied, keeping her alive in his mind.

"Is she still missing?" the librarian asked. "We could put up a flyer and ask our patrons to look for her if she is."

"Thank you, but I'd hate to put up flyers the way people do for a lost dog."

Sandra checked in the ghost books and set them aside on a rolling cart to reshelf later. "I wouldn't look at it that way. The more people who are searching for Faye, the sooner she ought to be found."

"True. I'll think about having some flyers made." He stepped away, and then turned back. "I just lost a friend and wonder if she had any books checked out that need to be returned. Her name was Pearl LaFosse."

"I don't recognize the name, but we keep all the requests for a card, so let me check our files." She looked under the Ls first and then the Fs. "I'm sorry, but I can't find her. Any library books she had would be stamped with the branch library's name."

"Thank you." It had been a long shot anyway, but maybe she'd bought all the books she wished to read. He went home and checked her copy of *Lust for Life* and found a bookstore name on the price sticker. "Yes!" he shouted. Mr. Cuddles' eyes shot open, and Hal apologized for disturbing his nap. "This is the first clue we've found, so don't give me your damn evil eye, buster."

The bookstore was located near the theater they'd visited on Sunday afternoons, and he nearly ran he was so excited to reach it. The clerk was a tiny gentleman seated on a tall stool \ reading a thick book. Hal waited for him to mark his place before he introduced himself.

"A good friend gave me a copy of *Lust for Life*, and I thought I might buy a book for her. I'm hoping you'll know what she bought recently so it won't be a duplicate. Her name is Pearl LaFosse."

The little man's eyes lit with delight. "Ah, yes, Miss LaFosse stops in here often. I believe her last purchase was an Agatha Christie mystery, *The Body in the Library.*"

"Yes, she mentioned it. Perhaps you can suggest something similar she might enjoy."

The clerk slid his glasses up his nose and considered the question thoughtfully. "We have a large selection of books in the mystery section. Let me show you where it is." He jumped down from his stool to lead the way. No more than five feet tall, he hurried along with a breezy step. "Miss LaFosse has just begun reading mysteries, so anything that looks good to you would be appropriate."

"Thank you." Hal scanned the titles and chose *Murder on the Orient Express.* It appealed to him, and it didn't matter what Pearl might have thought because he'd be the one reading it. He carried the book to the counter. "It might be fun for her to receive the book in the mail. Do you have her address?"

The clerk frowned slightly. "She doesn't have an account with us, so I'm sorry, no. If you two are friends who share books, don't you know where she lives?"

"Yes, of course I do. I just didn't think to bring it with me." He paid for the book and carried it home. As he laid it on the coffee table, it struck him that Pearl's copy of *The Body in the Library* hadn't been in her trailer, so where could it be?

CHAPTER 11

When Hal arrived home, he found Detective Lynch standing on his front porch. "I saw your car in the garage and thought you had to be here," Lynch called to him.

Unwilling to reveal he was seeking answers of his own, Hal showed him the bookstore bag. "I needed something new to read." He unlocked the front door, and the detective stepped over the threshold without waiting to be invited in. "I can't believe you dug up the flowers when you wouldn't have found anything but dirt."

Lynch gazed about the living room. "No, we didn't, but your landlord said he didn't mind. You'd be surprised how stupid some people can be when it comes to hiding a body."

"You spoke to my landlord?" Hal was disgusted Eric Duffy had been bothered over nothing. He was a nice man, a gentleman, and he shouldn't have been dragged into Jacob Lynch's absurd investigations. "As far as we know, Faye is alive, and possibly a killer's hostage. What are you doing to find her? Has the newspaper story generated any valuable leads?"

"We've gotten quite a few tips from the crazies who'll confess to any crime, but nothing remotely useful as yet. Are you sure you haven't heard from your wife? Have you answered your phone only to have someone hang up without speaking?"

"I haven't been answering my phone." Hal laid the new mystery book on the coffee table. He compressed the bag into a tight ball Mr. Cuddles might like to play with, if the cat ever got off his cushion other than for meals.

The detective focused on Hal's hands. "You look tense, Mr. Marten. Are you sure there isn't something you'd like to tell me?"

Other than, *Go to hell*, Hal couldn't think of one. "Not a thing."

"You left this number when you called this morning. Are you taking time off from work?"

"I am," Hal responded. He stared at Lynch rather than admit he'd been put on leave. "I'm hoping we find my wife safe and soon."

Lynch turned toward the door. "Just go on thinking that, Mr. Marten, and I'll keep working on the case in my own way."

Hal locked the door behind him and thought good riddance. Lynch was never going to find Faye digging in her own garden. Sickened by the lack of progress, he went outside to replant the wilted pansies and snapdragons before they died. It would give him something to do for an hour or so.

He was watering the flowerbeds with the hose, when Eric Duffy called to him. Hal turned off the faucet and opened the gate. "Good afternoon," he greeted him, fearing the worst.

Eric Duffy was in his seventies, and he and his wife had once lived in the duplex where Hal and Faye now resided. He walked across the grass to get a better look at the flowers, and then came back to the small patio where Hal stood.

"You've been a good tenant," Eric began, "but when the police start excavating the flowerbeds, I have to worry."

"Me too. I assure you there's absolutely no reason to

believe I had anything to do with Faye's disappearance. We'll continue to be good tenants."

Duffy kept his white hair cut short, and he preferred a sports shirt and slacks to a suit and tie when he made calls on his tenants. His mood remained thoroughly business-like today. "Your lease runs through August. Let's wait to see how things stand then before we discuss renewing it."

August was months away, but Hal didn't like his landlord's tone of voice. This was just another blow, and he shrugged it off rather than appear as angry as he truly felt. "That's fair." They shook hands and Eric left. Hal remained silently fuming and thought maybe he ought to buy a punching bag to hang in the garage.

As a child, Joe Ezell had been to the fabric wholesalers' shops on Los Angeles Street with his mother. There were dozens of such venders, all claiming to have the best possible prices. There were also many wholesalers selling the latest fashions. He'd gotten only a quick glimpse of Pearl LaFosse as she'd left the Golden Bear, but her elegant suit would have come from a shop with designers' high-priced fashions rather than bargain housedresses.

He entered several such places, but received only confused stares when he gave the clerks Pearl's name and described her as a beautiful, sophisticated young woman. He was about to give up when a clerk at the fifth shop responded with a thoughtful nod. "Has she shopped here?" Joe asked.

"Lots of women come with their friends, but there is a pretty brunette who shops alone. She likes suits, but anything would flatter her figure." The young man winked and broke into a wide grin.

Joe hadn't mentioned Pearl had been murdered to avoid lengthy conversations that would surely lead nowhere he needed to go. "That might be Pearl. Do you have her address or telephone number?"

"No, we're a cash only business and don't collect numbers. If the woman I'm thinking of might be your Pearl, I've seen her go across the street to Helen's. She sells the type of hats the woman wears."

Joe chided himself silently for not going on a hunt for hats in the first place when far fewer places sold them. "Thank you for your time. I'll try there."

The clerk rested his arms on the counter. "I should have asked why you're looking for her before I answered your questions. I hope you don't wish her any harm."

"No, of course not. It's about an inheritance." That was a good story, and Joe had used it before. People became positively loquacious when they thought some of that inheritance might be coming their way. "Thanks."

Helen was an Asian woman with flowing black hair, carefully penciled eyebrows, and ruby red lips. She sat upon a stool behind the counter ruffling a red ribbon on a small red hat. "How may I help you?" she asked.

Joe looked around the shop. Helen had sorted her wears by color and style, and they ran the gamut from tiny veiled cocktail hats to wide brimmed straws with trailing ribbons. "Beautiful hats," he began, then felt foolish for stating the obvious. He described Pearl and a bright light of recognition brightened Helen's gaze.

"She never gave me her name, so she could be Pearl, but a lady like the one you describe comes in every month or so." She held up the hat she was decorating. "She bought one similar to this one not too long ago. She insists a hat have a flirtatious soul. I believe my creations have exquisite style, but she calls it soul. Did you wish to buy her a present? You must already know what she likes, or I can make suggestions."

"Thank you, but no. I'm looking for her because the family has lost touch, and there's a generous inheritance involved."

"Really? I hope she wishes to spend part of it on new hats." She giggled and then shook her head. "I'm sorry, but she never left her address or telephone number with me. Why don't you give me your card, and when she comes in, I'll give it to her."

While that would never happen, Joe pulled a card from his wallet. "Thank you, that would be very helpful." He debated buying a hat for Mary Margaret while he was there, but it struck him as too personal a gift, and he slid his wallet back into his pants pocket and left.

He looked up the street and a sign for another hat shop caught his eye. Neither of the clerks there recognized Pearl's name or description. The hats on display were not nearly as pretty as the ones at Helen's, and he left without wasting any more of their time or his.

He hated being stumped, and wished he'd learned something more useful than he had. Soon after getting his detective's license, he'd discovered when he grew frustrated with an investigation, it was time to quit for the day. He dodged this way and that along the crowded sidewalk to reach his car without being pummeled with shoppers' bags bursting with bargains.

The central library had copies of all the city telephone books, and he stopped by on his way back to his office. He flipped through them all, but didn't find a single LaFosse living in Los Angeles. He'd seen Pearl with his own eyes so he knew she existed, or at least had, but she was proving to be as impossible to track as Faye Marten.

Maybe a round of golf would help clear his mind, or at the very least, it couldn't hurt.

Hal was disappointed in Joe's report. He took the cup of coffee Joe offered, but he was in no mood to speculate on what to do next. "Maybe Pearl is so difficult to find because she wanted to be. I don't want to believe it, but what if she were an expensive call girl? Would she entertain her clients in her home, or meet them at hotels or private clubs?"

Joe rolled a pencil between his palms. "If she were a rich man's mistress, he would have paid for her apartment. If she shall we say 'entertained' more than one amorous client, I'll bet she met them at a nice hotel. Do you want me to make the rounds and see if any desk clerks will admit to knowing her? As for private clubs, they'll protect their members and won't admit a thing."

Joe took a yellow legal pad from a desk drawer to list hotels. He began with the Biltmore. "The Biltmore is a good possibility. The interior is damn near covered in gold leaf and the Academy Awards have been given out in their ballroom."

Hal nodded thoughtfully. "It's the last place Elizabeth Short was seen."

"The Black Dahlia? That story makes me shudder every time I see a reference in the paper. I'd rent a boat and drop a body at sea before I'd slice one in two."

"Or leave it in the mountains," Hal proposed. "Go far enough into the Angeles Crest Forest, and it wouldn't be found for years, if then."

"I'd keep that thought from the police detective who's been questioning you."

Hal straightened up. "I intend to. A woman as elegant as Pearl LaFosse would have looked at home in the Biltmore. What about the Beverly Hills Hotel?"

Joe put in on the list. "They have bungalows movie stars rent. If Pearl regularly met a wealthy man there, he might have kept a bungalow. I'm beginning to get excited now, how about you?"

"I understand what you mean, because any lead would be welcome. Los Angeles has a dozen or more expensive hotels, try them all if the first couple don't provide anything we can use."

"I will." Joe added the Hotel Normandie, Hollywood Roosevelt, and the Beverly Wilshire. "The way she dressed, it didn't look as though she'd spent the afternoon at the Georgian Hotel appreciating the ocean views, but I'll keep it in mind."

"Do. If she came by the Golden Bear Lounge on the way home, she could have lived near there. There are too many apartments to survey, so let's hope you find someone who knew her at one of the hotels. Then we'll need the name, or names of the men she met."

"That might be tough to get."

"Probably, but that's no reason not to try."

"What do you plan to do if we can link her to a man?"

Hal set the empty coffee cup on the desk and stood. "You needn't worry that I'll go after him myself. I'll pass along his name to Detective Lynch. I want to see the man who shot Pearl punished, but I'm hoping finding her killer will lead to news of my wife."

"I wished I'd had a photo of Pearl this morning, because this job would be a whole lot easier if we had one. Maybe you could describe her to an artist and get a good likeness. Do you know anyone who loves to draw?"

Hal thought a minute. "What you're describing is a police artist, and I'm not asking Detective Lynch for anything, let alone a drawing of Pearl, but I may know someone who could help. I'll call him and get back to you."

Joe rose to walk Hal to the door. "See what you can do, and I'll wait to start making the rounds of the hotels."

Hal thought Lou King might solve several problems. He'd know how to track bail jumpers, and could probably contact a portrait artist outside the police department. He called his office when he got home. Lou again wanted to meet that night at the Golden Bear Lounge, and Hal reluctantly agreed. He stretched out on the sofa and fell asleep. When he woke with a start, no more than fifteen minutes had passed. He went into the bedroom to set his alarm clock so he'd not be late to meet Lou, but now sleep eluded him.

He reached the bar before Lou, and waved to Mitch as he slid onto a stool. Mitch brought him a beer and set it down carefully in front of him. It was Saturday night, and the bar was crowded and noisy.

"Any word on your wife?" Mitch asked.

Hal shook his head. "I'm hoping she's still alive somewhere."

"I do too," Mitch replied.

Before the bartender could move down the bar, Hal stopped him. "How long had Pearl LaFosse been coming here, Mitch? I think whoever shot her might have grabbed Faye."

Mitch leaned against the bar. "Pearl might have been in a few times last fall, but this year, I saw her almost every Thursday night. You're the only one who ever succeeded in speaking with her, or even knew her name, so I can't help you with more."

"Thanks anyway," Hal said. He took a long drink of his beer and had just set his glass on the bar when Lou King walked in.

Lou took the stool beside Hal's. "You don't look good."

"I hear that a lot. I have a detective tracing Pearl LaFosse in hopes we can learn something about whoever might have taken Faye from what they know. How do you go after men who jump bail?"

Lou ordered a scotch on the rocks before he replied. "I don't do it myself. I have a bounty hunter go after them. He actually finds most of the people he's seeking at home, or their mother's house, or some favorite haunt. Most aren't difficult to find, but I'd rather spend my time on other things."

Lou was always well-dressed, and Hal readily understood that he wouldn't deign to dirty his well-tailored suits tackling runaways. "I understand, but when we know next to nothing about Pearl, it's difficult to find her family or friends."

Lou nodded thoughtfully. "I don't mean to insult the dear lady's memory, but I thought her a classy hooker."

Hal was already investigating that angle. "Do hookers usually look that good?"

Lou laughed. "The expensive ones do, and they rarely encounter any trouble with the law, so they don't often call me for bail."

Hal asked about hotels to keep the conversation going, and Lou was reminded of a hooker who'd had a variety of wigs so she could frequently ply her trade at the Coconut Grove nightclub at the Ambassador Hotel without being recognized by the staff. "The problem was, she was at least six feet tall and weighed maybe one hundred twenty pounds, so they could always see her coming no matter what she'd done with her hair. I believe she married one of her johns and moved to Oregon."

Hal smiled as though he were amused by the tale. "Do you know who in Los Angeles would have the money to keep a woman as refined as Pearl, and the means to have her killed if she displeased him?"

Lou shook his head. "I can think of one, and you don't want to go there. Governor Warren calls Jack Dragna the 'Capone of LA', and he's far too dangerous a man to question about Pearl, or for any other reason."

Hal finished his beer and paid for Lou's drink. "There have to be other men who...."

"Of course, many wealthy men who are looked upon as highly respectable are tied to organized crime. Other men simply have the wealth to pay someone they found in an alley to kill Pearl before their wife found out about her. Maybe the man did it himself, but if the police have no leads with their resources, Pearl's death will probably remain an unsolved crime."

"Just like the Black Dahlia," Mitch offered. He stood by the cash register making change.

Hal had to swallow hard. "All right, let's forget the men. What about the high priced call girls you know, Lou. Could any of them have been a friend of Pearl's?"

"They don't have a union," Lou remarked with a deep chuckle. He took a sip of his scotch. "I know a woman who keeps tabs on her competition. She'd be happy to meet with you, for cash, of course."

Hal doubted he'd have a job much longer and couldn't promise much. "Why not tell her I think someone is murdering prostitutes, and we want to get out a warning?"

"That would work, but you'll at least have to buy her dinner."

"I could do dinner. There's one other thing I need. We've no photo of Pearl, but a police artist could draw one that would be close enough for her to be recognized. Do you know how I'd reach one away from a police station?"

"I do. You have my card. Come by my office tomorrow around noon, and I'll ask a man who does sketches for the police to come by."

"Thanks, Lou." Hal left the Golden Bear still feeling as though he were fighting his way out of a maze, but clinging to the hope a new path would soon appear.

CHAPTER 12

Lou's office was located in a one-story concrete block building on Los Angeles Street, not far from the criminal courts building. The venetian blinds were pulled halfway up the front window where King's Bail Bonds was lettered in gold. On Sunday, the surrounding streets were nearly deserted, and Hal arrived and parked in the lot several minutes early.

Pearl existed vividly in his mind, but he doubted he'd be able to find the right words to describe her well. He watched a man enter the building carrying a paint-splattered briefcase and assumed he must be the artist. He followed him in the bail bondsman's door.

A lovely Chinese girl dressed in a pale green sheath met them at the counter. Her long black hair was tied back in a fanciful knot and secured with ebony chopsticks. "Hi, Eddie, and you must be Hal. Lou is expecting you." She led them into Lou's office and closed the door on her way out.

"My sister, Jade. I'll introduce you later," Lou promised. He stood and circled his desk. "Hal, this is Eddie Padilla. He's done sketches for the police for years and should be able to produce a drawing of Pearl for you."

Eddie was Hal's equal in height, with a stocky build. He had dark brown hair and eyes, and a flash of white teeth in his smile. His features were pleasant, if not truly handsome. He reached out to shake hands with Hal before he sat down, opened his briefcase, and pulled out a sketchpad and colored pencils.

"I like to begin with the shape of the face. Will oval do?" He crossed his legs and propped his sketchpad on his knee.

Hal glanced toward Lou before nodding. "Yes, she had classic features and wore her hair up with lots of curls."

"Blonde, brunette, redhead?" Eddie asked.

"Brunette," Hal and Lou replied. "Keep helping me," Hal encouraged.

"She was slender," Lou offered, "and had elegant posture. She moved as though she were someone important. Every man in the bar noticed her whenever she walked in."

"Eye color?" Eddie asked.

Lou looked at Hal. "I never saw her up close."

"She wore cocktail hats with veils that shaded her eyes, but they were neither dark, nor light," Hal explained.

Eddie shuffled his pencils in his hand. "Hazel, maybe?"

Hal nodded and watched the artist work. He had the hair perfect, and added a cute feathered hat atop her curls. "Yes, that's something Pearl might have worn."

"Good," Eddie answered. "Did she have pencil thin eyebrows like the movie stars, or fuller brows?"

"Natural brows," Lou and Hal again answered in unison.

"Long eyelashes?"

"With her veiled hats, it's difficult to say," Hal responded.

"All right, I'll just draw in some lashes, and they can be changed later. How would you describe her nose?"

"She had a nice feminine nose, it wasn't too big or too sharp."

Lonnie sketched in a nose. "Mouth?"

"She used to lick her lips," Hal offered, and had to swallow a sigh. Lou stared at him, as he supposed he deserved. "I just want to find Faye," he stressed. "Pearl's mouth fit her face, it wasn't too large or small. Occasionally she gave a slight smile, a mere quirk of a corner of her lips. She wore bright red lipstick, and I didn't see anything else when she talked."

Lou watched the artist draw a pretty woman, but it wasn't Pearl. "Can you tell what's wrong?" he asked Hal.

"I don't know, but I was afraid we couldn't do her justice," Hal answered.

Eddie set the drawing on Lou's desk. "Let's try again."

Hal picked up the sketch, drew up a chair, and sat beside the artist. "Can you make her cheeks a bit fuller?"

Eddie again began with an oval outline, highlighted the cheeks, and made the nose a bit longer. He widened the eyes, and gave the lips a better definition. He completed the drawing with the dark curls and feather hat. "Tell me if this is closer, and I'll add the veil."

"We're almost there," Hal assured him. He watched Eddie add a delicate crisscross over the eyes for the veil, and startled by how closely the drawing now resembled Pearl, he sat back and looked up at Lou. "What do you think?"

"That's her. Do you want Eddie to draw more than one?"

"Yes, my detective will need a copy, too. I hope it isn't too much trouble."

Eddie laughed. "This is what I do all day, and it's a lot more fun to draw beautiful women than battered thugs."

Lou pulled an empty file folder from the low file cabinet and handed it to Hal. "Keep them in this so they'll stay clean."

"Thanks." Hal watched Lonnie work with brisk pencil strokes and subtle shadings to create a copy of his first drawing. Hal had cashed a hundred dollar check on Friday so he had money to pay the artist and wanted to be generous. He stood and handed him a couple of twenties. "I can't thank you enough. Someone has to have known Pearl, and your drawings will be a great help in finding them."

"My pleasure." Eddie gave Hal the second drawing, and slipped the bills in his pants pocket. He packed up his pencils and sketchpad and was ready to go. "Call me any time, Lou."

"I will." Lou returned to the seat behind his desk, and Hal sat down opposite him. Lou maintained an office so neat it bordered sterile, but the potted philodendron with deep green leaves trailing across the low file cabinet made it look at least occupied. "I know you're in a hurry to find Faye," he began.

"Desperate is a better word," Hal offered. "I won't let my imagination go to what she must be enduring, but it has to be horrible."

Lou nodded thoughtfully. "I promised you a number. The girl's name is Crystal, and she might travel in the same circles Pearl could have. This is all conjecture, of course."

"Of course." Hal wrote the telephone number on the inside of the folder and rose to leave. "Thank you for everything. The sketch will make our search for Pearl, and I hope Faye, a whole lot easier."

"Don't try any heroics if you do find Faye," Lou cautioned. He stood and walked him into the outer office.

"I know, I should rely on Detective Lynch to free her, and I will." He met Jade formally on the way out, and thought her far too lovely a young woman to work for her brother when at least half their clientele had to be guilty. He was grateful he wasn't among them.

Crystal went by a single name. It wasn't the one her mother had given her, but she'd chosen it to better suit her naturally alluring personality. She was a striking redhead with a slim willowy figure and nearly all legs.

When Hal Marten had called, she'd been flattered Lou had given him her name, until she discovered the subject was murder rather than sex.

"I'm sorry, but that just doesn't sound like a fun evening," she responded. "Why don't you hire a detective?"

"I have, but he doesn't know the people you do."

"Probably not, but I'm discreet, Mr. Marten, and I don't kiss and tell."

"I don't care who you've kissed," he replied too sharply. "One woman is dead and my wife may be too. I'm looking for whatever help I can get, and Lou thought you might know something important."

"I've always liked Lou," she responded. "I'll probably regret this, but meet me at the Bar of Music on Beverly Blvd. in Beverly Hills at six o'clock tonight. The crowd will be light that early, but I expect you to be there when I come in. If you aren't, I'll leave, and you'll not get one word out of me, not ever."

"That's fair."

"I'll be the beautiful redhead. How will I recognize you?" she asked.

"I'll wear a gray suit to match my mood."

"You can do better than that," she teased before she recalled why they were meeting.

"I'm five feet ten with fair hair and blue eyes. Some women think I'm good-looking."

"Then I'm sure I will too, Hal. See you soon."

Hal went to the movies to get through the rest of Sunday afternoon, but ten minutes after leaving the theater he couldn't recall what he'd seen. He showered and put on a gray suit as promised. He'd never even met a prostitute, and he didn't consider their meeting a date, but still, he felt it was a strange way to spend a Sunday evening. He missed the usual roast chicken, and the thought of Faye's awful cooking broke his heart.

He arrived at the Bar of Music half an hour early. The

front of the building had a rounded shape that struck him as more bloated than modern. He sat down at the bar, and ordered a beer. The bartender was a young man who didn't look at him twice, and Hal wished he'd asked Crystal to meet him at the Golden Bear.

There was a piano at the end of the bar, and a man dressed in a tux played a lazy rendition of Frank Sinatra's hit, "I'll Never Smile Again". Faye had loved Sinatra and a new burst of sorrow swept through him. A bowl of peanuts on the bar gave him something to do, and he cracked off the shells with a vicious crunch. When Crystal spoke to him, he nearly tossed the bowl into the air.

"Sorry, I didn't mean to startle you. Come, let's move to a booth."

Hal brushed the peanut shell dust from his suit jacket and followed her to a back booth. He wondered if the location held any significance. She was wearing only light make-up and a demure navy blue dress with a high neck and long sleeves rather than the tight sequined outfit he'd imagined. She was gorgeous by any standard. Her eyes were a warm golden brown, and her long lashes looked real rather than fake.

He checked his watch. "You're early."

"I am, but I wouldn't have penalized you had you not been here yet." The bartender sent over a gimlet without her having to ask, and she took a small sip of the pale green cocktail. "Now tell me your story from the beginning."

Hal sighed and tried to make sense of what made no sense at all. When he finished, the curious light remained bright in Crystal's eyes, and he hoped she'd remain sympathetic.

"You've really fallen down the rabbit hole, haven't you, Hal?"

"You could say that, but it's more of a snake pit." There was a bowl of peanuts on their table, and he reached for one to snap open. He offered her the newly shelled nuts.

"Aren't you sweet," she observed. She scooped the peanuts from his palm with a slow caress, and he jerked his hand away. "Sorry, I didn't mean to do that, habit I guess."

Hal clasped his hands in his lap. "No, I'm just jumpy."

"With good reason." She ate the peanuts and sipped her gimlet. She drew a finger across her sweet apricot tinted lips. "I've been invited to parties where men bring their mistresses rather than their wives. They're rather common here in Hollywood. That's how I've met the type of woman you believe Pearl might have been, but frankly, I don't recall anyone of that name."

Hal pulled out the folder he'd tucked into his jacket and showed her the drawing. "She was a pretty brunette who wore beautifully tailored suits and cute little cocktail hats."

Crystal's red curls were piled atop her head in the style heroines in Western movies favored. She poked a stray wisp into place. "My hair is my best feature, so I'm not fond of hats, even tiny ones. That's beside the point, isn't it?" She studied the drawing a long moment, and then shook her head. "I'm sorry, I don't recognize her. Los Angeles is overflowing with pretty girls who've come to California hoping to break into the movies. Most of them fail, and some stay to make a living with their looks."

"Was that your dream when you came here?" Hal asked.

She responded with an indulgent smile. "I was born here, and had a few film roles as a child, but I prefer real life to make-believe and never caught the acting bug. They make a great roast chicken here on Sundays. Are you hungry? I haven't eaten all day, and you look as though you could use a good meal."

"I don't recall eating either." He'd not even bought popcorn at the movies. "Chicken sounds awfully good."

A waiter brought them menus, but they ordered without opening them. Hal spoke after the waiter walked away and immediately regretted it. "You're not what I expected. I'm sorry, that didn't sound right, did it?"

She lowered her voice to a near whisper. "You imagined some brazen hussy in a low cut dress, hair dyed blacker than midnight, and an overwhelming dose of near nauseating perfume?"

Hal laughed in spite of his dark mood. "That's close, but you're much kinder than I'd thought you'd be."

"Thank you. You're such a nice guy, and I'm whatever you need me to be. I wish I could help you, but even if Pearl were involved with anyone I knew, I never met her. When affairs come to an end, and I'm being generous referring to them as such, most men buy a girl an expensive gift, offer her an envelope of big bills and say good-bye. They don't resort to murder when they want to move on, unless..."

Intrigued, Hal leaned forward. "Unless what?"

She frowned pensively. "Maybe she broke it off. That's another story. Some men can't bear to lose their pretty toy and turn violent."

Hal fought to suppress a cold shudder. For an awful moment, he thought Pearl might have given him a gentle push. "Can you give me names?"

"No, it wouldn't be wise for either of us, but the detective you mentioned must know who they are. They have reputations for being rough with women, and the smart girls avoid them."

"You impress me as being a very smart woman, Crystal."

"So why am I doing what I'm doing? Is that the next question? Let's just say I'm too restless to settle down, and I'm awfully fond of male company."

"I understand, but you've not met a man who wouldn't let you walk away?"

"No, and I don't intend to. Are you thinking I'd make a poor prospect for life insurance?"

He shook his head. He'd called the office on Friday to speak with Lorraine and she'd assured him his salesmen were getting along just fine and not to worry. She would probably have said the same thing even if the office were in total chaos. "If I can't find my wife, I may no longer be in insurance, so you needn't worry I'll urge you to buy a policy."

"I like you, Hal. You seem so damn normal, and I don't see many men like you."

Hal took normal to mean just plain dull, but Crystal continued to talk with him as though she wouldn't rather be somewhere else, and he was too grateful to ask why.

Detective Lynch came to Hal's home so early Monday morning he had to answer the door still wearing the blue pajamas Faye had made for him. "Do you have news of Faye?" he asked as he welcomed the detective inside. He hadn't slept well, yet again, but didn't care how weary or ridiculous he might appear in his baggy new pajamas.

Lynch swept him with a narrowed glance. "I need you to come to the station with me. I'll wait here while you dress."

"You didn't answer my question," Hal complained. "Have you found Faye?"

"No, but we've other matters to discuss. Hurry and dress, and call your attorney to meet us there."

There was a uniformed officer standing outside on the porch, and Hal's mood slid a couple of notches further into dread. He hoped he wouldn't need to call Lou King to cover his bail. "I'll call her."

Gladys Swartz was already at the station when they arrived. She was dressed in a black suit and wore such a serious expression Hal feared she might have been on her way to a funeral when he'd called. She stepped forward to greet them and introduced herself to the detective.

"Let's get this farce over with quickly, shall we?" she asked.

Hal loved the way she had instantly gone on the attack, and bit his lip to hide his smile. They were shown into the same dreary interrogation room, and he hoped this second interview would be as brief as the first.

The muscles clenched along the detective's jaw as he grit his teeth rather than spit on the floor as he surely must have wished to. "This is no farce, Mrs. Swartz. Mr. Marten, you were seen going into the Bar of Music in Beverly Hills yesterday. Are you aware it caters to a mob clientele?"

Gladys rested her hand on Hal's knee and squeezed slightly. The table blocked Lynch's view of the gesture, and Hal understood he should admit as little as possible. "I'd no idea. Their roast chicken on Sundays is especially fine."

Lynch dropped into the chair opposite them, opened a manila folder and quickly closed it. "Who did you meet there?" he asked, his tone darkly accusing.

"A friend."

"We already know her name," the detective countered. "She's a favorite of known criminals. First you're involved in a brutal murder, and then your wife disappears. Now your visiting mob haunts and meeting with a woman no man would introduce to his wife. Your behavior has become increasingly suspicious, Mr. Marten."

"That's enough," Gladys quickly responded. "Mr. Marten was an innocent bystander to Miss LaFosse's death, and his main concern is his wife's whereabouts. That's all we'll discuss today. What news do you have of Faye Marten?"

"None, but she isn't the issue at present."

"I say she is," Gladys countered.

Hal knew she would decry Lynch's every stupid move, but he had to speak up too. "Faye's disappearance appears to be linked with Pearl's murder. I've been trying to learn more about Pearl to see who might have wanted her dead. That's why I was at the Bar of Music."

"You fancy yourself a detective?" Lynch snorted, clearly discounting the idea as absurd.

"Why not when he might actually get some results?" Gladys offered quietly. "We're ready to go." She'd placed her briefcase beside her chair and leaned over to pick it up.

"Wait a minute." Lynch demanded. "We're still searching for Pearl LaFosse's family. It was clear she didn't live in a mobile home at Starlight Park, but she must have lived elsewhere and someone has to know her." He flipped open the folder. "There's nothing left of her face, but she did have a distinctive birthmark on her right shoulder. I'll release that much to the press, and maybe a relative will come forward."

He turned the folder around so Hal and Gladys could see the photograph of the cat head birthmark. Hal recognized the familiar silhouette instantly and pulled the photo close. He couldn't catch his breath, and the room swirled around him at a dizzying speed. "I'm going to be sick," he mumbled.

Lynch jumped to his feet and yanked open the door. "The restroom is at the end of the hall. Hurry. I won't have you puking in here."

Hal rose on trembling legs and balanced his weight against the corridor wall as he made his way to the rest room. In danger of tripping over his own feet, he pushed open a stall door and vomited what was left of last night's chicken dinner. The toilet's flushing roar couldn't drown out the fierce scream in his head, and shaken to the marrow, he rested against the side of the stall so long Gladys came to find him.

She took his hand to pull him to the row of white porcelain sinks. "Rinse your mouth, splash some water on your face, and then tell me what you found so sickening."

Hal leaned over the sink and splashed water until he had to stop to breathe. "Faye has the same birthmark, so either Faye and Pearl were twins, or the dead woman is my wife."

"You can't be serious," Gladys replied, but his stricken

expression couldn't be mistaken. She handed him several paper towels to dry his hands and face and took his arm to guide him to the interrogation room. "Mr. Marten isn't able to continue today."

Hal nearly fell into his chair. "No, wait. I want to see Pearl's body. My wife had a similar birthmark, but I can't believe she's the one who's dead."

"What?" Lynch cried. "This case gets crazier by the minute. I know there are men who ask their wife to dress up like a French maid, but were you and Faye playing some kind of crazy game where you pretended to be strangers meeting in a bar?"

Hal shook his head. "No. Just let me see the body." He listened as Gladys and Lynch argued the matter until he wanted to scream for them to stop. "Just let me see her," he urged between clenched teeth.

The Coroner's office was in the basement of the Hall of Justice. The air held an eerie chill, but Hal welcomed the cold and followed the attendant down the hallway to a viewing room. The body's head was wrapped in white gauze so he didn't have to look at that horror again, but he needed to see the birthmark up close to make certain the dead woman really was Faye.

He took her hand first. Pearl had always worn gloves, but he'd held Faye's hand so often he knew the slender fingers were hers. "Did she have a wedding ring?" he asked.

The attendance checked the file. "No, only a watch. We're saving it for the next of kin."

Faye had always worn a pale pink polish on her toenails, and he recognized her pretty feet. He forced himself to ask the attendant to lift her body so he could see the birthmark, but he already knew he was looking at his wife, his late wife.

Detective Lynch and Gladys were in the hallway watching him through the glass. He turned and nodded. He'd been in the insurance business long enough to know what steps had to be taken, but he simply stood by Faye's body and fought not to make a pathetic spectacle of himself by breaking down and weeping.

Gladys entered the small room to take his arm. "We'll sign to claim the body and a mortuary will come for her. Let's go, Hal. There's nothing more to be done here."

Hal hesitated only long enough to squeeze Faye's cold hand, and he left feeling equally dead.

CHAPTER 13

Gladys Swartz drove Hal home. His hand was shaking so badly she had to take his keys to unlock the front door. "You needn't stay," he mumbled.

She watched him lurch through the door and followed him inside. "I'll leave when I'm certain you'll be all right."

He fell into his easy chair. "How do I look?"

"Despondent," she responded. "That's why I'm here. You've had an awful shock, and Lynch is sure to find a way to turn it against you. Can you swear to me you had absolutely no idea Pearl was your wife?"

Mr. Cuddles rose from his pillow to stretch and leaped down to the floor. He rubbed against Hal's legs and gave a plaintive, "Meow."

"Give me a minute, cat." Hal closed his eyes and let the memories of his few conversations with Pearl flood through him. "Pearl was so completely another woman, no one who ever met Faye would have guessed they were one and the same. Pearl's gestures, her language, and her voice held a low sexy edge. She didn't resemble Faye in any way."

He reached for the file folder on the coffee table. "I had an artist make a drawing of her yesterday. She was an elegant orchid of a woman, Faye was a charming girl."

Gladys sat down on the couch and leaned close to study the sketch. "I see what you mean." She pulled a notebook from her briefcase. "Tell me more about how they were different. It's important, or I wouldn't ask." She opened the notebook and drew a line down the center of the page to create two columns.

He left the open folder on the coffee table, leaned forward and clasped his hands between his knees. "Faye had a natural beauty. Rather than visit beauty salons, she'd bend over and fluff her curls with her fingers before we went out. She had such beautiful skin she didn't need make-up other than a blush pink lipstick. She was very sweet and kind. I never heard her say a negative word about anyone, or anything. Let me show you her clothes."

He led the way into the bedroom and opened the closet. "As you can see, she loved colorful fabrics. She often sewed a new dress in a week, and she was very proud of her work. I always found a way to compliment her, but it was often a real challenge."

She touched one of the dresses. "This purple and yellow number looks as though it could jump right off the hanger and make its own way to the garden."

"True." He remembered how Faye would model her fashions and couldn't believe someone so pretty and full of life was gone. He closed the closet door rather than stand there and wallow in his memories. They returned to the living room.

"Now tell me about Pearl," Gladys coaxed.

"I noticed her the first time I stopped by the Golden Bear Lounge."

"Tell me why."

"She was the only woman there that night. She was wearing a suit and little cocktail hat. That's how she was always dressed, in beautifully tailored suits and tiny hats with veils that shaded her eyes. She wore such bright red lipstick, it was difficult to focus on her other features. She always wore black leather gloves, so I never saw her hands."

"And when you came home, Faye was always here?"

He glanced out the front window and was surprised to find such a lovely day. "Yes, until the night Pearl was shot, or Faye rather. She had dinner nearly ready that night. Pearl never stayed long at the Golden Bear, and she always left before I did. I usually came home half an hour or so later than usual on Thursday nights. She must have had our car that night, probably every night she was there, so she could have driven home and turned herself back into Faye before I walked through the door."

He caught Gladys's gaze and held it. "Why would she have done such a thing? She hired a detective to follow me simply because I'd wanted to shake up our routine. Maybe she didn't trust me and wondered how far I'd go with Pearl. But if she were Pearl, she'd already know. None of this makes any sense."

"No, it doesn't, and from what you've told me, Faye seems as though she would have been the trusting sort."

"I'd always thought so. She was positive there were ghosts because she'd read about them in books. We were going up to the Gold Rush country and see if we could find one. Now I don't know if I ever knew her." He leaned back in his chair and closed his eyes.

Gladys rose. "The cat's hungry, and so am I, aren't you? What do you have to eat?"

He opened one eye. "I've gotten used to the fact that Pearl is dead, but I've just discovered I've lost my wife."

"Yes, I know that's why I'm here, but you need to eat or you'll get sick and be in worse trouble than you already are."

"Impossible."

"Where's the cat's food?"

"Mr. Cuddles eats on the back porch. There's a can of his tuna open in the refrigerator, but don't give him too much."

"Come on, Cuddles." Gladys scooped him up, and he

leaned into her arms rather than spring from her grasp. "Heavy little guy, isn't he?"

Hal was surprised the cat hadn't scratched her. "Be careful, he doesn't take to strangers. Better put him down."

"He's purring as loudly as a motorboat, so he likes me, or the prospect of tuna." She carried Mr. Cuddles into the kitchen, put him down and opened the refrigerator. "You've got bread and eggs. Why don't I make us some scrambled eggs and toast?"

"Will you bill me for it?"

"No, my house calls are gratis. I'll take that as a yes." She lured Mr. Cuddles out onto the back porch with the bowl of tuna and closed the door behind him. "You keep a very neat house, or Faye did."

She went back into the living room to add the trait to her list for Faye. "Every detail is important. Please keep thinking about her."

"I can't think of anything else."

Hal thought Gladys's coffee was some of the best he'd ever tasted. He carried it into the dining room. "You make a fine cup of coffee."

"Thank you, it's a rare gift." She set a plate of scrambled eggs and two pieces of toast in front of him. She'd made herself a similar plate and spread strawberry jam on her toast as soon as she joined him at the table. "Now hurry up and eat so we can get back to work."

He salted and peppered his eggs. "I can eat and think." The eggs were light and fluffy, delicious really. He swallowed another bite. "I can't understand how Faye turned herself into someone as sophisticated as Pearl."

"Let's turn it around. Could Pearl have pretended to be Faye?"

He needed another swig of coffee to even consider such a far-fetched prospect, but it would have been much easier for a sophisticated woman to pretend to be naïve than the other way around. "What would have possessed her to do so?"

She caught herself before she gestured with a slice of toast and placed it on her plate. "Maybe she didn't want to be found."

"Why?"

"A man probably," she responded, "undoubtedly a dangerous one."

"So she married me and pretended to be a happy housewife to escape him? He could have been the one who killed her."

"Seems likely. Maybe she felt secure enough with you to be herself briefly on Thursday nights and go to the Golden Bear for a drink."

He pushed his empty plate away. "There was nothing fake or forced about Faye. She wasn't acting a part, she really was an innocent sweetheart."

"And Pearl?"

He wiped his mouth on his napkin. "The lady was as smooth as silk. There was nothing fake about her either. People are going to think me a fool, aren't they? Especially if I try to explain there weren't two women, but only one."

She reached for his hand. "I don't think so."

He squeezed her fingers. "But you're being paid."

"That's a cynical way to look at it." She pulled her hand from his, picked up their plates and carried them into the kitchen sink. "I don't do dishes, so you're on your own there."

Her manner had turned chilly, and he was quick to apologize. "I'm sorry. I didn't mean to insult you, but I once had such a pleasantly dull existence and now my life has become utterly unmanageable."

"And you're paying me to keep it from going completely off the rails. I need to use your telephone to call my office. Keep adding to our list of differences while I do. You may think of something that will make everything fall into place."

"The phone in the living room has a long cord, take it into the bedroom."

"Thanks." She carried her briefcase into the bedroom with her. Hal did the dishes and put them in the drainer to dry. The window above the sink offered a clear view of the pretty spring flowers they'd planted, and he had trouble catching his breath. When Gladys rejoined him, he leaned back against the counter.

"How am I going to have a funeral when it will be obvious to everyone that I barely knew my wife?"

"You needn't concern yourself with that today," she advised softly.

"I can't leave Faye in the mortuary indefinitely. I'll have to have her body cremated and scatter the ashes. I couldn't bury her at Forest Lawn with two names on her tombstone."

"Maybe we've done enough for today and you simply need to gather yourself to better cope with what's happened. Why don't you call the detective you hired to let him know what's happened? Maybe he'll have some helpful ideas."

He nodded. "I should call my boss and tell him my wife's been found dead."

"That's a step, even if it will be a painful one. Don't provide any details. I'll call you later."

He walked with her to the front door. "Thank you for making breakfast."

She squeezed his arm. "My pleasure. Get some rest."

"Rest," he echoed. "I vaguely remember sleep." He closed the door and watched her drive away from Mr. Cuddles' favorite window. He'd forgotten all about the cat and let him off the back porch.

Joe stared at Hal wide-eyed. "Let me get this straight, Faye and Pearl were the same woman?"

"Yes, and if it strikes you as too absurd to be true, imagine how it sounds to me."

Joe got up to pour them each a cup of coffee. "Unbelievable, but no matter what her name was, her death is tragic."

Hal nodded. The coffee Joe brewed tasted bitter and was too strong, but he didn't care. "You met Faye. Did she seem like an actress playing a part?"

"No, she was a gentle soul who adored you and was greatly worried she might lose you. What are you going to do?"

Hal shrugged. "Have her body cremated and find a place to scatter her ashes. I can't bear the thought of putting her in the ground. We'd never talked about what we'd do if one of us died. Couples ought to make plans, even if it is a stressful subject. I give the same advice to people purchasing insurance. It's important to plan ahead so you won't be blindsided, but I didn't take my own advice."

"Have a funeral for her. Your friends will come," Joe urged.

"A funeral is to celebrate a life, and I don't even know who Faye was. That will make for a very short obituary."

"Nevertheless, you should write one." Joe reached for a yellow notepad. "Faye Renee Marten, beloved wife of Harold Marten, passed away on, what was the date?"

"The third. I don't know where she was born, or grew up, or who her parents were, so there's nothing more to add. We'd been married less than a year, but that's still pathetic, isn't it? I should have learned those things while we were dating." He gave up on the coffee and placed his half-filled cup on Joe's desk.

"We could say she'll be remembered for her beautiful smile and pleasant manner," Joe suggested.

"Yes, that's true. She loved to sew, but she wasn't very good, and we can't say that."

"How about she loved to sew and was known for her sweet smile and pleasant manner?"

"That's good." Hal stood and began to pace. "Maybe I should have some sort of a memorial for her at our home, my home. There's no need to include that information in the obituary. Lord knows who'd turn up if I gave my address."

"That's wise. Saturday afternoon would be good. Let me know when you decide the time, and I'll be there. I did meet Faye, after all, and I'm so sorry she's gone."

"Thank you. I'll let you know." Hal left with the obituary they'd written, and he'd call the paper to have it printed. It was so little to say about Faye, but sadly, he'd not known anything more. He felt sick clear through. It didn't matter that Faye hadn't been what she'd seemed. She'd been his wife, and he ached for her loss.

Joe made notes of their conversation, but the case had taken such a bizarre twist, the summary lacked even a hint of sense. When CC came by that afternoon, he had to share what he'd learned. "You're not going to believe this," he began.

"What's that, sir?" CC picked up the wastebasket beside Joe's desk and waited to hear.

"The little lady who disappeared, the one who was so worried about her husband and another woman, she was that other woman."

CC frowned and shook his head. "I don't understand. How could she have been two people?"

"It beats me, and while I hate to speak ill of the dead, she must have been badly confused, or just plain crazy."

The janitor responded with a blustery sigh. "Don't that beat all. She sounded perfectly sane to me."

Joe sat forward and rested his arms on his desk. "I didn't realize you'd spoken with her."

"No more than a word or two." He emptied the wastebasket in the big trashcan in the hall and returned it to its place. "Bet you'll remember this case, Mr. Ezell."

"It's definitely going in my book, if I ever write one."

"You have yourself a nice afternoon now." CC closed the door on his way out.

Tuesday morning, the *Los Angeles Times* again ran the pretty high school photograph of Faye that Hal had given Detective Lynch. The headline read, "Murdered

Housewife Led Double Life". Her gruesome death was briefly described, and the remainder of the article focused on the puzzling nature of her double identity. The reporter painted her as a talented actress who had fooled her husband into believing she was two separate individuals. *Or so her husband claimed.* Hal tore up the whole paper and dropped the confetti-sized bits into the trash. The telephone soon began to ring. He didn't answer.

His doorbell rang, and looking out he saw two men, one holding a camera. He ignored them as well. Carmen came to his backdoor in tears, and he welcomed her in.

"Oh Mr. Marten, I'm so sorry. Faye was such a delightful girl. How can anything they said about her in the *Times* be true?"

"I'm as confused as you are, Carmen. You were a good friend to Faye, and I want you to remember her as the charming young woman you knew. Reporters have come to my door, and I'm not speaking with them. If they bother you, please don't reply to their questions or Faye's story may become even more distorted."

She nodded. "I won't say a word to them, it's none of their business. I just don't understand how Faye could have been someone else too."

"None of us do. I'm sorry I've nothing to offer you."

"Oh no, I don't need anything. I'll bake some cookies and bring them over so you'll have them should someone you want to see come by."

"Thank you, that would be very nice."

When she left, he picked up the list he'd made and checked her name. He'd put off calling George Sharp, and his secretary, and now he doubted that he needed to. He decided to do it anyway. George's secretary put him right through.

"Hal, I saw your name in the paper with a preposterous story about your wife. That's not good for California West's business. You know that."

Hal counted to ten before replying. "I'd like to take off

the rest of this week, and return to work next Monday."

"Well, I don't know, Hal. I'll give it some thought and call you later in the week. Good-bye."

Hal hung up the phone and checked off George's name. He called Lorraine Adams, and she burst into tears. "Oh, Mr. Marten, the story in the paper is so awful. I kept hoping, everyone in the office did, that your wife would be found safe. Is there to be a funeral? I want to come."

"Thank you, Lorraine." He told her he planned only a simple memorial on Saturday afternoon. "You have my address."

"I'll tell everyone. While we're on the phone, you were right about Mr. Sharp. He hasn't come by to speak to your salesmen even once, but they've been doing their best work for you anyway. Will you be able to come back to work soon? Is that an awful thing to ask?"

"No, not at all. I'm afraid it's up to Mr. Sharp, but I'm hoping for next Monday."

"Don't you worry, Mr. Marten. I'll give him a talking to."

Hal covered the phone so she'd not hear him laugh. "Thank you, Lorraine, but I don't think it would help."

She whispered, "Sharp is a stubborn fool, if you don't mind my saying so, but he can't argue with your sales figures. We have him there."

"Thank you, you've made my day." He said good-bye and checked off her name.

He needed to get out of the house, if he could sneak by the reporters who'd soon gather like sharks. He went out his back door, and through Carmen's back yard to go out her gate. He walked up the block and then turned down the way he wanted to go at the next corner.

He'd not met Fiona until Faye disappeared, but she'd known her, and he invited her to come to his home on Saturday afternoon.

"Faye was one of my best customers, and I'll be there," she promised. "I don't believe anything they said about her in the *Times*. They just want to sell papers."

"You're right." He left the fabric shop sorry he'd not had a chance to come there with Faye. He went to the library next, and found the librarian equally sympathetic.

"I enjoyed knowing Faye, and I'll have someone cover my shift and come over for a few minutes. We don't have any mysteries on our shelves that are as complicated as the story in the *Times*. Is any of it true?"

That wasn't an easy question for Hal to answer. "Only that my wife is dead, that much is true."

"Oh, I'm sorry. I didn't mean to sound so insensitive. I'll look for a poem to read at the memorial. Would that be all right with you? I'm thinking something sweet about life or nature."

He hadn't thought of what he'd say himself, and welcomed her idea. "Thank you. That would be a nice touch." He left thinking he ought to invite the men who'd known Pearl at the Golden Bear Lounge, but none of them had really known her. Lou King had been helpful, and he'd let him know. He bought some vanilla ice cream on the way home and wondered if he should serve some on Saturday.

Mary Margaret waved a copy of the *Los Angeles Times* at Joe. "Was Faye Marten your client who disappeared?"

He'd been careful not to reveal Faye's name, but now a few details wouldn't matter. "She was. It's the strangest case I'm ever likely to have, and I have a sinking feeling it isn't over."

She refolded the paper. "I feel sorry for her poor husband. I know what it's like to be lied to, and it's no fun."

"Faye didn't lie to him. She simply led two lives and left him out of one. Crazy dame. I can't tell you how wonderful it is to fall for a woman who is sane."

"Is that supposed to be a compliment?" she asked. "I'd say it's the bare minimum. I'm making the last pot roast until fall. I hope you're not tired of it."

"Does anyone ever tire of your wonderful pot roast?"

He stood at the kitchen door and watched her finish the last of their dinner preparations. "May I help with something?"

"Take the butter out of the fridge, would you, please?"

"Be happy to." He set it on the counter for her. She was a treasure, and he knew he ought to propose, but not tonight over a pot roast. That wouldn't be romantic at all. "Hal is having a memorial for Faye at his house on Saturday afternoon. Would you like to go with me?"

She looked over her shoulder. "You're inviting me to a memorial?"

"Is that insulting?"

"No, not at all," she responded. "Saturday is my day off and I'd love to meet Hal, but I'll pretend you never whispered a word about him to me."

"That should work. I'll set the table." He felt as comfortable in her cozy apartment as he did with her. He really ought to do something about it, but not tonight.

Detective Lynch came to Hal's home Wednesday morning, and waited impatiently as Hal checked out the front window before letting him in. "Have you quit answering your telephone?" he asked.

Hal hadn't again been caught in his pajamas, but the detective had come close. He gestured toward a chair. "I didn't want to encourage the reporters by answering. Would you like some coffee, what about the man you left in the car?"

Lynch remained standing. "No, neither of us wants coffee. That's not why I'm here."

Hal bit his tongue rather than respond with his first thought. "If you have more questions, I'm all out of answers." He walked into the kitchen to pour himself a cup of coffee and took his time rejoining Lynch in the living room.

The detective paced with a restless stride. "I keep wondering how a man can be so oblivious he didn't recognize his own wife when she'd simply changed her clothes. It keeps going around and around in my mind like a dog chasing his tail."

Hal gave a noncommittal shrug and sipped his coffee. "I didn't think you'd come to pay a condolence call. You mentioned clothes, and I'd like to have the ones you took from Pearl's trailer."

"No, Pearl's things are still part of an open investigation, as is Faye's photo. Dispensing sympathy isn't my job. Solving your wife's murder is. I still think you're hiding more than you're admitting."

"You've just called me too oblivious to recognize my own wife, so how can I possibly know anything of value?" Hal was sick of the man's hostile opinions, and he didn't need Gladys there to back him up.

"I think you're simply being clever."

"How can I be both oblivious and clever? Make up your mind."

Lynch looked around the room and saw the Agatha Christie book on the coffee table. "Maybe you got the idea for a perfect murder from a book."

"I want the killer caught even more than you do," Hal countered. "Someone wanted Pearl dead, and maybe they had no idea she was also Faye Marten."

"Unlikely," Lynch responded with a barely contained snort. "I suggest you start answering your phone, otherwise people might think you've left town."

"Is that why you came by, just to see if I'd be here?"

"No, I wanted you to know your wife's murder is an open case I intend to solve."

"I'll cheer when you do. I hope to return to work next week. Call my office if I'm not here."

The detective regarded him with an accusing glance. "Going back to make certain you receive the insurance money you're owed?"

Hal sucked in a deep breath. He'd not been in a fistfight since junior high, but he was sorely tempted to slug Lynch before the man could pull his hands out of his jacket pockets. He chose sarcasm instead. "I'm so relieved you're not in my family, so I don't have to see you during the holidays."

The detective yanked open the front door. "You're not half as glad as I am."

Another car had already pulled up at the curb, and knowing it had to be another reporter, Hal closed the door behind Lynch and left it locked the rest of the morning. Another far more interesting story had to grab the reporters' attention soon, and he'd ignore both the doorbell and ringing telephone until then.

CHAPTER 14

———◆———

Wednesday evening, Gladys came by with take-out boxes from a Chinese restaurant. "I tried calling you earlier, and when you didn't answer your telephone, I was afraid you might have fainted from hunger."

Hal took the white bags from her and carried them into the dining room. "Are you this concerned with the welfare of all your clients?" He filled Mr. Cuddles' bowl with tuna and shut him on the back porch.

"Of course. Will you get some plates? I refuse to eat out of the little cartons."

He smiled as he opened the cupboard. Clearly she believed she could just come in and take over, and he wasn't in the least bit offended. "I'll bring forks too. I never could get the hang of eating with chop sticks."

"It's like everything else, it takes practice."

The sly teasing note in her voice reminded him of Pearl. He brought the plates, napkins and forks to the table. "I've been working on the list of differences between Faye and Pearl, and Pearl would have made your comment in a low breathy voice. Even if her words weren't overtly suggestive, she'd make them so. Faye would have simply said she was no good with chop sticks either."

"That's a helpful observation. Frankly, I'm amazed by

Pearl. She existed for only a few minutes a week at the Golden Bear Lounge, and yet she seems to have impressed you deeply. Was it only that she was so different from your wife?"

He watched her empty a noodle dish onto their plates. She added fried shrimp and green beans. He waited for her to sit down and then joined her. "I'd never met anyone like her. She looked like a model from a magazine come to life."

"Maybe that's what she was, a creation of her own imagination with a little help from Vogue."

"Maybe." He bit into a fried shrimp. "These are really good."

"They are. What did your boss say when you called him?"

He told her. "I'm not sure I want to go back to work for California West. This might be the best time to look for another job elsewhere."

"Are you talking about a different company, or new location?"

"Maybe both."

She gave a noodle a lazy swirl around her fork the way she had in the Italian restaurant. "I'd advise against making any changes in the near future. You've been through a terrible ordeal, and you should take time to get your bearings before you launch into something new. You also don't want to look as though you're getting out of town just ahead of the posse."

The green beans were crisp and flavored with garlic. He used his napkin rather than lick his fingers. "It will be impossible for the police to find any evidence that links me to Faye's death, but you think I should still give them time to forget me before I move?"

"Faye's case may remain open, like the Black Dahlia's."

That was the worst news imaginable. "Does that mean I'll remain under suspicion forever if Lynch can't find who shot Faye?"

She nodded. "If you keep your job and remain in your home, you'll look like the responsible citizen you are. That's the image you must project."

"My boss may fire me."

"I'll tie him in a knot if he tries."

He laughed and nearly choked on a green bean. "I should have made tea. Would you like some?"

"Yes, thank you. I'm not fooling, Hal. We'll sue California West if they even hint you ought to look elsewhere for work. How long have you been with them?"

"It'll be two years in the fall," he called from the kitchen.

"And you've received good performance reviews?"

He put the kettle on the stove and came back to the table. "Excellent in fact. Will that help my cause?"

"Yes, most certainly. You've not been accused of any crime, and you won't be, so there's no legitimate reason not to allow you to continue in your job. If your boss gives you any trouble, I'll come to see him."

She had a fierce gleam in her eye, and he believed her. "Charlie Sharp is as round as a bowling ball, but I'd still love to see you tie him in knots."

"Don't laugh, it may be only metaphorically speaking, but I'll do it."

"Thank you." He got up when the kettle whistled and returned with two cups of tea. "Do you take sugar?"

"No, this is fine. Have the last shrimp. You were slim to begin with, and now you're too thin."

He shrugged. "It's not my main concern."

"I suppose not. Have you thought about what you want to do with Faye's belongings?"

"No. I suppose I should."

She reached into the last bag for the fortune cookies and handed him one. "I know it's difficult. I'll always miss my husband, but it's his memory I cherish, not his old clothes. I packed them all up and gave them to a charity thrift shop. Is there someone who can help you with Faye's things?"

He snapped open the fortune cookie. "My neighbor will, but I'll wait until after the memorial on Saturday afternoon. I've no idea what I'm going to say, just toast her memory I suppose." He pulled the small paper strip from the cookie. "*New horizons await.* That's timely, isn't it?"

She rolled her fortune through her fingers. "*Mysterious man may bring sorrow or joy.* That's rather creepy."

"Let's hope for the joy." He caught her gaze and held it. He was too bruised emotionally to flirt, but damn, he sure wanted to. "I'll get the dishes."

"Fine. We need to keep working though. I can't help but feel Faye isn't through surprising us."

Fearing she was right, he stopped in the doorway. "I'm beginning to wonder if she even lived in the boarding house where I used to pick her up for our dates. She'd meet me out front, so I never went to the door or met anyone else who lived there."

"Feel like going for a drive?" she asked.

"Right now?"

"Why not? The owner should be home, and the dishes can wait. My car's in front so I'll drive."

He grabbed his jacket. She had a gray Chevrolet sedan, and he slipped into the front seat beside her. They left his street, and she pulled into the traffic on the thoroughfare so smoothly he ceased worrying about riding with a woman driver. He gave the directions as he recalled them.

"Faye told me she'd had Mr. Cuddles for four years. Do boarding houses allow their residents to have pets?" he asked.

"Some may. Did you leave him on the back porch?"

"I did, and I should have let him out. He sleeps in the laundry basket, so he won't be uncomfortable, but I didn't mean to forget him."

"Do you plan to keep him?"

"I don't know. If I stay where I am, and the landlord may not renew my lease, he'll have a home. If I move, I might not be able to take him with me."

"I love cats, and haven't had one in several years. I could take Cuddles home with me tonight, but I think you need the company."

"Oh yeah, he's great company. He's either sound asleep or demanding to be fed. Do you really want him, or are you simply providing more of your sympathetic service?"

She laughed. "I'm not nearly as sympathetic as you believe." She turned on the radio and the lively Andrews Sisters' song, "Rum and Coca-Cola", was far too silly for their errand, and she quickly turned it off.

"I don't mind the music," he told her, but she left it off.

The passing streetlights lent her hair a golden sheen, and he thought again of how totally inappropriate his growing attraction to her was. She had impressed him at first with her focus on the law. Now that he'd gotten to know her, well, at least begun to know her, he found her far more warm and appealing.

Pearl had initially caught his attention with her stylish suits and frivolous hats. But she'd kept it with her beauty and seductive conversation. His insides began to twist with shame at how easily she'd fooled him.

"It's right ahead, the shingled two-story with the bright porch light," he directed. "Faye may have referred to her landlady by name, but I've forgotten it if she did. There's a room to rent sign in the window."

Gladys pulled into a parking place at the curb. "Good, it will give me an excuse to ring the bell. I'll say Faye recommended the place and see what the landlady can tell me about her. Please wait here."

He nodded reluctantly. "Her name would have been Faye Bell then, or that was the name she was using when we met. Wave if you need me."

"I will." She left the car, straightened her suit skirt and walked up to the front door. She rang the bell and a teenage boy came to answer. "Hello, I wonder if I might speak to the landlady about a room."

He yelled over his shoulder, "Grandma, someone's here for you."

A buxom woman came to the door with a dishtowel in her hands. "I'm Florence Reese, and I own the place. If you've come about a room, I do have a vacancy, but it's on the small side."

"May I please see it anyway?" Gladys asked.

"Well, I suppose." Florence handed the dishtowel to her grandson. "Dry the dishes before I come back downstairs."

"Aw, do I have to?"

Mrs. Reese's expression turned grim. "Do you enjoy eating? Go on with you." She led the way up the stairs. "He was such a sweet little boy, but now he tries my patience severely."

"I'm sure he'll grow up to be a fine young man."

"Quite an optimist, aren't you?" Mrs. Reese asked.

Gladys wouldn't describe herself as such, but she was playing a part. "Most of the time, yes." She was shown to a room in the rear of the house. It was barely large enough for the twin-sized bed and dresser. The closet was tiny, and a single chair was wedged in the corner by the window. The hideous wallpaper with gigantic pink roses made the room appear even smaller. Faye would probably have loved it.

"A friend of mine used to live here, a year or so ago. Perhaps you remember her, Faye Bell?"

Florence pursed her lips thoughtfully. "I hate to say the name doesn't ring a bell, but it doesn't. Let me check my log. I keep track of everyone who moves in and where they're going when they leave so I can forward their mail. What do you think of the room?"

"I'm afraid you're right, and it really is too small for what I need. Thank you so much for showing it to me."

"It's no trouble, and you gave me a chance to stick my grandson with the dishes." They went downstairs to the living room, and she took a dog-eared log from her desk. She ran a finger down the column of names. "Most girls who move in stay long enough to be remembered. I don't see her name though."

Florence turned to a dark-haired girl curled up on the sofa reading a magazine. "Hazel, do you remember a girl named Faye Bell living here?"

The girl's eyes widened. "No, but isn't she the one who went missing and then turned up dead as someone else?"

Mrs. Reese regarded Gladys with a skeptical eye. "I'd forgotten the name, but now I recognize the story. What are you doing, walking up and down the street searching for where the dead girl lived?"

"No, not at all," Gladys assured her. "I'd been told she'd lived here, and I wanted to verify it, that's all."

"You with the police?"

"No, I'm an attorney with an interest in the case. I'm sorry to have bothered you." Gladys regretted not bringing a photo, but smiled as she swept herself toward the door. "Thank you both. Oh, by the way, Mrs. Reese, do you allow your residents to have cats?"

"No pets allowed," Florence insisted firmly. "Stink up the whole place and leave the furniture covered in filthy fur."

Gladys found Hal leaning against her car. "No one named Faye Bell ever lived here, and the landlady doesn't allow pets. I should have thought to ask you for a photo of Faye to bring with me."

"I need to get back the one I loaned to Lynch that ran in the *LA Times*, but he's keeping it for the time being."

"We'll get it back," she promised. They got into her car, and she rested her hands on the steering wheel. "If Faye had you pick her up here, she must have lived close."

"For all we know, she could have ridden a motorcycle here from Santa Monica."

She laughed at the thought. "I doubt it, but she did love you, Hal, or she wouldn't have been so terrified of losing you that she'd hire a detective to follow you."

He looked toward the rooming house. All the lights

upstairs were lit and the house nearly glowed. "You didn't like the room?"

"Don't change the subject. The woman you married, whether her name was Faye Bell or Snow White, truly loved you."

His life was such a twisted mess, he wouldn't even go there. "It's getting late."

She waited a long moment, and then started the car and drove him home where only a pudgy Persian cat waited.

Hal went to the Golden Bear Lounge Thursday night. No one appeared to be particularly surprised to see him, but the bar no longer held its former appeal. He sat down beside Lou King and Mitch brought him a beer.

"How are you doing?" the bartender asked. He rested an arm on the bar, getting comfortable for a chat.

Hal took a drink of his beer, and shook his head. "Things could be better."

Lou raised his scotch in a silent toast. "I understand completely."

Hal glanced over at the last booth. He'd not thought to add up the minutes he'd spent with Pearl, but they were probably less than an hour. He focused on the foam on his beer. "Have the police come in here again asking about me, Mitch?"

"No, that one time was all," the bartender responded. Someone signaled him from a booth, and he walked away to serve them.

Lou lowered his voice, "Was Crystal any help to you?"

"Not really, but we had a nice dinner together anyway."

"That's a plus at least. Are the police still crowding you?"

Hal shrugged. "It's only Detective Lynch, not the whole department, but he's got no other suspects. Whenever a woman is murdered, isn't her husband at the top of the list?"

"Rightly so," Lou agreed. "But that's just sloppy police work in this case."

"I wish I'd never come in here."

Lou touched his sleeve. "You're forgetting Pearl came in here first. Someone from her life, strange as it must have been, shot her. Don't blame yourself for stopping at her favorite bar. She would have died whether you were here that night or not."

"I hadn't looked at it that way, but it doesn't help," Hal murmured. "I wanted a few minutes to myself, not to become involved in some grisly noir drama." Damned *New Horizons*, he thought, and finished his beer without tasting a drop. "I'm having a memorial at my home Saturday afternoon, although I've no idea what to say."

Lou studied their reflections in the mirror behind the bar. Dark and light, they could have been posed for a painting. "Something will occur to you."

Hal nodded, but he doubted it.

Gladys was the first to arrive on Saturday afternoon. She carried a beautiful hydrangea with puffy white blooms. "I was tempted to wear a cocktail hat with my suit, but decided it would be in very poor taste."

"It might have gotten you shot, so it's a good thing you didn't." Hal took the potted plant into the dining room where he'd set out the cookies Carmen had baked. "Thank you for this, I didn't expect anyone to bring anything."

"You're welcome," she replied. "I thought if you stayed here, you could plant it in the yard. Where's Mr. Cuddles?"

"On the back porch where he won't bother anyone who doesn't like cats. As for staying here, I'd rather not. Faye loved it, and it doesn't feel right to remain here without her."

"I understand, but please stay put for now."

Joe Ezell arrived next and introduced Mary Margaret as his girlfriend. "I hope you don't mind my coming today," she offered. "I'm so sorry you lost your wife."

"Thank you," Hal responded. He still had no plan for the memorial and hoped everyone didn't come believing he needed abundant sympathy. He introduced Gladys, and got them something to drink. It was the first time he'd had liquor in the house, and it suddenly struck him that Faye would have preferred he serve a fruit punch.

"I'm lost here," he whispered to Gladys. "Faye didn't drink, but Pearl liked martinis."

She squeezed his arm. "Don't worry, neither of them is here to complain. These sugar cookies are wonderful. Did you bake them?"

Hal introduced Carmen as the baker when she arrived. Fiona came with several women who'd met Faye in the fabric shop. Sandra Sloan, the librarian, carried the book of poetry she'd promised. Lorraine Adams arrived with four men from his office. He shook their hands and hoped they weren't counting on furthering their careers by being there.

As Lou King came through the door, he whispered in Hal's ear, "I thought someone ought to be here for Pearl."

Hal missed both women, and now that his living room was becoming crowded, he had to begin. He brought chairs from the dining room to provide extra seating. "Thank you all for coming here this afternoon to remember Faye. She was a darling young woman who deserved to live a long and happy life. Miss Sloan has a poem she'd like to read."

Sandra opened the book to her place and read a poignant selection about the beauty of love lingering long after loss. "I'll remember Faye for her curiosity and desire to learn."

Fiona raised her hand. "What I recall about Faye is her love of creating something new from fabric and thread. She took a real joy in it."

Before anyone else could offer a thought or memory, there came a loud pounding on the door. Hal hurried to answer and found Detective Lynch standing on the porch. "Can't this wait? We're having a memorial for Faye."

"They can finish without you. Hal Marten, you're under arrest for conspiracy in the murder of your wife, Faye Marten."

Hal looked over his shoulder. Gladys and Lou were already on their way toward him. "I'll meet you at the station," she called.

Hal left as Carmen offered to lead a prayer, and he hoped she would include him as well as Faye.

CHAPTER 15

"Anyone can see that dear man didn't have anything to do with his wife's death," Carmen proclaimed. "He gave me a spare key in case of an emergency, and this surely is one. I'll lock up after everyone leaves. Please take some cookies with you."

"Please remember to feed Mr. Cuddles," Gladys called on her way out. Lou caught up with her on the walk.

"Tell him not to worry, I'll cover his bail. I saw Pearl maybe half a dozen times, and she looked nothing like Faye's photo in the *Times*."

Gladys paused on the sidewalk. "I can't help but wonder why Detective Lynch is so eager to charge Hal with murder. Do you suppose he's the one who shot Pearl?"

Lou laughed in spite of his best effort not to. "That could very well be the reason. I didn't like him on sight. Give me a call if you need me in court."

Hal remained silent as he rode in the back seat of the squad car to the Hollywood station. Gladys had warned him not to say anything rather than have something to regret, but a conspiracy charge was so unexpected he could barely keep still. There were reporters and photographers waiting outside the station, and he turned away from the blaze of flashbulbs and ignored their shouted questions. He could easily imagine tomorrow's headline in the *Times*: "Husband Arrested In Murder". His career with California West would be over, and his landlord would probably call the sheriff to evict him forthwith.

He had no personal property on him other than his watch and wallet and signed for them at the bottom of the form. When Detective Lynch took him into the same smelly interrogation room, he regarded him with an icy stare rather than curse the bastard in the filthy language he deserved.

"You know why you're here, so you might as well admit the truth," Lynch began. He waited for Hal to choose a seat and then stood with his arms braced on the back of the wooden chair opposite him.

Hal looked around the dreary room. "I've no idea why I'm here."

"Let's not stretch this out any longer than we have to. We've an informant who heard you offer a man money to kill your wife."

Gladys came through the door before Hal had time to do more than offer a startled gasp. "Who is this informant?" she asked. "Someone with a name like Leroy Slick who's hoping to get out of jail free by swearing to something that never occurred?" She sat down beside Hal and reached for his hand beneath the table to give his fingers an encouraging squeeze.

"He doesn't have to be named now," Lynch countered.

"Because no such witness exists," Gladys answered. "I'm beginning to believe you knew Pearl, and had something to do with her death."

"What?" the detective nearly shrieked.

"See how it feels," Hal asked. "What do I have to do to get out of here?"

"If you have some paid snitch you plan to have testify in court, think again," Gladys warned. "I'll speak to the

DA's office within the hour and inform them of the way you're persecuting Mr. Marten and demand an apology for this ridiculous outrage. Plus, you interrupted a thoughtful memorial for his late wife. What in the world were you thinking?"

Lynch had turned a most unflattering red. The color flamed in his cheeks and spread down his neck. "No one believes he didn't know his own wife," he muttered between clenched teeth.

"I do," Gladys replied. "Now either book Mr. Marten so we can go to court and request bail, or I'll ask a judge for a writ of habeas corpus to keep Mr. Marten from being unlawfully held. It's your choice. Hurry up and do what's right."

Lynch regarded them both with a viciously controlled stare. He paused a long moment, as if deliberately making them wait. "I'll not book him today, but it's coming, don't think it isn't."

Gladys stood. "Let's go."

Hal left with her without offering his own opinion of the way Lynch had treated him. He picked up his wallet and watch. Gladys took him out a side door so they avoided the reporters who had been so eager to yell at him as he'd entered. He waited until they were in her car before he spoke.

"I thought something was off when they didn't take my fingerprints or photograph me. Isn't that routine with an arrest?"

"Yes, it most certainly is. Lynch was just bluffing in hopes you'd confess."

"Which I never will. Do you think we could actually make a link between Lynch and Pearl?"

She responded with a triumphant grin. "I doubt it, but it shocked him into releasing you, so it worked. Police are fond of using paid informants, but juries don't value their testimony."

"Do you think this is actually going to trial?"

"Not if I can help it."

"For a conspiracy charge to stick, don't they have to say who I supposedly paid to kill Pearl? Shouldn't he be tried for murder?"

"Of course, but you didn't pay anyone, did you?"

"No, I'd no reason to kill Pearl, or my wife. The whole situation is ludicrous, but isn't it easier to prove that someone committed a crime rather than that he didn't?"

"My business is defense, Hal, and I'm very good at convincing juries of my clients' innocence."

"I'm sure you are, but..."

"Do you want to go home, or come to my office? I'll call my contact in the DA's office and see what's behind Lynch's vendetta against you."

"Your office so you don't have to repeat the conversation. Vendetta is a good term. How about a vicious vendetta?"

She maneuvered through the light Saturday traffic to reach her office building, pulled into the underground parking, and found her space. "That's perfect. Let me do all the talking, or I'll lock you out of my office."

Hal laughed at the thought. "I promise not to scream and yell in the background."

Her building was eerily quiet on Saturday, and their steps echoed with a hollow ring as they crossed the marble-floored lobby. "We have to use the stairs on the weekends, do you mind?"

"I could use the exercise," he replied.

She climbed the stairs slowly. "I used to run up the stairs, and then had to rest before I could speak. So I gave it up as counter-productive."

He knew she was doing her best to keep him from thinking past the present moment, but he carried too large a knot of worry for her kindness to matter. He could still appreciate her shapely legs as he followed her up the stairs, however.

"Thank you for all you're doing for me."

"Don't forget it's my job."

She'd brushed off his compliment as though it were a

spot of lint, but he'd been sincere. He dreaded the inevitable conversation about costs, and feared he'd already run through his savings. Thoroughly depressed, he followed her into her office and sat down in one of the leather chairs meant for clients. He glanced out the window, and was surprised to find the sun still shining.

"Would you like coffee? I could make some," she offered.

"No, thank you. I refuse to get drunk, but if you have a bottle of whiskey in your bottom drawer, a drink would be awfully tempting."

"One wouldn't be nearly enough, and then you'd wake up tomorrow with a brain-pounding hangover and blame your suffering on me."

"You speak from experience?"

"I'll take the advice I give my clients and not admit a thing."

He got up and walked to the window to look out while she called her contact. Even hearing only one side of the conversation, it was plain things weren't going his way. When she hung up, he still fully expected her to twist her news into something positive. He was wrong.

"This is worse than I feared," she began. "The police are under enormous pressure to find the Black Dahlia's killer, but with no suspects, they're out to defuse the bad press by solving every other murder they possibly can."

He looked over his shoulder. "With phony informants?"

"It's nothing new."

He drew in a deep breath. "Then we have to solve the crime ourselves. I'll have to canvas the street where I thought Faye lived, and see if I can find out something, anything, about her. As for Pearl, there's only the trailer where she must have only changed her clothes, and no leads elsewhere."

She rocked back in her chair. "You're still separating them in your mind?"

"What else can I do? Pearl is the one who was

murdered, but she has no more substance than smoke. We spoke once about ghosts, and she said there were people she intended to haunt. I wonder how she's doing."

She got up and reached for her handbag. "I'll take you home."

"No, thanks, I'll ride the Red Car and maybe get off somewhere I've never been."

"Don't do anything foolish," she warned firmly.

He regarded her with a solemn gaze. "I doubt my reputation can sink any lower." He meant it.

Joe Ezell and Mary Margaret waited to leave Hal's apartment when Carmen Espinoza returned to her side of the duplex. Mary Margaret held half a dozen cookies neatly wrapped in wax paper. "Thank you again for the cookies."

"You're welcome," Carmen responded. She stood on her porch for a moment to survey the street, and finding no one lurking about, went on inside.

"What an absolutely astonishing afternoon," Mary Margaret whispered as they walked to Joe's car.

"I won't forget it anytime soon. I just hope Hal's attorney is as good as she looks."

Mary Margaret waited for him to open her door and slid into the front seat. When he got behind the wheel, she couldn't hold her tongue. "I don't suppose he hired her for her looks, but clearly most men would call her beautiful."

"Come on, Mary Margaret, it was only an innocent observation."

"It didn't sound very innocent to me. Just drop me off at my house."

"I will not," he argued. "Let's do something fun, like go to the zoo."

She checked her watch. "There's not enough time left before it closes."

"Let's go tomorrow then. I haven't seen a hippopotamus in years. I'm fond of giraffes too. Did I ever tell you that? They have the most amazing long black tongues."

"You're just trying to distract me."

"Of course I am. I don't suppose you noticed that Hal is a good-looking man?"

"Is he?" She glanced out the window at the passing scene.

"Most women would think so," he replied in his best imitation of her tone, and he was relieved when she responded with an adorable giggle. There was really no comparison between a cute little redhead and a statuesque blonde, but that's a thought he'd keep to himself now that he was ahead.

A photograph of Hal entering the Hollywood Station was in the Monday morning edition of the *Los Angeles Times*. According to the reporter assigned to the crime beat, Hal had been questioned and released, but that he'd already hired a defense attorney clearly indicated he had something to hide.

He swore a long and particularly vile string of curses he'd learned in the Army, and threw the paper in the trash. While he doubted he'd be allowed to stay, he dressed in one of his new suits and went into the California West office early to greet each salesman as he arrived. Some appeared embarrassed, others surprised, and the four who'd come to the memorial wouldn't meet his eye. Lorraine Adams nearly wept when she saw him.

"That interruption on Saturday was so awful and unnecessary," she began. "Will you have another memorial for your wife?"

Hal took her arm and led her to her desk. "Not until we find who killed her," he whispered. He looked over her head and watched to see which salesman reached for his telephone first, most probably to tell George Sharp he'd dared to show his face there. When several grabbed their telephones, he went on into his office and waited for George's call. When in a few minutes the vice president appeared at his door wearing a look of barely suppressed rage, Hal wasn't surprised to have garnered such quick attention. He rose to welcome him.

"I thought I'd come by to see how things are going. I hope my salesmen haven't caused you any concern."

George closed the office door behind him. The glass top half gave the whole office a clear view, even if their conversation couldn't be overheard. He spoke in a harsh whisper, "I thought I'd made it plain you're not to come into the office. How could you have misunderstood?"

"I'm not in the least bit confused," Hal countered. "I intend to find who killed my wife because the police obviously don't know where to look, but that doesn't mean I can't give my office force the attention they deserve."

George's eyes narrowed to tiny sparks as he continued to fume. "I've always liked you, Hal, so leave now before you force me to let you go. Don't think I won't do it."

Hal's voice remained calm and low, "Do you have some complaint with the way I'm doing my job?"

"No, of course not, but that was before your got yourself tangled in your wife's murder."

Hal circled his desk to face him. He was taller and looked down at his boss with a carefully schooled expression. "My attorney assures me you've no grounds for my dismissal, so you ought to think carefully before you invite a law suit that would cost California West a whole lot of money and probably end your career."

George spit out the question, "Are you threatening me?"

"No, I'm merely sharing information. Now is there anything you need me to handle before I leave?"

George nearly strangled on his own spit. "No, just go, and I'll overlook the way you've disregarded my wishes today, but wait at home for a direct summons."

Hal opened the door for him and spoke loudly enough for everyone in the office to hear. "Thank you for your sympathy and support, sir. It's deeply appreciated."

The vice president had a swaying rolling walk, and his arms brushed his sides as he strode down the aisle separating the salesmen's desks. He looked neither to the right nor left. Hal closed his office door behind him and smiled at his secretary. "I need to go. Thank you for handling everything."

"It's my pleasure. I hope you'll be back soon, Mr. Marten."

"So do I. Good day, gentlemen. California West is grateful for your continued excellent work for the firm." Certain he'd impressed George Sharp sufficiently to keep his salary coming for the next few weeks, he left with a far bouncier step than when he'd arrived.

Hal had just gotten home when the telephone rang. He debated answering before picking up. "Hal Marten," he said, an office habit.

Her voice was whisper soft, "This is Crystal. We met at the Bar of Music."

"Yes, I remember you." He crossed his fingers and hoped she'd learned something useful.

"You showed me a drawing of Pearl when we met. If she used two names with you, she might have gone by others. Someone might recognize her from the sketch, and I should have asked to take it with me."

He also still had the one he'd meant to give Joe Ezell, and he was sorry he hadn't asked Eddie to draw more than two. "Do you want me to bring it to the Bar of Music?"

"Could you?"

"Yes, do you want to meet again at six?"

"Could you make it earlier, five?"

"See you then." Hal hung up and wondered if Detective Lynch was still having him followed, but he didn't really care.

He fed Mr. Cuddles so the cat wouldn't starve to death before dinner. He still hadn't grown fond of him, but he owed it to Faye to take the best care of her pet that he possibly could.

He really ought to know which vet had seen the cat and began a search through the drawer where they kept household receipts. He was surprised to find a photo taken by a restaurant photographer soon after they'd gotten married. Faye looked so happy, and his grin was equally wide. He remembered the evening clearly. They'd eaten prime rib, and she'd laughed often at his jokes. She'd always been such an appreciative wife, and he wondered how much of it had been an act. He'd meant to buy a frame for the photo and left it on top of the dresser. There was no receipt for a veterinarian in the drawer.

Joe Ezell studied the drawing with an intense gaze before looking up at Hal. "In the photo you gave me to show around, your wife's smile is as radiant as sunshine, but here there's only a hint of a smile. As Pearl, she looks far more worldly. Maybe it's the little hat, or the provocative gaze."

"Provocative is a good word. Faye deserved an Oscar for the parts she played. I want you to take the new sketch of Pearl with you to the hotels. She could have called herself Petunia Smith for all we know, but when she played Pearl, she would have resembled the woman in the sketch closely enough to be recognized."

Joe closed the folder and set it aside. "I understand why you're so curious, but we've talked before about what dangerous characters we might bump up against. I don't carry a gun, and I don't want to run into anyone who does."

"I don't blame you. If you've had enough, just say so, and we'll settle your bill. I can make the rounds of the hotels on my own."

Joe leaned back in his swivel chair. "No, I'm too eager to discover just who your wife was, but we need to rely on the police if we get even a whiff of who killed her."

Hal raised his hand. "I promise I'll have my attorney pass any suspicious names to her contact in the DA's office. I need to know where Faye lived when she wasn't with me, or before we met. There has to be an apartment somewhere filled with her things I've never seen. She didn't live at the boarding house she called home, and while you show the sketch in the hotels, I'll canvas the neighborhood where she pretended to live. I'll need the photo you have of Faye."

Joe handed it over and opened a drawer on his desk to give Hal a small spiral notebook. "People will be more talkative if you take notes. It makes them feel important."

"Thanks. I have a pen." He waited to tell Joe about Crystal until he knew whether or not she'd be of any help. He stood and looked around the stark office.

"You could use a plant. Philodendron are good. They're showy and no trouble." The one he'd taken from Pearl's trailer was thriving on his coffee table.

Joe rose and followed him to the door. "I lean more toward cactus, but you're right, a green plant would give the office some color."

Hal shook his hand and walked the short distance home. When he found his landlord standing on the front porch talking with Carmen, his heart fell. "Good morning, Mr. Duffy," he called as he moved up the walk.

Duffy checked his watch. "It's nearly noon, but good morning anyway. We need to talk." He wished Carmen a good day and followed Hal into his side of the duplex. He dismissed Mr. Cuddles with a quick disinterested glance.

"I couldn't tell from the article in the *Times*, but were you released on bail?" he asked.

"No, sir. I've never been arrested, and I had nothing whatsoever to do with my wife's death. I'll understand if you want me to move, and quite frankly, I'd like to go, but I should stay here for the time being."

Duffy appeared unconvinced. "And why is that?"

"So I don't seem to be the shiftless bastard the police believe I am. No man should lose his wife in the awful way I did, but to be considered a suspect is nearly intolerable."

Duffy focused on the philodendron. "Carmen thinks

the world of you, but I've gotten calls from several of your neighbors. They're worried about how often the police have shown up here. I'd appreciate it if you moved out when your lease is up August first."

Hal had no reason to argue. "Fine, that should give me the time to prove my innocence and find somewhere else to live. I hope the neighbors aren't worried about a shoot out. I don't even own a gun."

"Let's leave firearms out of it."

Hal stood at the open door after Duffy had left wondering which of his neighbors were the nosy, fearful type. He knew a few just to wave to as he walked to the Red Car or back, but Carmen was the only one he'd ever spoken with. He'd not thought of inviting any of them to the memorial, and now he was glad he hadn't. He changed out of his suit into slacks with his dress shirt, made himself a sandwich for lunch, and was ready to go.

Hal drove down the street where he'd thought Faye had lived and noted a couple of big homes with signs of rooms for rent. That didn't mean others didn't rent rooms, but at the present had no vacancies. Determined to pry a clue out of the neighborhood if there was one to find, he'd work both sides of the block with Faye's photo to see what turned up.

The woman at the first house on the corner nearly swept him off the porch with her broom, but undeterred he went on next door. Some people were friendly and eager to chat even if they knew nothing helpful. He stayed only a minute longer than necessary to be polite and excused himself. He was already at the house at the end of the block before anyone provided anything helpful.

The gray-haired man wore a white dress shirt, loose fitting brown slacks held up by suspenders, and leather slippers. He studied Faye's photo and scratched his chin. "Mrs. Collins, right across the street there, had a girl living with her for a while. She looked something like this young woman, but I can't say for sure. Let me ask my wife."

Hal held onto the photo while the man called a pretty dark-haired woman in a housedress and apron with a touch of flour on her cheek. She wiped her hands on the apron before touching the photo. "First, tell me what this is about."

Joe had coached him. "There's an inheritance coming to her, but unfortunately, the family has lost her address. They knew she lived somewhere near here. Does she look familiar to you?"

The woman pursed her lips thoughtfully. "This looks like the girl who used to live across the street with Mrs. Collins. She hasn't been there for a while though. Now I think a young man rents the room, but I'm not sure. I'll warn you now, Mrs. Collins is hard of hearing so you'll probably have to shout, and I don't believe she sees too well either."

Elated to be on the right path, Hal broke into a wide grin. "Thank you both. I appreciate your help. I'd sure like to see the inheritance delivered soon." Looking at his late wife's photo, he nearly stepped in front of a diaper service van coming down the street, but caught himself in time to remain on the curb. He could easily imagine the reporters at the *Times* speculating he'd thrown himself in front of a truck rather than face prosecution. That it had been a diaper service van would make for a great punch line.

The Collins' house was a craftsman style one-story bungalow. Rose bushes that had had their spring pruning lined the walk and filled the flowerbeds bordering the house. He had the notebook and could write messages if Mrs. Collins didn't understand what he said, but if her eyesight was as poor as her hearing, they'd be stuck for a way to communicate.

A sandy-haired young man who looked to be of college age answered the door. "May I help you?" he asked.

"Yes, I'd like to speak with Mrs. Collins. Is she home?"

"Just a minute, I'll call her." He left the screen door latched while he looked.

A tiny little woman dressed in a ruffled pink dress that could have come from Bullock's children's department unlatched the screen door and looked up at Hal. Her white hair was spun atop her head in a hairdo that rivaled the whipped cream on a sundae. Her lips were as pink as her dress and slippers.

"What is it you want, hon?" she asked.

Hal loved her already. He introduced himself and showed her the photo of Faye. "Do you know her?"

"Well, of course I know her, and you needn't shout. I'm not nearly as deaf as I pretend to be when I'd rather not listen to someone jabber on. Now why are you asking about Renee?"

Hal had known her as Faye Renee Bell, but maybe she'd tired of her middle name. "It's a matter of a large inheritance, and her family has lost her current address. I'm hoping you'll be able to help me find her."

She inched her rimless glasses up her nose with a brightly polished pink nail and studied him more closely. "I'm the only family she has worth a fig, so don't you go lying to me about an inheritance. What's Renee done now?"

"You caught me." There was a padded rattan sofa on the porch, and he gestured toward it. "Would you care to sit with me while we talk?"

"Not particularly, but I'll do it anyway." She turned to the young man who stood close behind her. "If I disappear from my own porch, you call the police right away, Carl."

"Yes, Mrs. Collins, I will." He smiled at Hal over her head, clearly not worried that she'd meet with foul play.

Hal waited for her to make herself comfortable before he took a place beside her. "Renee was my wife. I'm very sorry to bring you the sad news of her death."

The little woman didn't even blink. "Well, Mr. Marten, there has to be a lot more to your story. Tell me how you met Renee and how she came to such an untimely end, not that it was unexpected, of course."

The dear lady didn't appear to be in the least bit stricken by the sad news, and he didn't know quite how to take it. "I met her in the spring of 1946 when we were both taking classes with UCLA's extension department."

She raised her hand. "She was living here with me then, and she may have said she was taking college courses, but she never finished high school. You might say higher education wasn't something Renee admired."

Hal added another lie to his mental list. "You obviously know more about her than I did. How were you two related?"

She crossed her legs and rested her folded hands on her knee. She wore several rings with large faceted stones set in gold. "She was my niece, my youngest brother Albert's daughter. Or at least Albert liked to believe she was his daughter, but I was never too sure. Patsy Bell wasn't what I'd describe as a high-class woman, you understand, but she was a sister-in-law, and I tried to get along with her. Didn't get much in return, I'm sorry to say."

Hal opened the notebook and pulled his pen from his pocket. "What was your brother's last name?"

"The family name is Stewart. I was wed to Jeb Collins, may he rest in peace. My given name is Mildred, which is too dreadful to speak, let alone carry around, and I've always gone by Millie."

Hal made a quick note that Renee's parents were Albert Stewart and Patsy Bell. "Did Renee have brothers or sisters?"

Millie shook her head. "No, one child with Patsy Bell was all Albert deigned to have. They divorced when Renee was still a little bitty thing, maybe two. Albert saw her often, but she never went to live with him and his second wife. Louise was a different story, not nearly as pretty a woman as Patsy, but chairman of the church guild," she confided with a telling dip of the head.

"Ah, I see. So Renee grew up in her mother's home?"

"Such as it was. Patsy married a couple more times, maybe had three husbands after Albert. It could have been four. I couldn't keep track of them when they came to pick up Renee after she'd spent a few days with me. They were all good looking men with easy salesman's smiles, but none struck me as having much depth. Of course, if they'd had much in the way of character, they wouldn't have married Patsy."

Hal had to rein in his thoughts before they went a dozen wild directions. "It sounds as though you were a good influence for Renee. Why weren't you surprised to hear that she'd died so young?"

Millie fiddled with a gold earring. "If you were married to her, you must know she wasn't well-acquainted with the truth. From the time she said her first word, she preferred telling a fanciful fib. Something was just twisted in her brain, I guess, or Patsy set such a poor example Renee simply didn't learn any better. She could be the sweetest little girl one day, and a sullen brat the next.

"She saw a psychiatrist for a while when she was in high school. I think my brother may have paid for that. He's gone now, sweet man. All the Stewart men have weak hearts, but the women have all lived into their nineties. I'm hoping to celebrate my one-hundredth birthday before I'm called to heaven. I'm looking forward to seeing my darling Jeb again, but not anytime soon."

"Of course not. Where did Renee go to high school?" he asked.

"She went to Hollywood High. She definitely had a flare for drama, but that was the only class she did well in. She was working as a file clerk when she last lived with me. What did she tell you?"

"That she did temp work and never stayed long in any office."

"Well, that much is true. She'd do good work, and then lose interest and ask for days off. Or else she just wouldn't return to a job after getting her first paycheck. So you came along last year." She nodded thoughtfully. "She used to go up to UCLA to meet college boys. She was exactly like her mother. If there were only one man left alive on the planet, Patsy could have found him within a half an hour."

She reached out to touch Hal's knee. "I'm sorry not to have better memories of Renee, but there's no point in lying about her now. Would you like some tea? I can't get through the afternoon without my tea and a couple of cookies."

"I don't want to put you to any trouble."

"Well, as I see it, you're a nephew by marriage. Just call me Aunt Millie when you come by. A cup of tea is no trouble at all." She pushed off the sofa with a near leap and hurried inside her house.

Hal wanted to see more of the charming little lady, and was grateful she'd given him such an important part of Faye's, or Renee's past. He still had more to tell her, and to ask, and he could use a cup of tea with a whole lot of sugar while he thought of a way to explain the mysterious existence of Pearl LaFosse.

CHAPTER 16

Joe began at the beautifully appointed Biltmore Hotel on Grand Avenue. Entering through the high arched doorway, felt like stepping into a Renaissance palace. Nearly overwhelmed by the gold leaf and marble, he made his way to the bell captain's desk. A slim gray-haired gentleman in a finely tailored uniform, who looked as though he'd held his post for a good many years, acknowledged him with a curt nod.

Joe introduced himself as a detective working for the family and showed him the drawing of Pearl. "She's inherited a good deal of money, but she's lost touch with the family. Do you recognize her?"

The bell captain regarded the detective with an icy glare. Joe hadn't worn one of his ill-fitting suits to melt into the crowd, but the guests of the elegant hotel were all more expensively dressed. "What leads you to believe she may have stayed here, sir?"

"As you can see, she's an elegant woman, one who'd be at home here," Joe answered. "Have you seen her?"

The bell captain surveyed the lobby rather than study the sketch. "Our guests appreciate our discretion, sir. May I suggest you try elsewhere?"

Joe was prepared to tip well for leads, but clearly any

bill he'd offer would simply insult the man. He thanked him and walked into the bar. The lighting was pleasantly dim, and the voices of tourists planning the rest of their day carried easily across the room. He walked up to the bar and waited for the stocky bartender to come to him. He imagined the burly fellow might lift beer kegs over his head for fun.

Joe held a ten dollar bill as he gave his detective speech and opened the folder with the drawing. "Do you recognize her?"

"Do you want a martini, sir?"

"Make it club soda." He waited until he'd been served a glass with a lime wedge garnish. "She may have come here from time to time."

The bartender leaned close and whispered, "I read the papers often enough to know she's dead. Unless you'd like to join her on a cloud playing the harp, you'll make a smart move and leave." He picked up the ten dollar bill and walked away.

Joe sipped his club soda slowly. Overcome with an itchy bad feeling, he realized the bartender had recognized Pearl from the drawing. Only her name had been given in the papers, and Joe hadn't said it. That meant Pearl had been there and clearly had associated with men who closely guarded their privacy. Everyone they came across would have been paid handsomely, or threatened, to guaranty their silence. He finished the last drop of his club soda and headed for his favorite golf course.

Hal walked into the Bar of Music at a quarter to five and waited for Crystal at the bar. The piano player was into bluesy jazz tunes, and kept up a running conversation with a little brunette seated on the nearby stool. Hal kept turning over the conversation he'd had with his new Aunt Millie, and thought of a dozen questions he should have asked. He looked forward to going back.

When Crystal entered, he escorted her to the last booth. She again wore a high necked and long sleeved dress, this time in a lush ruby shade. She'd gathered her hair into a clip at her nape and soft curls brushed her shoulders. She smiled as though she were glad to see him, but he supposed she greeted all men in the same way.

"I can't promise anything," she said after the first sip of her gimlet. "Maybe with the drawing, I'll have more success than I did simply using Pearl's name."

He handed her the folder, and she opened it to study the sketch. "There's something about her that draws you in, isn't there? Maybe it's her eyes."

He'd been drawn to all of Pearl's assets, and nodded thoughtfully. "You'd remember her if you'd ever met. I've found an aunt who remarked on her talent for drama, but if she'd ever wanted to be on the stage or in movies, she didn't mention it to me."

Crystal reached across the table to touch his hand. "That gives me a new direction to look. There are wealthy men who love to invest in films to meet pretty actresses. One of them might have known her."

"That's a good idea. Thank you. Do you want something more than a drink?"

"I'd love to stay and have dinner with you again, Hal, but I'm busy tonight. Maybe when I see you the next time."

"Fine. I do want to have the drawing returned."

She made an elaborate crisscross of her heart. "I promise." She finished her gimlet, and he walked her to a De Soto coupe parked out front. She waved before driving away, and he hoped she really would get back to him with a tangible lead.

He checked his watch, and wondered if Gladys would still be at her office. He went back into the bar to use the pay telephone in the hall by the men's room. When she answered, he asked her to dinner. "We could go to the Italian place near your office."

Her voice was cool, "Do you have something to report, or are you asking me on a date?"

The way she'd asked the question gave him his answer. "This is strictly business, Mrs. Swartz, and I've got plenty to report. Besides, I'm too recent a widower to consider dating anyway."

"Meet you in half an hour."

Hal had already been seated at the table they'd shared on their first visit when Gladys walked in. She was dressed in a pale lavender suit that looked too sweet for the courtroom, but it was gorgeous with her fair coloring. He would have complimented her, but thought it would be better to avoid anything so personal. Once they'd ordered, he told her he'd met Faye, or Renee's aunt.

Gladys ate a couple of breadsticks while she listened attentively to all he'd learned. "She didn't tell her aunt she was marrying you?"

"No, but she had a good reason when Aunt Millie would have known little of what Faye, or Renee, told me about herself rang true. Millie Collins didn't recall the name of the psychiatrist Faye saw, but I would love to read his records."

They'd switched their orders this time, with Hal enjoying the spaghetti and Gladys the ravioli. "Definitely pillows of perfection," she nearly purred. She waited until they'd eaten several bites before offering advice.

"Type up everything you've learned today because the more we know about your late wife, the easier it will be to build your defense. Let's keep calling her Faye because that's the name you knew her by. She may have been drawn to you because you're such a responsible man. It would have been a comfort to her when her childhood may have bordered chaos."

"But she thought I'd changed and hired a detective to follow me. That's where I hit the brick wall. Maybe she gloried in fooling me as Pearl LaFosse, but feared I'd want to meet other women."

"Maybe. We don't need special insight into her motives to prove you had nothing to do with her death, but every scrap of information helps."

"So we can overwhelm Detective Lynch, if nothing else?"

"I prefer the word eviscerate," she responded with a decidedly predatory grin.

"Good word, although one I seldom have occasion to use in insurance." They'd ordered a bottle of Chianti, and he refilled their glasses. "I have the detective Faye hired doing what he can to track Pearl. Her aunt had never heard the name. The dear lady gave up reading the papers during the war when the news was too distressing and knew nothing about the murder."

"Do you think she'd make a good witness if we had to call her?"

"Yes, she's sharp and doesn't shade her opinions. She said Faye's mother moved to Texas before the war, and she hasn't heard from her since. Faye said her parents were dead. We know Albert died, and maybe Patsy is gone too."

"Forget Patsy. Let me know if the detective learns anything new about Pearl."

"I will." He was reluctant to tell her he'd seen Crystal again, but thought he ought to before Detective Lynch called him down to the station over it. Gladys's eyes widened slightly when he mentioned Crystal's name, but she didn't stop him. "I'm relieved to have found something we can hold onto about Faye, but Pearl is still where we have to go. Or at least, I think so," he said.

"Crystal sounds like she's sincere. If she turns up anything useful, let me know immediately. Under no circumstances are you to attend any parties with her. Do you understand me? If she invites you, tell her you've come down with pneumonia, and can't leave the house. You've got to avoid becoming involved with the wrong crowd, and she's definitely well-acquainted with them."

"I understand." She was sympathetic, and provided

excellent advice as an attorney, but even heartsick as he was, he wished they could have more. There were a whole lot of things he'd have to accomplish first though. "My landlord wants me out of the duplex by August first. I need to decide where I'm going to work before I move, if I'm not in jail."

"Put the thought of jail out of your mind," she ordered sharply.

"All right. Maybe I could move in with my new Aunt Millie." He laughed and she laughed with him, but it wasn't an altogether bad idea.

When Hal came home and switched on the light, the first thing he saw was the bright red ribbon bow tied around Mr. Cuddles' neck. The cat leaped from his pillow to plead for dinner with his usual pitifully demanding meows, but Hal just stared at him. He bent down to see if there were a message tied to the bow, but found none. He untied the bow and drew the satin ribbon through his fingers. He'd locked the front and back doors before leaving that afternoon, but clearly someone had been in the house and wanted him to know it.

He fed Mr. Cuddles, checked to make certain all the windows were locked as well as the back door, and then went next door. "Hi, Carmen. Someone tied a bow on the cat. Did you see anyone who might have been in my apartment this afternoon?"

She frowned and studied the ribbon in his hands. "You know I have a key to your place, but I had no reason to go in today, and I didn't see anyone either. Do you suppose it's a threat?"

"I do. I'll call a locksmith in the morning and have deadbolts put on both the front and back doors. Someone got in today, but I won't make it easy for them the next time they try."

"Is anything missing?"

"I didn't notice anything out of place, but I'll look again. Good night." Hal went home and searched for any sign of an intruder. The police could have come in with a warrant he supposed, but Carmen would have seen them, and they wouldn't have tied a bow on the cat. He called Gladys at home.

"I'm coming to get him," she offered immediately. "Someone wants you to know they could have easily killed Mr. Cuddles, and they might do so if they visit again."

He silenced a near snort. "I hate to call Detective Lynch to report a bow on the cat."

"That isn't really the issue. Someone broke in. You need to report it."

"I will." He fetched the cat carrier from the garage and left it on the back porch. He made another slow tour of the house, and this time noticed the restaurant photo of Faye and him was missing. He checked to make certain it hadn't fallen behind the dresser, or sailed under the bed, but it was gone.

Gladys had changed into gray slacks and a white sweater and looked relaxed and even prettier than she had in her lavender suit. Hal turned down the heat of an all too admiring glance. "I just made coffee. Would you like a cup?"

"I'd love one." Mr. Cuddles had returned to his pillow, and she scratched behind his ears. His satisfied purr amused her. "I wish people were as easy to please. He loves his pillow. May I take it with me?"

"Sure, along with the cat box and bag of litter. I've several cans of cat food. Faye only bought one kind, maybe that's all he likes."

Gladys sat down on the sofa, and set her cup on the coffee table. "This is just a temporary arrangement, isn't it? Won't you want Cuddles back when you move?"

"Not if he's still in danger," he answered. He sat in his favorite chair and held his warm cup. "I left a photograph of Faye and me on the dresser, and it's gone. Whoever broke in might have taken it as proof he'd been here."

"It's possible he simply wanted a photo of her. Did you call the police?"

"It can wait until morning. Detective Lynch wouldn't be there this late in the day."

"Probably not, but he wouldn't handle break-ins." She leaned back, kicked off her shoes and folded her feet underneath herself. "I'd take it as a warning. Someone wants you to stop asking questions. Clearly you're poking a hornets' nest. If we didn't need to solve Faye's murder ourselves, by default, I'd insist you stop."

"I must be getting close," he mused aloud.

"It appears so. Did the police ever find Faye's purse?"

"No, she must have left it in the car when she went into the Golden Bear, and the kids who stole it would have taken anything of value and tossed the empty bag. She wasn't wearing her wedding ring when she was shot. I'd given her a gold bracelet she liked to wear, and it isn't here. Her jewelry might have gone to pawn shops, but neither piece was distinct enough to be recognized as hers now."

"It's a shame you don't have her ring." She sipped her coffee and looked up at him with a soft blue gaze. "Be prepared for Lynch to laugh at you. He might even say you made it up, but clearly you're getting more leads on your wife's murder than his whole department has."

"So what's the point of reporting it?" he asked.

"You want it on the record. He's annoyed you're pursuing the case, but we won't allow Faye's murder to remain unsolved. Whoever came in and tied the bow could have hidden and choked you to death with the ribbon. So you've got an additional worry now."

"I've already thought of that. I'm having dead bolts put on the doors tomorrow, so it will be more difficult to break in. As for Mr. Cuddles, I couldn't find Faye's record of his vet visits. If you want to take him to one, I'll pay for it."

"He looks plenty healthy, so I'll wait on that. Did Aunt Millie know about Cuddles?"

"Yes, she did. Faye brought him along the last time she

stayed with her. Millie said the cat slept so much of the time, she often feared he'd fallen into a coma, but he never missed a meal."

She placed her empty cup on the coffee table. "So he hasn't changed much, has he? This is a beautiful philodendron. Did Faye love plants?"

"No, Faye thought houseplants were too much trouble to water and dust. It belonged to Pearl. I'll get the cat carrier so you can be on your way."

"Thank you. I have an early morning court date." She stood to put on her shoes and pet Mr. Cuddles. The cat didn't see the carrier coming until Hal had eased him right on in.

"I'll carry him out to your car, and then bring the other things," he offered.

"I'll carry the rest, so you needn't make two trips." Mr. Cuddles had already begun to complain with long, loud mewing, and she looked into the wire mesh door and apologized. "Relax, big boy, I promise you'll get all the pampering you need at my place."

Hal handed her the bag with the cat box, litter, and cans of tuna. Even if it hadn't been a social visit, he wished he'd thought to play some soft music on the radio. He waved as she drove away, and looked up and down the street searching for someone who might have been watching the duplex, but there were only the familiar cars belonging to his neighbors parked nearby.

Once inside he locked the front door securely and hoped whomever had come in wasn't planning on returning tonight. He picked up the Agatha Christie book to read a while, but his concentration was shot. He could set booby traps to confound anyone who broke in that night, and provide himself with a loud warning, but that was the sort of thing the Marx brothers would do, or the Three Stooges, and he let it go and slept on the sofa.

Detective Lynch came to Hal's home soon after his call. "There was no sign of a break-in, other than a missing photo and a bow on the cat?" He glanced toward the front window. "Where is the cat?"

"He's staying with my attorney."

"Maybe you ought to stay with her too," Lynch offered. "The next guy who breaks in might want to make a more lasting impression."

"I know. The locksmith should be here within the hour to add deadbolts to both the doors. Do you know of any other cases where a burglar tied a ribbon on a pet?" He'd rolled up the ribbon and handed it to Lynch.

Lynch pulled an evidence bag from his pocket and dropped in the ribbon. "I've heard no mention of ribbons, but at first glance, this doesn't strike me as an ordinary burglary. What are you thinking, that he must have come knowing your wife had a cat?"

The thought had occurred to Hal in the middle of the night. "Yes, unless he carried a pocketful of ribbons just for the fun of it. Otherwise, it seems like an odd thing for a man to have."

"This whole case is odd," Lynch countered. "I don't see any point in looking for fingerprints if nothing was touched. I'll tell you again to let us find your wife's killer. You needn't hang out at the Bar of Music hoping to overhear someone admit to it."

"I like the piano player," Hal responded with a careless shrug.

Lynch had been more subdued than Hal had expected. The man hadn't accused him of murder even once. "There weren't any footprints in the flowerbeds. Whoever came in must have seen me leave, and didn't bother to peek in the windows before he picked the lock on the front or back door and came in."

"He probably came in through the back," Lynch adjusted the angle of his hat and went out onto the front porch. "You worry me, Mr. Marten. I'm not convinced there really was a break-in, when all you have to show for it is a ribbon you could have purchased yourself. If that's the case, then you're as nutty as your late wife."

"Are you hoping I'll punch you in the nose for that?" Hal asked. For some reason, the snide observation didn't bother him at all when he'd expected much worse from the man.

"I said nutty, not stupid. Let me know if you have another break-in, or worse. I'll advise you again, rather than put yourself in danger, leave your wife's murder to us."

Hal made no promises, and he watched the detective drive away. A woman up the block out watering her flowers looked his way. Lynch had arrived in a plain sedan rather than a police cruiser, but she looked mighty interested anyway. He waved to her before going inside.

He had nothing planned other than waiting for the locksmith, and that worried him. There had to be something he could do before someone dropped a red ribbon around his neck and yanked it tight.

CHAPTER 17

The locksmith was a gregarious gray-haired fellow who proved to be a lover of poetry. He'd recited Alfred, Lord Tennyson's "The Charge of the Light Brigade", while working on the front door. For the one in back, he chose Robert Frost's "The Road Not Taken". Hal hadn't expected such literate entertainment from a tradesman, but he enjoyed the selections thoroughly. He tipped the man generously and promised to keep his card should he again have need of a locksmith.

"That's the trouble with this business," the locksmith replied. "There aren't a lot of repeat customers, unless you're someone who owns an apartment house with a high turnover of tenants."

"People will recommend you to their friends," Hal offered.

"Yes, they do, and I'm grateful for it. If the locks give you any trouble, call me, and I'll come right over."

"Thank you." Hal had just closed the front door when the telephone rang, and he was slow to answer. "Hal Marten."

"Good morning, hon, this is your aunt Millie."

He was delighted to hear from a friendly soul, and at the same time, hoped she'd not make a habit of calling him daily. "Good morning, Aunt Millie."

"After you'd left yesterday, I got to wondering if Renee might have left something here with me. Didn't have a chance to look until this morning, but I found an old valise of hers in the hall closet. I haven't opened it, so it could contain old shoes for all I know, but I thought you might want to come and take a look at it."

Hal hoped it held answers for at least some of his questions about his late wife. "Yes, I'd love to see it. What's a good time for you?"

"Come for lunch at one o'clock."

"See you then."

Hal needed to check-in with Joe Ezell first, called him, and walked over to his office.

Hal had had enough of Joe's coffee to know he didn't want another cup, but he'd been there so often of late, he sat in his usual chair and felt at home. "I found Faye's aunt Millie living on the street where Faye had pretended to rent a room at a boarding house." He condensed what he'd learned about his late wife's troubled childhood. "Millie has invited me to come for lunch. Faye, or Renee, left a suitcase there when we married, and it might contain something to link her to Pearl. The aunt knows a great deal about her niece, but nothing about Pearl. What did you find at the hotels?"

Joe grinned and opened the case folder. "Finding a living relative is the first success we've had. Sometimes that's all a case needs to break apart in solvable pieces. Let's hope it's true here. Now for the hotels, the bartender at the Biltmore recognized Pearl from the drawing and knew she was dead. No photo appeared in the Times with the article about Faye's double identity, but he made the connection immediately. He also told me to get out. I think we were right about Pearl knowing someone who values his privacy. Whether he's a crook or not, I can't say, but I stopped there rather than visit any more of the hotels on our list."

Hal nodded thoughtfully. "That's probably wise. Someone broke into my place yesterday and tied a red ribbon bow on the cat. I took it as a threat and had deadbolts put on the doors this morning."

Joe gaped at him. "How did they get in?"

"Must have picked the lock, because Faye's keys were found in the car. They were returned to me at the police impound lot."

"Her house key is still on the ring?"

"Yes, but I suppose someone could have had a duplicate made."

Joe sat forward in his chair. "Probably not if they were just kids out for a joyride. They wouldn't have thought that far ahead and planned a break-in."

"I suppose not." Hal rose and stretched. "I'll call you if there's anything we can use in Faye's suitcase."

"Let me know either way," Joe asked.

"I will, but I don't suppose I'll find an envelope containing the murder's name that says, 'Open in the event of my death.' That would be too easy."

"Go and look," Joe encouraged. He made notes after Hal left and added them to the file. Aunt Millie was the first person who'd actually known anything about Faye, and he wished he'd found her rather than Hal.

Hal bent down to give Aunt Millie a kiss on her cheek. Today she was dressed in a pretty pink polka dotted dress that was cute even without ruffles. Her skin was powdery soft, and she wore a luscious perfume with a sweet floral scent that reminded him of candy. "I like your perfume."

"Thank you. It's been my favorite for a good many years. The suitcase is on the coffee table, why don't you take a look through it while I see to lunch."

"I could help you if you like."

She waved him off with fluttering bejeweled hands. "My maid, Bessie, is a wonderful cook, and no help is needed. Go on and look through the suitcase, and see what you find. We can talk about it while we eat."

The living room had finely crafted mission style furniture, precisely what the house required. The oak gleamed with polish, and each piece stood as straight and overtly simple as the day it had been fashioned. The sofa was covered in soft, brown leather, and a hand-woven Navaho rug in reds and browns covered the floor. It was a handsome room, and could have been included in a turn of the century museum.

The battered suitcase looked as though Faye had carried it for years while growing up. The worn leather handle was loose, and perhaps that was why she'd left it behind. He unsnapped the two brass locks and opened it carefully. The yearbooks from Hollywood High School immediately caught his eye. The years 1936 and 1937 were stamped in gold on the front.

He found Renee's freshman photo in the first book. She looked very cute, and had a wide, charming smile. In her sophomore year, she stared at the camera with a sullen frown. Clearly something had happened to her, and she'd left school after that year. There were no notes from friends scribbled in the books, and he laid them aside.

He found a diary she'd written at ten, with big loopy letters that covered only half the pages, and the rest of book had been left blank. He read a few lines and found what a ten year old would write about, her friends. One was being selfish, and another too proud of her beautiful white dog. Renee wished she could have a dog, but her mother had said no.

There was a copy of *Little Women*, and a worn deck of cards held together by a frayed rubber band. He wondered if she'd played Gin or maybe Go Fish with friends. There was a small porcelain Christmas angel wrapped in tissue paper. A little red box held a pair of hairclips with silver birds. There were several years of birthday cards signed by her mother tied with pink ribbon. A photo in a gold frame showed Renee at three or four in a pretty party dress and black patent leather shoes. She sat perched upon her mother's knee, looking up at her with an adoring gaze.

Patsy Bell wore her hair swept atop her head in a mass of curls. Her tailored suit gave her the appearance of a very proper lady. Her winsome smile struck Hal as all too familiar, and he carried the photo over to the window to study in better light. He recognized the tilt of her head and the grace of her pose. Had he not known the woman had to be Patsy, he would have sworn he was looking at Pearl. He took the framed photograph into the kitchen were Aunt Millie sat on a stool directing Bessie to add stuffed olives to their tuna salads.

Bessie was an ample figured black woman in a neatly pressed gray uniform. Her bright smile revealed a gap between her front teeth. Her gray hair was pulled back in a bun.

Hal nodded a greeting and showed his aunt the photo. "Is this Patsy with Renee?"

"Why yes, it is. She and Albert were no longer married by then, but she often had photos taken for Easter or Christmas and sent them to him. As I told you yesterday, she wasn't nearly as sweet as she looks. Did you find anything else of interest in the suitcase?"

"A girl's treasures. I wish she'd brought it with her when we married so we could have talked about her childhood."

"As I see it, she left it here to avoid having to tell you the truth."

Millie slid off her stool and led him into the dining room. The long oak table had tall slat-backed chairs, and she had a thick cushion on hers to manage a comfortable height. The table was set with heavy sterling silver in a baroque pattern and cut crystal goblets held ice water. Hal took the chair at her right and put the starched white linen napkin in his lap.

Bessie served their tuna salads on china with a delicate pink rose border. There were freshly baked rolls, and the salad was incredibly good. It was all lovely, but he was interested in so much more than a fine meal.

"This is all wonderful, Aunt Millie, but I'm ashamed by how little I knew about my wife before she died."

Millie reached over to pat his arm. "It wasn't your fault. It sounds as though you two were happy together. Try to concentrate on that."

His memories of Faye were now as mixed up as their salad, but he thanked her for the thought. Bessie served lemon sherbet for dessert with sugar cookies. When it was time to go, he thanked Millie for everything. "Do you mind if I take the suitcase with me?" he asked.

"No, it's yours. I'd forgotten it was here. If I find anything else Renee left behind, I'll give you a call. You take care now."

He kissed her cheek. "You too, Aunt Millie." He went into the living room to gather Renee's things and repack the suitcase. When he picked up the copy of *Little Women*, her bookmark slipped out, and he scooped it from the floor. It was a business card with a psychiatrist's name, Dr. Andrew Soule, and he nearly shouted for joy. If the man would talk about a former patient, and why wouldn't he now that Renee was dead? He tossed everything into the suitcase and carried it out to his car.

Once home, he dialed the doctor's office, hoped the number was still current, and that Dr. Soule didn't play golf on Tuesday afternoon. A woman answered, and in a soft mellow tone offered to make him an appointment in the following month. "No, my late wife was one of Dr. Soule's patients, and I need to speak with him about her as soon as possible. It's an urgent matter, truly it is."

"Urgent or not, Dr. Soule is attending a conference in London, and he won't be flying home until the weekend. He'll need to see his regular patients next week, not take on anyone new."

"I'm not a prospective patient," Hal forced himself to speak in a normal tone rather than shout. "This is about a murder investigation, and his information is vital. When will he be in his office?"

"Next Tuesday, but his schedule is full."

"I'll come early, or at the end of his day, but I must speak with him as soon as possible."

Perhaps the woman was used to handling excitable patients, and she continued in the same soothing tone, "Would you care to leave your name? I'll tell the doctor you called."

"It's Hal Marten, and my wife was Renee Bell."

"Renee? Why didn't you say so? I'll have him call you as soon as he arrives home."

"You remember Renee?"

"We don't discuss our patients over the phone, Mr. Marten."

"No, of course, not." He left his telephone number. If he didn't hear from Dr. Soule by Tuesday, he'd sit in his office until he finally became available.

He called Gladys next and told her about picking up the suitcase from his new Aunt Millie. "I found Faye's psychiatrist, but he'll be out of the country until next week. He ought to know far more about her than I've been able to discover."

"If I can work it into my schedule, I'd like to go with you. Did you call Detective Lynch?"

"I did, but frankly, he appeared more bored than interested in a reported break-in and didn't stay long. I'm not sure he believed it actually happened. How's Mr. Cuddles?"

"He made it through the night without a single meow of complaint. I placed his pillow on a table by a front window, and he'll have his usual entertainment today."

"Thank you." He wished he could think of something more to say, or a reason to get together before Dr. Soule returned home, but his mind went blank. "Good-bye then."

"Hal, you need to get out of the house, go shopping, go to the movies, don't sit there and wait for additional evidence to fall into your lap."

Surprised by her scolding tone, he quickly defended

himself, "I went out knocking on doors to find Aunt Millie, and that contact led me to the psychiatrist. I'm not just sitting here working crossword puzzles in my underwear."

"Of course, you're not," she replied. "I'm sorry. It's been a difficult day. Want to meet for dinner?"

Perhaps she felt sorry for him, and he didn't want her sympathy. His first impulse was to say no, but he didn't argue with himself for long. "We'll talk about my case?"

"Of course, don't we always? Come to my house so you can check on Mr. Cuddles."

He made a note of her address. "What can I bring?"

"Ice cream if you like."

The memory of how Pearl had described her favorite ice cream in a seductive purr was almost more than he could bear. He leaned back against the wall. "Do you like chocolate, or chocolate chip?"

"Of course, who doesn't? I've never thought vanilla was worth eating."

"It was Faye's favorite," he replied softly.

"I'm sorrow, I didn't mean to insult her."

"I thought the same thing. See you later." He hung up the telephone and left to get ice cream rather than sit at home and analyze their conversation until his head exploded.

Gladys's home in West LA was a one-story English Tudor design with a steeply pitched roof and ornamental half-timbering. The lead-paned front window glowed with a welcoming light, and a deep flower border added to the home's charm.

Hal arrived carrying both double fudge and chocolate chip ice cream from Aunt Lucy's Ice Cream Parlor. Gladys unpacked the bag and put the ice cream into her refrigerator's freezer.

"I love Aunt Lucy's," she exclaimed. "I haven't been there in years, but I'll bet it's still the best."

"It is. This is a pretty house. It looks as though it could

have come from an English village."

"Thank you, that's why I love it. I haven't owned it long, and it's furnished with odds and ends. I haven't had time to worry over the décor, and there's been no rush."

She showed him into the living room where Mr. Cuddles was stationed on his pillow peering out at the street. "I'm sure he's missed you," she said.

"Are you kidding? He probably won't remember who I am." He gave the beautiful cat a playful scratch behind the ears and Cuddles leaned into his hand.

"See, he knows you."

"Only because I had the can-opener," Hal argued. "It would probably be best if you kept him."

"It's not something we need to decide tonight. I baked a chicken. It's one of the few things I do well." She picked up Mr. Cuddles to feed him on the back porch.

"I love baked chicken," Hal answered. He followed her into the kitchen and kept out of her way as she fed the cat and served their plates. "The mortuary called this afternoon. They want me to pick-up Faye's ashes tomorrow, but I don't know what I'll do with them. I don't want to keep them in an urn on a mantel."

"The war turned my husband into ashes in the Pacific, but I wouldn't have wanted him on the mantel either. Is there someplace she loved where you could scatter her ashes?"

As soon as they'd sat down at her dining table, he apologized, "I'm sorry. Ashes don't make for pleasant dinner conversation. I shouldn't have bothered you with them."

She savored a bite of butter drenched mashed potatoes before replying. "Hal, we wouldn't be acquainted had your wife not been murdered, so anything relating to her makes perfect sense for discussion. We're talking about business tonight, remember?"

She was observing him with a thoughtful glance, but he knew she didn't mean it anymore than he did. "I do." The chicken was baked to perfection, and he said so.

He'd finally tossed out Faye's last meatloaf, but Gladys didn't need to hear about that. He doubted he'd ever want to eat another one.

"What does that sly smile mean?" she asked.

"It's nice not to have to eat my own cooking, that's all. What do you hear from the DA's office?"

"Not a thing, which worries me. Detective Lynch may not have threatened you today, but I'll bet he sure wanted to. Maybe he's attempting to lull you into a careless complacency."

"Probably. That's why I'm anxious to talk with Faye's, or Renee's psychiatrist. He has to know something important."

"If he's any good he will," she proposed.

"Of course, there's a possibility he'll prove worthless." He'd removed the photo of Renee and her mother from the frame and pulled it from his pocket. "Take a look at this. It's Renee and her mother, Patsy, who looks very much like Pearl. Do you remember the sketch I showed you?"

"Yes, I do." She wiped her hands carefully on her napkin before taking the photo. "She's lovely, and Renee was a very pretty little girl. There's definitely a resemblance between them. Many little girls admire their mothers, but could your wife have created Pearl to better pretend to be her mother?"

"Who knows? I'll ask the psychiatrist when I see him. Tell me what went wrong for you today." He slipped the photo back into his breast pocket.

"I wish I could, but my clients' problems are off-limits, remember?"

"Yes, but I thought you might make an exception." The dinner tasted so good, he didn't speak again until he'd finished eating. "I should probably be working on my résumé and begin looking for another job. Insurance is an important field, but I'm not certain I want to spend more of my time on it. You told me to hold off on a job change, but let's face it, California West may still be paying my salary, but I'm out of work."

She crossed her knife and fork on her plate. "What do you want to do?"

"I don't know. It's too late to go to medical school."

"Not if you really want to go."

He shook his head. "I don't, and if people think I killed my wife, it would be difficult to build a practice anyway."

"Stop it. What you need is a bowl of ice cream." She got up to carry their plates into the kitchen, and he followed her. "Maybe I'll apply at Aunt Lucy's. I did well in chemistry in college, and there has to be some involved in making ice cream."

She set their plates on the counter and washed her hands. "There must be, and there are sure to be lots of delicious combinations Lucy hasn't even thought of as yet."

"There have to be." He watched her take the bowls from the cupboard. She had plain white dishes, nothing with a dainty rose trim for her. They looked like they could have come from a restaurant supply house. She was dressed in slacks and a sweater, and he concentrated on the pattern in the linoleum rather than her trim figure. He'd have one bowl of ice cream and leave before he embarrassed them both with a request for a whole lot more. He had once been such a sensible sort, and now he could barely hold himself together.

She put the coffee pot on the stove. "You've become awfully quiet. Do you want the chocolate or chocolate chip, or some of each?"

"Both sounds good." Once back at the table, he watched her lick her spoon. She'd chosen the chocolate and ate it with a near delirious abandon. "Clearly you love ice cream."

"I do, and this is incredibly good. Thank you for bringing it. How's yours?"

He looked down at his bowl and tried not to think of how excited Faye had been to take ice cream home. She'd always had a childlike wonder of the world, and he'd miss that about her. He should have said so at the memorial, if he'd had the chance.

He took a sip of coffee to clear away the sad thoughts. "It's as good as I remembered. I should really go to Aunt Lucy's tomorrow and apply for a job."

"Maybe you ought to begin with vanilla ice cream at home and do some experimenting to see what you can create with it. Then you'll have new flavors to tempt Aunt Lucy where other men are just looking for work."

"Terrific idea. There are pastry chefs, but I've not heard of ice cream chefs, but there must be some. Maybe I should enroll in a fine cooking school so I'll have a fancy certificate to wave."

She glanced away so quickly he knew her thoughts weren't on ice cream either. It wasn't simply lust either, but a stronger pull he didn't dare acknowledge. "Let me help you with the dishes."

"No, you needn't stay. I enjoy working out my cases in my mind while I clean up the kitchen."

"Really?" He didn't believe her, but he thanked her for the dinner and went to the front door. "When I come up with a new ice cream flavor, you'll be the first to taste it."

She held the door open. "I'll look forward to it. Good night, Hal. You take care."

She'd said his name with such sweet longing, he went down the walk so lost in thought he didn't notice the dark sedan parked behind his Packard until a big man wearing an overcoat and hat tipped low got out and came toward him.

It was too warm a night for an overcoat, and Hal instantly recognized trouble. Maybe his questions about Pearl had finally shaken someone out. He had a second or two to avoid him and leap into his car, but he waited on the walk. He was a lot tougher than he looked, and he doubled his hands into fists. The man might be carrying a gun, but his hands were thrust deep into his pockets, and that was a huge mistake.

CHAPTER 18

Gladys waited at the window to watch Hal depart. Alarmed by the approaching stranger, she feared Hal might suffer some terrible harm right there in her front yard. She flung open the front door, but before she could threaten to call the police, Hal slugged the man with a hard right and dropped him flat.

She ran down the walk. "My God, who is he?"

"I've no idea, but he didn't look friendly." Hal bent down to search the man's overcoat pockets and withdrew a gun. He tossed her the man's hat. "Call the police. If you have some clothesline or rope, let's tie him up before he wakes."

"I've got it!" She raced into the house and quickly returned with a silk sash. "This will have to do." She twisted the length of fabric into a makeshift rope and lashed the man's hands together behind him. "Silk is strong, and it will hold. I'll go call the police."

"Ask for Detective Lynch too." He grabbed the collar on the man's overcoat and hauled him up to the porch. He didn't want to hold the gun, and laid it inside on the hall table. The man had begun to groan. With his hands in his pockets, he'd not been able to catch himself when struck. But rather than the force of Hal's blow, the goon had probably knocked himself out when he'd hit the sidewalk. Hal rubbed his knuckles ready to punch him again if he had to.

Several neighbors came out their front doors, but cautiously remained on their doorsteps or lawns to observe. Hal offered no commentary before the police arrived, and the officers waved the spectators back into their homes. Still curious, they pressed their faces against their front windows to see what they could.

Gladys had seen everything and described how her guest had been accosted on the sidewalk as he'd left for home. Hal nodded and allowed her to explain how he'd defended himself, as any citizen would. It made perfect sense, and Hal would never admit he'd punched the man before he'd been verbally threatened. The man had come toward him in a menacing fashion, and that had been threat enough for him. He'd been armed, so clearly his intentions hadn't been good.

The man came around when a policeman replaced the silk sash with handcuffs. He nodded his chin toward Hal. "He's the one who ought to be in cuffs. He attacked me, it wasn't the other way around."

"Do you have a permit to carry a gun?" the officer asked.

"It's in my wallet. I went out for an evening stroll, and he slugged me."

Noting the obvious size difference between the two men, the taller of the two officers regarded Hal with a questioning glance. "Do you want to add anything to your story?" he asked.

Hal shook his head. "No, I don't." He turned when Detective Lynch entered the house. The officers weren't from his station, and he showed his badge and introduced himself as a homicide detective assigned to a relevant case.

"Do you know this man?" Hal asked.

"Sure, that's Bobby Mund. Sometimes calls himself Ralph Goode. He's one of Jack Dragna's boys."

"Never heard of him," the cuffed man responded.

"Yeah, sure. He'll swear he never heard of you either." Lynch regarded Hal with a troubled frown. "Is it impossible for you to stay out of trouble?"

Gladys stepped to Hal's side and repeated the story she'd given to the policemen. "Pearl LaFosse has to be the reason Jack Dragna sent a man after Hal. He might even have shot her himself."

"Never heard of her," Mund muttered.

"Looks like you don't know anyone tonight. Get him out of here," Lynch ordered. "I'll take his gun in for testing."

One policeman hesitated. "We should take the gun, sir."

Lynch handed them one of his cards. "Have your captain call me in the morning if he wants to argue about it."

The officer appeared convinced, and he and his partner marched Mund down the walk and into the backseat of their patrol car.

"Didn't you want to question him?" Hal asked.

"Waste of time. He wouldn't have admitted anything, and one of Dragna's attorneys will have him released before sunrise. The gun is the only thing that matters. If it proves to be the weapon involved in your wife's death, we'll pick him up again."

"If he's still in town," Hal mumbled under his breath, and Gladys squeezed his arm.

Once Lynch had departed, Hal again turned toward the front door. "I hope to have better luck getting home this time."

"Now that my neighborhood has become so dangerous, I'd rather you stayed," Gladys responded softly.

Tempted, Hal leaned against the doorway. "That's not a good idea for either of us."

"Of course not, but so what?" she countered, but she remained several steps away.

He'd love to feel the soft swell of her breasts pressed

against his bare chest, but she'd be Pearl in his mind, and that wasn't right. Ashamed to admit how easily, no, how readily he'd use her, he started down the walk and turned back to wave.

"Good night," he called, but she'd already shut the front door and didn't hear him. Too late, he thought he could have at least kissed her. Even if the kiss had tasted of regret, it would still have been wonderful. In too dark a mood to drive straight home, he stopped at the Golden Bear.

He recognized a few of the Tuesday night crowd, and the man with the bushy white eyebrows nodded a hello. Whiskey straight up might have been what he needed, but he ordered his usual beer. Mitch set the glass in front of him, and he took a long swallow.

"How did you tear up your knuckles?" Mitch asked. "You know I don't allow any fighting in my mom's place."

"Yes, I do. It was the first thing you told me. Did you give Pearl the same warning?"

Mitch laughed. "No, I just welcomed her right on in. I miss seeing her."

"So do I," Hal responded. Mitch moved away to serve the others at the bar, and once he'd finished his beer, he was ready to go.

He hadn't taken more than two steps out the door when two men as huge and broad shouldered as Bobby Mund grabbed his arms and lifted him right off his feet. Certain this wouldn't end well, he saved his strength rather than struggle, and they shoved him into the back seat of a Cadillac parked at the curb. He was surprised when they remained outside the car, but then sensed he wasn't alone. The man beside him sat veiled in dark shadows, and Hal didn't recognize his deep voice when he spoke.

"You're a difficult man to see, Mr. Marten."

"You should have called my office. My secretary books my appointments."

The man's laughter rolled around the inside of the car.

He slapped Hal on the thigh. "I admire a sense of humor in a man."

He leaned forward into the light thrown by the streetlamp, and Hal saw the deep lines at his nose and mouth giving him the droppy jowls of a bloodhound. He wore thick black-rimmed glasses, and his hair was a silvery gray. Hal was afraid he had to be Jack Dragna, but he hadn't been shot, so things didn't look too bad for him, as yet.

"Was there something in particular you wished to say?" Hal asked.

"Yes, that's why I sent Bobby to bring you to me, but somehow you misinterpreted his intentions."

"Perhaps."

Jack opened a manila folder holding the sketch Hal had given Crystal. "Do you mind if I keep this? I met Pearl a couple of years ago at a party, I've forgotten whose it may have been. She had a way of passing through a crowd, glancing around as though searching for a friend, and then she'd disappear. I saw her only a few times when I was with other women. When I wanted to find her, I had no luck." He sighed softly. "She was the kind of woman a man wants to be seen with, and now she's gone. I'm sorry we missed the chance to become better acquainted."

Joe Ezell had the other copy of the sketch, and Hal thought it would be wise to be generous. "Keep it. Do you know who killed her?"

"No, or he wouldn't still be breathing. You and your detective friend have been asking too many questions, nosing around in the wrong places, and should look elsewhere. No one I know would have hurt Pearl, and if you'd been part of it, you wouldn't have come looking for me. That would have just been plain stupid, and you don't strike me as a stupid man."

"Thank you. I hope nothing untoward has happened to Crystal."

"No, I like her a lot. She'd asked around about Pearl,

and we had a conversation about it. A man ought to take good care of a beautiful woman. They're national treasures, and there are far too few of them. Your attorney is sure a looker."

Uncertain how to respond, Hal swallowed hard. "She's a fine attorney, and that's what I need."

"You want the DA to look elsewhere for suspects? You got it," Jack offered. "It's the least I can do for a friend of Pearl's."

Corruption in the Los Angeles city government and law enforcement was well-known, but Hal doubted he'd benefit from encouraging it. "I just want to find out who killed Pearl, and to see that he's punished."

"You'll find him a lot sooner if you'll stop looking in my direction. You need a ride home?"

"No, I have my car." He had one last question. "Did one of your men put the bow on my cat?"

Jack's rolling laugh again echoed in the car. "That was a good one, wasn't it? Take my card, and if you find out who offed Pearl, call me, and I'll take care of him."

Hal took the business card. He wanted the photo of Faye and him taken in the restaurant returned, but wouldn't push his luck. He got out at the curb and held his breath until the two thugs who'd picked him up like a stuffed bunny got into the Cadillac and drove away. He pocketed Dragna's card, walked to his car, but didn't turn the key. He remembered Gladys's suggestion he keep careful notes, and just as soon as his hands stopped shaking, he'd drive home, and do just that.

CHAPTER 19

Joe broke out in a sweat just hearing about how Hal had met Jack Dragna. "You knocked out one of his thugs?"

Hal rubbed his sore hand. "He was a clumsy sort, and I can't take full credit."

"Still, the police arrested him."

"They did. Lynch called me this morning, and the man's gun wasn't the murder weapon. I didn't think it would be after Dragna insisted he'd had nothing to do with Pearl's death. He'd know who'd killed her if it had been someone in his circle. I don't know where to look now."

CC came to the door, rapped lightly, and looked in. "Excuse me, gentlemen, but something Mrs. Marten said keeps worrying me."

Joe gestured for him to come in. "I thought you'd only exchanged a few words with her."

The janitor stood just inside the door. "That's right, we did, but she asked where to find a hit man, and...."

"What?" Hal nearly shouted. "Why didn't you tell us this sooner?"

CC shrugged. "She was crying, and I didn't think she really meant it. You know how when you're mad at someone you might say you'd like to kill them, but it's just talk. But if Mrs. Marten and Pearl LaFosse were the same woman, hiring a hit man doesn't make any sense at all. That's the thought I can't shake."

"Thanks for telling us," Hal said. "If you remember anything else she said, please don't keep it to yourself."

"There's nothing more," CC promised. "I'm sorry you lost your wife. She was a sweet lady."

"Yes, she was." Hal felt as though he'd been punched in the stomach. He waited until CC had closed the door behind him to speak. "Every time I think things can't get any worse, they do. Where could Faye have found a hit man around here? I assume they don't run a storefront operation."

A single idea rolled around in Joe's mind. "There's only one dive I can think of, the Square Deal Café. Do you suppose someone hanging around there could have offered to kill Pearl?"

Hal stood. "I'll go and see. I have the small photo of Faye and maybe someone will recognize her."

Joe rose from his chair. "You realize it's a crime to solicit murder, don't you?"

"I should hope so. I'm not looking to hire anyone, just to get some information. You don't have to come with me. I'll just go in and have a beer and see what the bartender knows. I doubt many women go in there, and he'd remember Faye."

"Sure he would. She was upset when I reported on my investigation, but hiring a hit man is a damn odd way to commit suicide."

"We all thought Faye and Pearl were two different women, maybe she did too."

"How could anyone be that confused?" Joe asked.

"Damned if I know." Hal stepped to the window overlooking the street. "I didn't really know my wife, Joe. If she'd screamed and thrown pots at me, this all would have ended differently, but she kept the fact that she'd hired you a secret."

"Look, maybe Faye didn't find a hit man. CC might be right, and it was all talk."

Hal shook his head. "No, it's just strange enough to be true about Faye. I'll talk to you later." He hadn't shown Joe Jack Dragna's card, but it had only his name and a telephone number. If the man had a legitimate business of some sort, other than simply extortion, he'd not given it.

Hal stopped next at the mortuary. The white building had a stately columned front and soft organ music blended perfectly with the dim lighting to create a sacred mood. An attractive brunette in a simple black dress approached him as soon as he'd come through the door. Her nametag read Mrs. Adele Anderson in delicate italic script.

"I'm Hal Marten, and I've come to pick-up my wife's ashes."

The woman introduced herself and nodded thoughtfully. "Please step into our parlor while you wait. You'll need to arrange for payment for our services and to sign for the remains. Then I'll bring your wife's ashes," she promised in a hushed whisper.

The parlor was located on the left, and from what he could see, a nice sized chapel took up the building's right wing. The carpet was thick, the well-cushioned sofa and chairs inviting, and he took the wing chair she indicated. She produced a long printed form attached to a clipboard and gave him time to review it. Gladys had called the mortuary when they'd discovered Pearl was Faye, and he'd not cared about the details or cost. It wasn't unreasonable, and he signed and wrote a check. He again blessed California West for keeping him on the payroll.

"Thank you, Mr. Marten. I'll bring you a receipt." She nearly floated out of the parlor with soft, light steps.

A book of floral displays suitable for a funeral sat on the coffee table. He flipped through the pages, and again thought Faye deserved far more than the brief memorial service he'd given her. He was badly embarrassed by how Detective Lynch had ruined even that small tribute.

Mrs. Anderson returned carrying Faye's ashes in a box enclosed in a green velvet bag. She handed him his receipt in an envelope. "The box is sealed so you'll not lose any of the precious ashes before you wish to scatter them, but we have a beautiful selection of urns should you wish to select one."

He took the bag from her, and it proved to be heavier than he'd anticipated. Still, for the lovely young woman Faye had been, it didn't seem nearly heavy enough. "No, this is fine."

"Thank you for allowing us to serve you at this sad time. We are so sorry for your loss."

"Thank you." Hal appreciated the thought even if she said it to everyone who came through the door. He drove home with the box of ashes on the passenger seat, and once there, he placed them on the upper shelf in the bedroom closet and closed the door.

Not knowing quite what to expect, Hal waited until late in the afternoon to stop by the Square Deal Café. The air was thick with cigarette smoke, and the jukebox blared a raucous tune at an ear-numbing rumble. Four men were playing poker at a table in the rear, and three more were strung out along the bar, each protecting his space with widely placed elbows. He took the stool closest to the door and ordered a beer. He'd worn a dress shirt and slacks rather than a suit and tie and fit in.

The bartender was a tall, thin red-haired man with pale pink skin and bright blue eyes. "Haven't seen you in here before."

"No, I haven't had the time, but I'm out of work and nobody cares what I do." Hal had made that up on the walk over. He didn't have to act to appear miserable, when it was already too close to the surface. He pulled Faye's photo from his pocket.

"I think my wife may have come in here."

The bartender leaned over to look at it and shook his head. "Maybe, but it might have been on my day off."

The wiry little man seated the closest got up to check the photo himself. "Sure I remember her. She came in all sad and crying, and Mothball bought her a drink."

"Mothball?" Hal asked. He couldn't help but visualize a man battling a giant moth, and he quickly shrugged off the goofy image.

The bartender laughed. "We don't call him that to his face, but he works for a tailor, and sometimes he smells like the mothballs they use to protect their bolts of wool. Which is a better aroma than some of the guys coming in here have."

"Do you know his real name?" Hal asked.

"Jerry something," the bartender answered. "Our patrons don't usually exchange formal introductions."

"My name's Fred," the wiry man offered his hand, and Hal shook it.

"Hal." He took a long swallow of his beer. "When does Mothball usually come in?"

Fred frowned slightly. "It's Mondays I think. The tailor shop is closed that day, and he likes to play cards, but I didn't see him this week."

"I'm off every other Monday," the bartender said. "But I was here this Monday, and he didn't come in."

"Mothball's name isn't Jerry, it's Roger Yates," one of the men playing cards offered in a voice loud enough to carry over the music to the front of the bar.

"No, it's Mathew or Mark, one of the apostles," one of his buddies argued. "But you're right, his last name was Yates. I heard him say it a time or two."

"How old a man is he?" Hal asked.

"Maybe thirty," Fred responded, "but he could be a few years younger, or older, give a few."

Hal nodded thoughtfully. A thirty-year-old tailor's apprentice nicknamed Mothball didn't sound like a hit man, but he'd let Detective Lynch worry about the improbability of that. First, he wanted to see him.

"Where's the tailor shop?"

"It's right around the corner," the bartender answered. He looked up at the clock over the bar. "Might be closed by now though. Mothball just bought your wife a drink, that's no crime."

"No, it certainly isn't." Hal smiled, and there was nothing threatening in his manner. He had already paid for his beer, and left as soon as he'd finished. He found Pierce Custom Tailoring had closed at five o'clock, so he was too late to meet Mothball today. He'd go in tomorrow and ask about having a suit made. It would get him in the door without looking like a fool, as he feared he did too often now.

His telephone rang when he came through his front door, and he made a quick grab for it. "Hal Marten."

"It's Gladys, and…"

"I'm sorry about last night," he apologized quickly.

"So am I, but that's not why I needed to speak with you. My contact in the DA's office just called to tell me that you're no longer a suspect in your wife's murder. Detective Lynch is probably spitting bullets, but you're in the clear. Why do you suppose the DA's office lost interest in you so suddenly?"

The way she'd asked the question made him suspect she already knew. "I might have an idea, but let's not talk about it on the phone. Let's meet in China Town, you pick your favorite place for dinner."

"The Lotus Garden is near the East Gate on Broadway. Meet me there at seven."

"I'll be there," Hal replied. Now all he had to do was add to his notes and hope they made sense before he spoke with her.

Bright green neon piping gave the East Gate to China Town an eerie glow. The roof-line had an Oriental upward lift, and the structure looked ready to take flight. Hal arrived early and strolled around the center courtyard. An organ grinder with a monkey drew a small crowd, and a little boy handed the monkey a coin. The monkey doffed his cap and slipped the coin into his purse, much to everyone's delight.

Hal tossed a dime into the wishing pond, and hoped he'd soon return to a life he'd recognize as his own. He saw Gladys approaching the gate in a black suit she must have worn for court. He met her at the door of the Lotus Garden, one of the more elegant restaurants in China Town. They were greeted by a smiling host, and shown to a red leather booth bathed in a golden light. Hal ignored the seductive setting and shoved all thought of romance from his mind.

Gladys surveyed the menu. "I didn't have a chance to eat lunch, and I'm starved. Do you want to begin with the fried prawns, or the barbecued ribs?"

"Let's order both. How's the chicken with toasted walnuts?"

"Everything's good here. Let's order that and the lobster with fried rice. Will that be enough for you?"

Hal thought he'd had breakfast, but he didn't remember lunch. "Sure, it's fine." He gave the order to their waiter, and while he'd worried about how this conversation might go, he dove right in.

"As I understand it," he began, "an attorney has to report a crime if she knows of one, doesn't she?"

She picked up the white porcelain teapot and poured freshly brewed tea into their little cups. "Dare I ask what you've done now?"

"Not a thing," he swore. "I may know who directed the DA's attention elsewhere, but LA is so rife with bribery and criminal interference, I could be completely wrong. Let's just accept it as good luck and let it go."

"All right, if you insist. I'd rather think it was my spirited defense that influenced the DA."

"Of course, that had to be the major factor. I haven't received a single bill from you as yet, and I must owe you more than a few dinners."

"It hasn't even been three weeks, Hal, and my firm

bills monthly. Besides, I've only gone to the police station with you a couple of times, and we weren't there but a few minutes on either occasion."

"Your advice has been worth a great deal, and I expect to pay for it."

"I'll note it on the bill," she replied. Their waiter brought their appetizers, and they both reached for the same rib. "Go on, you take it."

He laughed, and was surprised that he could. "No, it's yours." He took a fried prawn and chewed it slowly. He liked her enormously, but limited his focus to murder. "Faye asked the janitor in my detective's building where she might find a hit man."

She stared at him, replaced the rib bone on the plate, and wiped her hands on her napkin. "Before we draw any conclusions about how crazy that sounds, we need to speak with the psychiatrist who treated her. Faye seemed normal to you, didn't she?"

"Yes, completely. If anything, she might have been too agreeably sweet."

"Then it's unlikely she could suddenly have become so depressed she'd plan her own death."

"Highly unlikely." He reached for another prawn. "However, if she did convince someone to shoot Pearl, I may have a line on who he is."

"Tell Detective Lynch please. I'll warn you again not to go after the culprit yourself."

Now that he'd come to the tricky part, he chose his words with care. "Let's say I discovered who killed Faye. It won't be easy to convince Lynch, but I may have met someone who'd handle the situation without the bother of a trial."

"Stop right there, Hal," she cautioned. "I assume this is the same person who might have influenced the DA in your favor. If you've actually met such a person, forget you know them. I'd rather not defend you on a charge of conspiracy to murder."

He admired her fierce determination, and yanked his

mind away from what he'd like to see from her in a dimly lit bedroom. "Would it still be a conspiracy if the man is guilty?"

"Yes! If you become entangled with the baser element of this town, they'll soon come demanding favors you won't want to grant. Don't think of what might be convenient now, when you'd have a lifetime of regret."

He already carried a heavy burden of regret, but he could deal with it. "I understand. I sell insurance, and know how to convince people that being prepared is the best way to protect themselves from unexpected problems. Unfortunately, no one foresees the real catastrophes until they smack them in the face." He paused to eat a rib, and found the spicy sauce incredibly good.

"I'm definitely getting out of insurance."

"And going into ice cream?"

"Maybe. I'd like to try mixing in peanut butter, but I'm afraid it would chill into solid clumps. I might have to bake peanut butter cookies and break them up into vanilla ice cream."

"That does sound good. Have you been giving this a lot of thought?"

"Since last night?" He hadn't spent a second thinking about ice cream until a minute ago. "No, but I liked your idea of beginning with vanilla ice cream and seeing what I can conjure up with it before I hit Aunt Lucy up for a job."

He was relieved she didn't appear to be upset with him for walking out on her last night, and he kept the conversation light while they lingered over dinner. When they cracked open their fortune cookies, he found his amusing. "All women are pretty in the moonlight."

"That might be a stretch with some," she replied. She showed him her fortune. "Love answers all questions."

"Probably, but I forgot to ask them. Forgive me, I don't mean to sound sorry for myself."

"You usually don't. In fact, you've shown remarkable

strength of character in the time I've known you."

He managed an embarrassed smile. "Thank you, but I don't feel as though I'm out of this unholy mess yet." He paid their bill, and left a generous tip. "Let me walk you to your car." She took his arm rather than his hand, but he counted himself lucky. She'd parked on the street rather than in a lot, and he had only a moment to tell her good-bye before she got in her car and drove away. He wished again that he'd kissed her last night when they'd had plenty of time, and was sorry he'd no such opportunity tonight.

"Love answers all questions," he muttered under his breath, but he knew absolutely nothing about love.

Thursday morning, Hal walked into Pierce Custom Tailoring wearing a dress shirt and slacks. A male mannequin in a beautifully tailored navy blue suit immediately caught his eye. "Good morning," he called to the dark-haired man seated behind the counter. "What does a custom tailored suit as handsome as this one cost?"

The man closed the open ledger he'd been working on and slid it onto the shelf beneath the counter. "Frankly, it all depends on how much you annoy me."

"Really?" Hal couldn't tell if he were joking or not. The fellow was perhaps fifty-years-old, and was dressed in dark slacks, and a white dress shirt and tie. A measuring tape hung loosely round his neck.

"Really. I'm Samuel Pierce. Forgive me if I've shocked you, but you appear to be a reasonable man, and you'd be easy to fit. You'd be surprised if you saw some of my clientele. I'm discreet of course, and never reveal names, but when a man would be more comfortable in a loose tent, it's difficult to create a suit that will flatter him."

"I know the type." Hal was immediately reminded of George Sharp, and wondered if he patronized Pierce Tailoring. "A young man recommended you. His last name was Yates, I believe."

"Lord help us," Samuel returned to his stool behind the long counter. "Phillip is my sister's son, and he works for me between stints in jail, I'm sorry to say."

There had been an apostle named Phillip, so one of the card players in the Square Deal Café had been right. "That's very generous of you. I hope it wasn't anything violent."

Samuel shrugged. "My sister married a thug, and her son is just like him. His main job was to keep the shop swept and clean, but now he's quit, as usual without giving notice."

Hal studied the woolen fabric swatches on display. "The shop looks fine. When did he leave?"

"He didn't come in on Tuesday last week, and I haven't heard from him since. Enough about him. Custom suits vary in price according to the fabric selected. How much did you want to spend?"

A week ago Tuesday, the *Times* had printed the story about Faye's double identity, and if Phillip had had something to do with her death, it could have hit him hard. It was definitely a suspicious time for him to leave his uncle's employ.

Hal stayed to talk with the tailor and convinced he would like to own a custom tailored suit rather than another off a rack, he promised to return when he had his finances in order. He went by Joe Ezell's office, but heard him speaking to a client and preferred not to interrupt or wait.

Once home, he glanced toward the window expecting to see Mr. Cuddles yawning a bored greeting. He felt foolish for missing the damn cat, and at the same time, he was enormously grateful Gladys had taken him in. He made a fresh pot of coffee, and drank a cup slowly while he debated how to go about giving Detective Lynch a lead on who had killed Faye.

Lynch answered his phone on the second ring, and listened quietly as Hal gave him a name of a possible shooter. "I know Phillip Yates. He's been in trouble since he turned thirteen and began robbing newsstands. He isn't the type to do good deeds for a lady, but if it involved murder, he might have. I'll follow up on it."

"Please let me know what you find," Hal answered.

"If we make an arrest, you'll read about it in the *Times*," Lynch countered and hung up.

Hal had expected as much. George Sharp hadn't called, so he couldn't go into the office. He looked around the apartment, and with nothing that needed doing, it was time to ask Carmen to help him pack up Faye's belongings. He'd need some boxes first though, and would see what he could pick up behind the grocery store. The afternoon was settled in his mind, but in a dark melancholy mood, he just couldn't get up and get on with it.

CHAPTER 20

Dr. Andrew Soule telephoned Hal Sunday afternoon just as he was preparing to go to the movies. Elated to hear from the psychiatrist, he agreed to meet with him that same afternoon. He called Gladys, and when her phone continued to ring, he feared he'd missed her. He was about to hang up when she finally answered.

"Sorry, I was outside playing at gardening," she apologized in a breathless rush.

"Dr. Soule is home and can see us this afternoon. Do you still want to come with me?"

"Are you kidding? Of course I do."

"He lives near you. I'll pick you up in half an hour."

"Make it forty-five minutes. I've got to rinse off the dirt."

He had never showered with Faye, which struck him as a sad failing. It wasn't the afternoon to offer to clean-up with Gladys either, but maybe someday it would be. "You have it."

Gladys dressed in dark slacks and a cream-colored sweater rather than her usual professional attire. "Let Dr. Soule assume whatever he'd like, but don't introduce me as your attorney. If he thinks there's a chance he'll have to testify in court, he might not be nearly as forthcoming as he'd be with us otherwise."

"Good plan. Do you ever miss anything?"

"Not much." She pulled a small leather-bound notebook from her purse. "You ask the questions, and I'll take notes."

"Fine, but ask any questions I miss."

"Will do."

Dr. Soule lived in a stately brick two-story home that appeared to be losing a battle with the lush green ivy growing in profusion up the north side. The psychiatrist opened the door on the first ring of the doorbell and ushered them into his book-lined den. He was of medium height with a chunky build and had the thick silver hair of film actors playing politicians. A neatly trimmed mustache and goatee framed a wide friendly smile. He was dressed in tan slacks, a pale blue shirt, and a forest green vest that might have been knit by someone who loved him.

"Here, take a seat on the sofa, and I'll pull a chair up close. When I heard you'd called about Renee, I was deeply saddened to learn of her death. May I extend my sympathies for your loss. If it wouldn't be too painful, would you please tell me how it happened?"

"Thank you." Hal hadn't expected him to be so open to a discussion about Renee, and while he welcomed it, he also found it somehow unsettling. "I'll tell you what I know of her story, but what you know about Renee, should come first."

"Then we'll be here a long while. Would you care for coffee or tea?" When Hal and Gladys politely refused refreshments, the psychiatrist got comfortable in his chair and began. "Renee's father brought her to me when she began having trouble in high school. She'd gone from being an A student, to one barely passing her classes. She wouldn't confide in her father, and he hoped I'd be able to discover what had gone wrong and correct it. Of course, it's impossible to fix anyone the way you would tune a car, but I recognized the girl's potential and agreed to see her.

"She was very shy, and did indeed appear to be troubled. I thought hypnosis might enable her to speak of her problem more easily. Curiosity may have prompted her to agree."

"So you hypnotized her?" Hal asked.

"Yes, I did, but rather than gaining significant insights into her falling grades as I'd hoped, hypnosis revealed something astonishing." He leaned forward. "Permit me a quick aside. Around the turn of the century, ending in 1904, a twenty-three-year-old woman referred to as Christine Beauchamp became a patient of a Boston neurologist, a Dr. Morton Prince. Under hypnosis, Miss Beauchamp revealed three distinct personalities, and none had any knowledge of the other. It's a classic case discussed in medical textbooks, but it's rare, and I'd not encountered such a patient until I met Renee."

Dumbfounded, Hal asked, "Are you saying she had more than one personality?"

"Indeed she did. Emotional trauma can be a cause and while she never admitted it directly, she may have been abused by one of her mother's gentlemen friends."

Gladys exchanged a quick perplexed glance with Hal. "So you met with Renee, and under hypnosis, another personality emerged?"

"Yes, she called herself Pearl and was insistent that I speak with her. She wanted to be a model, and had no interest in finishing high school. She was far more sophisticated than Renee, but she appeared only when I'd hypnotized Renee. I couldn't contact her otherwise, but from the way she spoke, she convinced me that she had a distinct life separate from Renee's. Unfortunately, her father died. Her mother regarded psychiatry as expensive foolishness, and removed her from my care. It was most disappointing, I assure you."

"Did you talk to Renee's mother about her second personality?" Hal inquired.

"No, she wouldn't have been receptive to the idea, and while I took slow measured steps with Renee, she didn't appear to fully grasp what I told her. I'd hoped she would come to see me again once she'd turned eighteen, but she didn't. Now please tell me your parts of her story. I'm anxious to hear it."

Hal drew in a deep breath, and released it slowly, but his thoughts remained in a painful jumble. He'd wanted answers from the psychiatrist, but what he'd learned had left him all the more confused. He repeated what Aunt Millie had told him about Renee's quixotic temperament as a child.

"I knew her as Faye Renee Bell, not Renee Stewart. She created a history for herself that bore no relation to the truth. We met, got along well, and married last summer." He described how he'd met Pearl after the first of the year.

"Now it looks as though my wife may have died in a murder for hire she'd arranged herself. It sounds impossible, but she may have been desperate to get rid of Pearl without realizing she'd be killing herself."

Like many silver-haired men, Dr. Soule's eyebrows were dark and each twitch and dip accented his dismay. "Remarkable in all respects," he murmured. "Of course, we all see the tragedy in her death, while I'm fascinated by how different her separate lives had become. I could have studied Renee for years, but sadly the opportunity is lost." He shrugged and sighed unhappily.

Gladys studied her notes. "So Renee could have hired someone to kill Pearl and been completely unaware that she'd also die?"

"Yes, although I know it stretches belief. If she had any other psychiatric care, I'm unaware of it. If only Renee's mother had let her continue to see me, we might have had a much better result."

"It's difficult to imagine a worse one," Hal interjected. "Would Pearl have planned Faye's murder?" Hal asked.

Dr. Soule sat back in his chair and knit his fingers over his chest. "I was hired to treat Renee, but Pearl seemed the stronger personality of the two. She was more confident and self-assured. She wouldn't have regarded Renee as a threat. This is all conjecture, of course, you realize."

"Yes, I understand. Thank you for your time." He stood and offered Gladys his hand to help her rise. "May we contact you again if we have more questions?"

The psychiatrist walked them to the front door. "Yes, please do. There's still a great deal more to be learned from Renee's life."

"I'll keep in touch," Hal promised.

Gladys whispered as they walked down the brick path to their car, "Do you mean that?"

He shook his head and unlocked the Packard's passenger side door for her. "Yes, but only if I have to. He regarded Renee as a lab rat, and it doesn't matter to him that she's dead. She was a fascinating case, and reporting on her would embellish his reputation as a psychiatrist. It was plain he didn't really care about her."

Once they were both seated in the car, he gasped as though all the air had been sucked from his lungs, and quickly rolled down the window. "We've found a psychiatrist who will attest to our belief that Pearl was a separate identity, and I'll give his name to Detective Lynch and let him pursue it."

Gladys reached for his hand. "I've had enough for today and could use some of Aunt Lucy's ice cream. How about you?"

"It won't be a bit of help, but why not?" Hal squeezed her hand and then took her to Aunt Lucy's. He needed to make fresh memories rather than fret over his wife's tragic death. Maybe Pearl was haunting him without the bells or cold mists or music coming from a piano while no one played. He ordered double fudge and thought of her with every single bite.

Monday morning, Hal practiced by telling Joe Ezell what they'd learned from Dr. Soule before he contacted

Det. Lynch with the psychiatrist's name. "Does that make any sense to you?" he asked.

Joe gestured helplessly. "I met the same Faye you married, a sweet girl who loved you. All this other stuff about Pearl, or hiring a hit man, it's difficult to believe."

"If it's difficult for you, imagine how impossible it is for me," Hal countered. "I may have found the hit man, and I've given Detective Lynch his name. He's a young man who's been in trouble since he was a kid. I'm still curious about Pearl and wonder about her life, but we'll never wrap up the details. It's time to end the investigation. Go ahead and total up my bill."

Joe carried a small notebook to keep track of the hours he spent working on each case and pulled it out of the top drawer. "Give me a couple of days to type up a bill. While your wife's case defies logic, I've enjoyed working with you. Most of the guys I grew up with have moved out of the area or didn't make it home from the war. I'd hate to miss a chance to find a golf partner. Do you play?"

"I played a few rounds in college with a fraternity brother who was on the golf team, and that's it. I may have a lot of time on my hands, so I probably should take up the game."

"I could give you lessons," Joe offered. "I'd once thought of becoming a golf pro, but that ship has sailed."

"Lessons would be good," Hal responded. He'd not admit it, but he was short on friends as well, and Joe knew his story so he wouldn't have to repeat it to anyone new. "I need to get back to work, if I still have a job. I'll talk to you soon."

Joe stood with him. "I'll mail your bill."

As Hal walked home, the idea of taking up golf became increasingly appealing. The top executives of California West played together, and he ought to be ready when, and if, he reached their level. He called his secretary to check in, and found her nearly hysterical.

"What's happened, Lorraine?"

"It's Charlie Sharp," she rushed to explain. "He had a

heart attack at a relative's wedding over the weekend, and died before they could rush him to the hospital. The whole office is in a state over it. Can you come in?"

"Of course, I can." Hal dressed in a favorite suit and took the Red Car to work as he had so many times. The familiar routine was a welcome release, and a couple of his salesmen cheered as he came through the door. "Good morning," he called. "We'll meet in fifteen minutes to plan the rest of the week."

Lorraine nearly cried she was so glad to see him. She followed him into his office with the notes she'd kept. "If you'll excuse me for saying so, the last couple of weeks without you have been hell. There's a good chance you'll get Mr. Sharp's job, and I know you're ready for it."

Hal had come too close to being fired to hope for a promotion but swallowed a chuckle rather than laugh out loud. "Thank you for the vote of confidence. Let's wait and see what happens." He reviewed her notes quickly before the meeting he'd called began. Overall, his salesmen had behaved themselves and sold insurance. Now he'd have to inspire them to sell even more.

First he needed to contact Detective Lynch with Dr. Andrew Soule's name. "This should be my last call," he began, but the detective interrupted him.

"You were right about Phillip Yates. We arrested him, and he confessed to your wife's murder. He'd seen himself as her hero until the news broke that Pearl and Faye were one and the same. He was drunk and hysterical when we picked him up, and his gun proved to be the murder weapon. So your wife's case is closed."

Hal was relieved, as well as grateful, but he refused to thank Lynch for his work when he'd been so damn misguided. He gave him Dr. Soule's name, but doubted the detective would follow up now they had made an arrest. As he saw it, the LAPD might never have solved the case without Phillip Yates' name. He'd gladly allow Lynch to take the credit, however, and hope he'd never have any need to see him again.

* * *

That night, after Hal had eaten what could pass for a dinner, he called Gladys at her home. He let her know Detective Lynch had arrested the man who'd shot Faye, and his wife's case was closed. "Are you ever going to send me a bill?" he asked.

"Yes, eventually, of course. How's the ice cream coming?"

"It'll have to wait. I've gone back to work, just to keep myself sane. By the fall, I should be able to decide what I really want to do."

"That's a good plan, Hal. Mr. Cuddles sends his best wishes."

"I miss him. Are you free for dinner Saturday night?"

Her reply held a wistful note, "Your case is over, Hal. We shouldn't endlessly rehash it."

"I agree. I'll pick you up at your place. It will give me a chance to see Mr. Cuddles."

After a long silence, she whispered, "What are we doing, Hal?"

His voice dropped to a husky edge, "Whatever you want. I'll see you Saturday."

She laughed as though he were merely teasing. "Fine, about seven?"

"Seven it is." He hung up before she changed her mind.

All he needed to do now was decide where to scatter Faye and Pearl's ashes. He sat back in his chair to think, and the idea came to him in an instant. One beautiful young ghost already traipsed around the Hollywoodland sign, and she'd be sure to welcome a couple of new friends. He'd go in August when the nights were warm and still to bid his wife and Pearl a last loving good-bye, while it would surely take a lifetime to forget them.

Turn the page for an

excerpt from

STAIRWAY

TO

MURDER

A Detective Joe Ezell Mystery

Book Two

P.J. Conn

Los Angeles, Summer 1947

Monday morning, Joe Ezell started up the stairs to his second floor office carrying a copy of *The Los Angeles Times*. Focused on the headlines, when he slipped, he fell hard, hit his chin on a step and actually did see stars the way cartoon characters do. He sat where he'd fallen to gather himself. Feeling like a clumsy fool, he wiped his chin on his handkerchief, but the blood on the stairs wasn't his.

Cleotis Cotton, the custodian of the building, entered right after Joe had fallen. "Oh my goodness, Mr. Ezell, let me help you up. Do we need to call an ambulance?" He picked up Joe as easily as he would a bag of groceries, and set him on his feet at the bottom of the stars.

Joe took a deep breath to clear his head. His chin hurt like hell, and he felt thoroughly rattled, but he'd not complain. "No, CC, I'm fine. But something is definitely wrong at the top of the stairs."

Cleotis followed Joe's glance and took a quick backward hop. "Oh my Lord, there's blood dripping halfway down the steps. Does a body hold much more than that?"

"No detective worthy of the name faints at the sight of blood, so I'll go up and investigate. You wait right here and if this is as awful as it looks, I want you to go into the drug store and call the police."

"Yes, sir, I'll wait right here."

Joe avoided the blood-spattered steps as he went up, this time with a firm grip on the brass railing bolted to the wall. He needed to go up only halfway to see the woman sprawled on the landing. Her throat had been cut from ear to ear, and he was terribly afraid she was his nine o'clock appointment.

"Call the police, CC," he called, "a woman has been murdered."

CC bolted out the door without asking if she was anyone they knew. Joe stood frozen on the stairs. He had met Georgia Dixon only once, when he'd picked up his girlfriend, Mary Margaret McBride, at the VA hospital in West Los Angeles where both worked as nurses. He recognized Georgia now from her curly brown hair. She'd kept it in a coiled bun for work, but going out the door at the end of the day she'd shaken out the tight curls and let them bounce upon her shoulders.

They had spoken briefly when Mary Margaret had introduced him, but he remembered her when she'd called to make an appointment. Unfortunately, she'd not revealed the cause of her concern, but clearly someone hadn't wanted her to see him that morning. She lay with her arms flung wide and her legs crumpled beneath her. Her black handbag had fallen open and the contents were spilled near her feet.

Rather than be accused of tampering with evidence, Joe left the purse untouched, and took great care to retrace his steps to the bottom of the stairs and sat down. He rested his head in his hands, and took in great gulps of air. He'd opened Discreet Investigations as soon as he'd passed the test for a private investigator's license. He'd studied the subject and felt fully qualified to follow men cheating on their wives, and vice versa, or perhaps catch an office thief or a clerk pilfering from the till, but murder, with one notable exception, was way beyond his realm of experience.

Max Broderick, a dentist with an office across the hall from Joe's, pushed through the heavy door at the entrance of the building and came to an abrupt halt. "What's wrong, Joe, are you ill?"

Joe looked up and nodded toward the gruesome evidence trickling down the stairs. "A young woman's been murdered.

The police have been called, and you better stay right where you are. Believe me, you don't want to see her."

"My god! A murder in our building?" Max gasped. A man in his fifties with thinning hair and thick glasses, he hadn't served in World War II and had no experience with dead bodies. His knees felt weak, and he leaned against the wall. "My patients are all scheduled for the afternoon, do you think the police will have cleared the scene by then?"

As always, Max was meticulously dressed, the handkerchief in his jacket pocket matched his tie. He wore handsomely-tailored suits to his office even though he'd slip off his jacket and wear a white coat to see patients. He seemed to be a nice enough fellow, and they often exchanged hellos in the morning, but neither had been inclined to linger for a full conversation.

"You'll probably have to re-schedule today's appointments," Joe advised. "The police aim to be thorough rather than fast."

"I could go up the back stairs to reach my office," Max replied.

"Better wait. If the police find you upstairs, they might suspect you know more than you actually do."

"Oh right. I'll stay right here then. Maybe I'll go into the drugstore and get a cup of coffee at the counter."

Joe nodded. "Go right ahead."

CC held the door for Max as he went out. "The police said they'd be right here. I told them we'd come into work and found a gruesome murder. That's the word, isn't it?"

"It's gruesome, all right." Joe wondered if Mary Margaret knew why Georgia had wanted to see him. If so, he hoped it wouldn't put the woman he loved in grave danger.

———◆———

STAIRWAY TO MURDER
available in
print and ebook

A native Californian, P.J. Conn attended the University of Arizona and California State University at Los Angeles where she earned a BA in Art History and an MA in Education. Her Historical Romance and Science Fiction novels, written under Phoebe Conn, have won many awards.

Phoebe is the proud mother of two grown sons and two adorable grandchildren, who love to have her read to them.